"It's Time For Us To Have The Discussion We Should Have Had Months Ago, Gillian."

"It doesn't matter to me what you want," she told him. "You are not a part of our lives and you aren't going to be."

"Like hell!" Devlin grabbed her, turned her toward him. "Now that I know I have a child, I'm damn well going to be a part of her life. A big part."

Gillian was trapped, and her fighting instincts surged to the fore. "There is no—"

"I'm Ashley's father!" Devlin's voice rose. Hearing the admission from his own lips sent a new surge of shock waves through him. He was a father! He felt a peculiar stirring in his chest and wondered if it was the kindling of that primal patriarchal bond or pure and simple rage at Gillian for her deception.

"Why, Gillian?" he asked. "How could you do this? Do you hate me so much?"

Dear Reader,

February, month of valentines, celebrates lovers—which is what Silhouette Desire does *every* month of the year. So this month, we have an extraspecial lineup of sensual and emotional page-turners. But how do you choose which exciting book to read first when all six stories are asking *Be Mine?*

Bestselling author Barbara Boswell delivers February's MAN OF THE MONTH, a gorgeous doctor who insists on being a full-time father to his newly discovered child, in *The Brennan Baby.* *Bride of the Bad Boy* is the wonderful first book in Elizabeth Bevarly's brand-new BLAME IT ON BOB trilogy. Don't miss this fun story about a marriage of inconvenience!

Cupid slings an arrow at neighboring ranchers in *Her Torrid Temporary Marriage* by Sara Orwig. Next, a woman's thirtieth-birthday wish brings her a supersexy cowboy—and an unexpected pregnancy—in *The Texan,* by Catherine Lanigan. Carole Buck brings red-hot chemistry to the pages of *Three-Alarm Love.* And Barbara McCauley's *Courtship in Granite Ridge* reunites a single mother with the man she'd always loved.

Have a romantic holiday this month—and every month—with Silhouette Desire. Enjoy!

Melissa Senate

Melissa Senate
Senior Editor

Please address questions and book requests to:
Silhouette Reader Service
U.S.: 3010 Walden Ave., P.O. Box 1325, Buffalo, NY 14269
Canadian: P.O. Box 609, Fort Erie, Ont. L2A 5X3

BARBARA BOSWELL

THE BRENNAN BABY

SILHOUETTE *Desire*®

Published by Silhouette Books

America's Publisher of Contemporary Romance

SILHOUETTE BOOKS

ISBN 0-373-76123-6

THE BRENNAN BABY

BARBARA BOSWELL

loves writing about families. "I guess family has been a big influence on my writing," she says. "I particularly enjoy writing about how my characters' family relationships affect them."

When Barbara isn't writing and reading, she's spending time with her *own* family—her husband, three daughters and three cats, whom she concedes are the true bosses of their home! She has lived in Europe, but now makes her home in Pennsylvania. She collects miniatures and holiday ornaments, tries to avoid exercise and has somehow found the time to write over twenty category romances.

One

"At least have the grace to admit it, Dev," said Devlin Brennan's sister Kylie as she staggered into his new apartment, weighted down by the towering stack of compact discs in her arms. "You knew you'd be moving into your new apartment this weekend and that's the only reason why you invited Cade and me to visit. To help you move all your stuff!"

"Well, there is that, of course." Devlin's blue eyes gleamed.

He and his brother-in-law, Cade Austin, were holding opposite ends of the long slate-gray sofa they'd hauled up four flights of stairs, having bypassed the endless wait for the busy elevator. Many new tenants were moving into the building this weekend, and all the noise and activity gave the place the feel of a college dorm at the beginning of the term.

"But I also wanted to spend some time with you, little sis," Devlin added. He and Cade set the sofa down in front of the window.

"That's the same smarmy tone you used to trick me into investing my allowance in your comic book collection back when we were kids," Kylie said dryly.

Devlin cast an affectionate glance at her. Kylie was not one to be fooled, but he didn't intend to stop trying. "How about this, then? I hoped the three of us could spend some time, uh, *bonding*. And what better way to bond with your family than while moving?"

"Feels more like bondage to me," Cade growled.

Devlin ignored him. "I missed you two. After all, I haven't seen you since your wedding, and that was—what?—a couple months ago?"

"Our wedding was July first and today is September first, so it's exactly two months ago." Kylie was precise. "I wish you'd come visit us in Port McClain, Dev. We could bond there just as well as here. No, even better because in Port McClain we wouldn't have to lug furniture from building to building. Our house has—"

"Have I told you how great you both look?" Devlin offered his most winning smile, determined to divert her before she began making plans for his future visit. He was in no hurry to visit Port McClain. The small Ohio town where Kylie and her husband lived was filled with other Brennans—a host of aunts, uncles and cousins—and Devlin didn't want to get entangled in the sticky web of extended family. "Marriage must agree with you," he added gallantly.

"Absolutely." Cade's eyes met Kylie's and she smiled at him.

Dev stirred uncomfortably. The smile his sister gave her husband was a private one, of such intimacy and warmth that he felt almost guilty witnessing it. He hoped they weren't going to launch into an appalling display of mushy marital baby talk. Devlin eyed the door, lining up his possible escape route at the first sounds of it.

"Dev, have you given any thought to getting married?" Kylie asked instead, turning her earnest blue eyes on her older brother.

Devlin groaned aloud. He would've preferred the romantic gobbledygook to The Question. "Sure. I've thought about it. And here's what I think—I don't want to get married."

"Not ever?" Kylie was worried. "You're just kidding, right? Seriously, Devlin, you do want to settle down sometime and—"

"Jeez, Kylie, you sound like Mom! Since the day of your wedding, she's been asking when *mine* will be. Dad's even starting to get in on the act. The last time I talked to him he actually said, 'Well, son, met that special girl yet?'" He did a passable imitation of their father's flat Midwestern tones.

"Well, have you?" Cade drawled.

Looking pained, Dev turned to his brother-in-law. "No offense, Cade, but before Kylie married you, the folks tended to focus their dreams of marriage and grandchildren on *her*. I was spared. But since Kylie's taken the plunge, the heat is on me. Suddenly Mom can't understand why I'm thirty-one and unattached. She worries about me eating right, she worries about me growing old alone. She fears I might follow in the footsteps of our late uncle Gene and turn into an irascible old bachelor. Every Sunday without fail, I get maternal angst long distance from Florida. Those weekly calls to the folks are driving me nuts!"

"Driving others nuts is a Brennan specialty," Cade murmured. "Uh, present company excluded, of course," he added when Kylie playfully socked his arm in protest.

"Cade and I aren't entirely off the hook, Dev," Kylie confessed. "Mom has let us know in no uncertain terms that she's ready to be a grandmother and she hopes we won't make her wait too long."

"Nine months is about as long as your mother wants to wait for her first grandchild," Cade added, amused. "But Kylie and I have decided to be a couple for a while, before we become a trio."

"Good for you!" Devlin offered his endorsement. "I'm definitely not ready to be Uncle Dev yet."

Him, an uncle! The idea boggled his mind. He pictured uncles as dull, somewhat grouchy older guys like his uncles Guy and Artie and the deceased Gene. No, he was not yet ready to play that role for the next generation. It was hard enough to remember that he was now somebody's brother-in-law!

His sister's marriage had affected him more than he cared to admit. He had always taken Kylie's presence in his life for granted. She was his little sister, who both adored him and fought with him. During their peripatetic childhood as "Navy brats," they were steadfast pals and allies—and occasional bitter enemies. But whether in positive or negative phases, theirs had been an exceptionally close connection over the years and across the miles. They were first in each other's lives.

Not anymore. Cade Austin, her new husband, came first with Kylie now. Which was as it should be, of course. Devlin was happy for them, yet as he looked at the pair kidding affectionately with each other, he felt left out.

He shook off the feeling. All those calls from his parents, warning him against the pitfalls of dying a lonely old bachelor, must be taking their toll on him.

"I'm perfectly happy with my life the way it is, and I don't want or need to make any changes, not for a long, long time," he announced, startling himself. He hadn't realized that he'd spoken his thoughts aloud.

"Famous last words." Cade smirked as he headed toward the door. "Come on, Dev, we still have half that van to unload."

Cade was the chief executive of BrenCo, the family-owned company in Ohio. His voice and his demeanor were conducive to giving orders—and having them promptly obeyed. Devlin automatically started to follow him out the door.

Kylie, in the midst of slipping the CDs into individual slots in the six-foot-high revolving storage case, snickered.

Devlin stopped dead. "What?"

"If you thought you could get out of hauling stuff by having Cade on hand to take over, you thought wrong, brother. Cade is even better at giving orders—and seeing that they're carried out—than Daddy."

Which was no small talent, as Devlin knew. Their father, Wayne Brennan, was a retired Navy captain who excelled in orders.

"Does that mean you jump to Cade's every command, Ky?" Devlin needled her. "Now there's a sight I'd like to see."

"Cade doesn't order *me* around," Kylie was quick to assure him.

"Yeah, right. Not much." Dev chuckled. "Who would've ever believed it? When Cade Austin speaks, my little sister—the former formidable feminist—not only listens, she does exactly what she's told, just like a good little obedient dimwit."

"Devlin! That van isn't going to unload itself!" Cade's voice sounded impatiently from the stairwell at the same moment that Kylie tossed a CD at Dev.

He moved with catlike speed and precision, avoiding the flying missile while racing out into the hallway, laughing.

Where he almost smashed head-on into a young woman holding a baby in her arms. Dev managed to avoid the collision by centimeters, his finely tuned co-ordination serving him well. Taking a deep breath, he leaned against the wall and looked at his near-miss, who was standing in the middle of the hall.

"Hello, Devlin." Her voice was cool and clear.

Dev's dark blue eyes widened. He knew her. Oh, yes, he knew

her quite well! "Gillian." He cleared his throat. His voice sounded oddly thick.

"Mama, mama, mama," the baby chattered, squirming in the young woman's arms.

"So that's your baby," Dev said, recovering somewhat. "A little girl?"

Gillian nodded her head.

"Good guess on my part, huh?" Dev smiled wryly. The baby's mop of dark brown curls with the pink barrette clipped in one thick lock was a dead giveaway to the child's sex. The pink ruffled sunsuit and little pink sneakers with lacy socks were other conspicuous clues. No unisex fashions for Gillian's kid. Nobody could mistake this little girl for a little boy.

Dev's eyes slid over Gillian as he gave her his routine once-over. Though she was dressed in loose-fitting jean shorts and a blue T-shirt, she was as unmistakably feminine as her small daughter's little pink togs. Her red hair, which usually hung nearly to her shoulders in a neat bob, was pulled high in a scarf-tied ponytail. She was petite, just five-one, the top of her head not even reaching the shoulder of his own six-foot frame. Her figure was still curvy and rounded in all the right places; childbirth hadn't changed that. Dev's eyes lingered on her chest. Maybe her breasts were bigger....

His eyes happened to stray to her face and he realized that she was watching him stare at her chest. She lifted her brows and nailed him with her pale blue eyes.

Dev felt awkward, a condition he rarely experienced. "What's the baby's name?" he heard himself ask, even as he mocked himself for finding the need to make inane small talk. Gillian certainly didn't.

"Ashley." She shifted the wiggling baby to her other hip.

"Ashley," Devlin repeated. "I treated a lot of Ashleys during my pediatric rotation in med school. I've often wondered what inspires one out of every three mothers these days to name their daughters Ashley. An interesting phenomenon, yet to be explored."

"Sorry to be so unoriginal. If I'd known you hated the name, I'd have chosen something else," she added, her tone caustic.

Dev smiled slightly. "I didn't say I didn't like the name, just that there are a lot of Ashleys around."

"Her name is Ashley Joy Morrow. Case closed."

Devlin recognized the note of finality in her tone. She sounded like an officious bureaucrat, which he decided, she might well be. After all, she was a medical social worker who worked in aftercare patient placements at the hospital. Didn't her position place her firmly within Officious Bureaucrat Realm?

In that case, how could he resist baiting her? It would be positively un-American not to.

"Morrow. Then that would currently make you Gillian Morrow, wouldn't it?" He gleefully reopened the name game and watched her stiffen in response. "Of course, I knew you as Gillian Bailey back in your wild and crazy single days."

He felt a perverse pleasure at her frown of annoyance. Gillian had been the polar opposite of wild and crazy while he'd known her. Conservative and stable would be apt, but she would consider that a compliment and right now he was set on riling her.

"I still use Bailey. I was divorced right after the baby was born so I never got around to changing my name," Gillian imparted the information reluctantly. "And I was never wild and crazy," she added, stung. She'd spent her whole life trying not to be, though she'd certainly acted that way around Devlin Brennan during the three months they'd been together.

"Divorce?" Dev appeared genuinely surprised by the news. "Well, that didn't last long, did it?"

"If you mean my marriage, no, it did not." Gillian looked at the ground, then smoothed the baby's thick dark curls with her fingers.

He noticed every nervous gesture she made. Clearly, her brief marriage was a sore subject for her. Being Devlin, instead of tactfully letting it go, he pressed her on it. "What happened? And where is Mr. Morrow now? Completely out of the picture—or simply off to one side?"

"I think you'll understand if I don't share the details of my divorce with you," Gillian said frostily.

"Mama!" Ashley roared.

"She's getting restless, I have to go inside." Gillian moved toward the door on the right, exactly across the hall from the door of Devlin's apartment.

"You're visiting someone who lives there?"

"*I* live there. We moved in yesterday."

Devlin felt winded, as if someone had kicked him in the belly. "You're joking."

"Why would I joke about that?"

A mirthless smile tilted the corners of his mouth. "Because I'm moving in there." He pointed to his apartment with his thumb. "Right across the hall from you."

They exchanged looks of mutual dismay, which each quickly attempted to conceal with a facade of cool unconcern.

"Well, if you ever need a baby-sitter, don't call on me," Dev said glibly.

"Don't worry about that. I don't want you near my baby."

She sounded a bit too fervent. Dev was insulted. "You don't think I could baby-sit? I happen to be great with kids."

"I'm sure your superficial charm is as effective with children as it is with women. But that isn't what—"

"Devlin, you are a dog," the booming masculine voice interrupted her in midsentence. At that moment Cade rounded the bend, carrying an enormous cherry-red BarcaLounger recliner. His dark brows narrowed in an expression of disapproval at the sight of Devlin, lounging against the wall. "You knew if you wasted enough time, I'd drag this monster up here myself."

Gillian moved quickly to stand against the opposite wall, ceding the right-of-way. Little Ashley made a loud crowing sound of delight, as if the sight of the big red chair pleased her.

Cade cast a startled glance at the child, and the baby smiled at him. Suddenly the chair slipped precariously in his hold. Devlin rushed over to grip the other side before it hit the floor.

Cade didn't seem to even notice. "Is that your baby?" he asked Gillian, who nodded her head.

"How old is she?" Cade demanded to know.

"Eleven months." Gillian began to inch away.

She appeared to be unnerved and Devlin couldn't blame her. He found Cade's insistent interrogation to be vaguely embarrassing, not to mention peculiar. Then again, maybe it wasn't peculiar to Cade, Dev conceded. He didn't know his brother-in-law all that well; maybe the man quizzed everybody in his path as a matter of course.

"Any other information you need to know, Cade?" Dev asked jokingly, trying to ease the tension that seemed to emanate tangibly from Gillian. He didn't want her to be scared of his brother-in-law! "The kid's birth weight, her blood type? Maybe her cereal preference?'' He smiled at Gillian, inviting her to share in the humor. She did not smile back.

Cade's frown deepened.

"Gillian, this is my brother-in-law, Cade Austin." Dev felt obliged to make an introduction as an explanation for all the questions. "Cade, Gillian Bailey."

"A close friend of yours, I presume," Cade intoned darkly.

A delicate shade of pink colored Gillian's cheeks. "I wouldn't say that we're friends," she murmured.

"More like ex-acquaintances who decided to pass on friendship." Dev was flippant. "She is also my new neighbor. Gillian just told me that yesterday she and the baby moved into the apartment across the hall from mine." He inclined his head toward Gillian's door.

She winced. She couldn't have made her displeasure with the situation more obvious if she'd shouted it aloud for all to hear.

Devlin frowned, irked. Though he was hardly thrilled by the prospect of living in such close proximity to an ex-girlfriend, he knew he could handle it. And if he could, so could she. After all, it wasn't as if he'd dumped her, turning her into a hurt and angry rejectee. *She* had been the one to break up with *him*. And shortly after, she'd married another man.

Not that he had been hurt or angry, not that he'd felt rejected, Dev assured himself. He had been surprised, yes, but he hadn't really minded. There were plenty of women here in the lively university town of Ann Arbor, more than enough women working within the behemoth medical center to give him easy access to Gillian replacements. He hadn't had a bit of trouble finding them, either, during the twenty months since their breakup.

Not that he was keeping count, of either the months or the women.

"You'll be living across the hall from each other?" Cade's gaze, laserlike in its intensity, traveled from Devlin to Gillian to the baby.

"Looks that way, doesn't it?" Devlin stated the obvious. He'd had enough of the conversation. "Let's get the chair inside." He began walking toward his front door. Since Cade held the other half of the chair, he either had to drop it or go along.

Gillian watched the two men tote the chair into Devlin's apartment, then quickly opened her own door and disappeared inside, clutching baby Ashley in her arms.

"We have to move!" She closed the door behind her and leaned against it, her face flushed, her knees suddenly weak and wobbly.

"Bite your tongue!" drawled the tall, blond young man, deeply tanned with sculpted muscles, who was sprawled across the sofa, sipping from a bottle of flavored iced tea. "We just moved you and the baby and all your stuff in here yesterday. Your next move isn't supposed to occur until the end of the millenium."

Ashley bucked and wriggled, and Gillian set her down on the floor. The baby stood alone for a moment, then took a few unsteady steps before deciding that good old-fashioned crawling provided the fastest means of locomotion. She took off on all fours at an impressive speed, heading for the small kitchen.

A voluptuous olive-skinned young woman with a thick mane of raven-black hair stood peeling carrots at the sink. She kept one eye on the approaching baby while studying Gillian. "What's the matter, Gilly? You look shook."

"Devlin Brennan is moving in across the hall, Carmen," Gillian managed to choke out the words in a tight little voice. "I can't stay here." She appealed to the young man for support, her blue eyes anguished. "Mark, you know I can't."

"But, sweetie, you've been on the waiting list for this place for nearly two years and you finally got in. The rent is right, the location is right." Mark's tone was a mixture of sympathy and practicality. "You can't just up and leave, not even if Satan himself is living next door."

"I agree with Mark," Carmen put in. "You can't leave the day after moving in, Gilly. Where will you go? All the decent places are taken by now and you know that rents anywhere else are a lot higher than what you'll pay here."

"After all, this building is subsidized housing for hospital employees," Mark reminded her. "And since you are one, you deserve to be here. Much more than Dr. Swoon across the hall," he added with a disdainful sniff. "That rich yango could live anywhere else. Why doesn't he?"

"He—he's not rich." Gillian automatically defended Devlin, without knowing why. "He's a resident doctor in orthopedics, still in training, and they get paid, but not all that much. Plus, he has loans to pay off from med school."

"My heart bleeds for him!" Mark exclaimed, giving his long blond hair a melodramatic toss. "After he finishes his residency, it will probably take one entire ski season, fixing bones broken on the slopes, for him to pay off his loans. Then he can start accumulating the typical yango props. The glam car, the ritzy golf club memberships, the palatial house. And let's not forget—''

"I want to forget everything about him, Mark," Gillian cut in. "Past, present and future."

Mark sighed. "That won't be easy with him right next door. Uh-oh, Carmen, watch out. Ashley is almost under your feet."

"Hi, Ashley! Did you come to see Aunt Carmen?" Carmen scooped up Ashley, who'd arrived in the kitchen and was circling her ankles. "What was Devlin Brennan's reaction when he saw the baby?" she asked, turning curious dark eyes toward Gillian.

"He wondered why every mother seems to name her daughter Ashley these days," Gillian said flatly.

"Not even a flicker of some kind of primal recognition?" asked Mark, his lips tightening in disapproval. "Honestly! The man has all the sensitivity of a Neanderthal."

"I forget—is a Neanderthal more or less sensitive than a yango, Mark?" Gillian teased in a blatant attempt to change the subject.

"This is no laughing matter, Gillian," Mark scolded.

"Then let's find a matter to laugh about."

"In Dr. Brennan's defense, he would have to be psychic to guess that Ashley is his daughter," said Carmen, sticking to the subject anyway. "After all, Gillian never even told him she was pregnant. Nobody would know who Ashley's father is, not even us, if she hadn't let us in on the deep dark secret."

Gillian sighed. "I wish I'd never mentioned his name to anyone," she muttered.

"You couldn't keep it to yourself, Gilly," Carmen said kindly. "And you did the right thing. As soon as you found out about the baby, you engineered that marriage of convenience to Mark."

Mark blew Gillian a kiss, and the mood in the room lightened considerably. "Anything to help my favorite foster sister."

"*She's* your favorite foster sister?" Carmen feigned indignation. "What about me?"

"Did I say she was my only favorite?" teased Mark. "You're both my favorites. Along with Debra and Stacey and Suzy and—"

"Okay, okay, we get it," Carmen interrupted good-naturedly. "You have lots of favorite foster sisters."

"I only hope I don't have to marry them all." Mark stroked his dimpled chin, looking pensive. "Even when it's on paper only, a marriage is kind of hard to explain to my friends back in L.A."

"I can imagine," Carmen said, with feeling. "Even a cover marriage makes me want to run away screaming."

"Gillian and I had a very amiable cover marriage and an equally friendly divorce," said Mark. "But, oh, the teasing I've had to take about it! You simply *can't* imagine!"

"Well, it's all over now, and I'm sure you won't have to endure any other cover marriages, Mark," Gillian soothed. "At our ripe old age of twenty-six, I'm surely the only one stupid enough to—"

"You weren't stupid, you were in love," Carmen cut in. "Don't be so hard on yourself, Gillian."

"Don't make excuses for me." Gillian crossed the room to flop down on the sofa beside Mark, her favorite foster brother who had done her the incredible favor of marrying her in name only to give her child a legitimate birth. As one who'd been born out of wedlock, Gillian had determined years ago that she would never let a child of hers bear that stigma. Mark had understood completely. His mother hadn't been married to his father, either.

"Well, stupid or in love or whatever, Devlin Brennan was definitely a willing participant, Gillian." Carmen's dark eyes flashed and she nuzzled the top of Ashley's silky head. "And it's not fair that you're assuming total financial responsibility for the baby. At the very least, that...that *yango* should be handing over a check every month to you for—"

"No!" Gillian exclaimed so forcefully that Mark jumped. "I don't want any charity from him. I've had enough of being a charity case, thank you very much. I have no intention of letting my daughter become one."

"It wouldn't be charity, but I know where you're coming from." Mark reached over to pat her shoulder. "Don't worry, Gilly. It's going to be okay."

How? Gillian wanted to cry. How could it possibly be okay if she had to contend with seeing Devlin Brennan every day, if she had to watch the parade of women through his apartment and his life? She stared fixedly at the olive green carpet until the weave seemed to blur and dance in front of her eyes.

The firmly suppressed memories escaped from the prison in her mind where she'd kept them locked away for the past twenty months. For a few moments she was swept back to the time she'd shared with Dev. Those three months had been the happiest, most exciting, thrilling, romantic time of her life.

But there had been a dark side that always shadowed that idyllic period. All during their too-good-to-be-true romance, she'd felt scared and insecure, not really believing that a man like Devlin Brennan could want a woman like her. Could want her! She'd always known their relationship was temporary, had been braced for the inevitable end. Something too good to be true generally turns out to be exactly that, and of course, her erstwhile romance with Dev had come to an abrupt end.

That she'd ended it herself was merely a technicality. She had read the warning signs and acted first, that's all. She was well aware that wanting something or someone you can't have was not only a waste of time and emotion, it was self-destructive.

She and Carmen and Mark and a few others among their many foster sisters and brothers had managed to develop a finely honed sense of their own self-preservation, but she'd seen far too many others who hadn't. When you didn't anticipate rejection, it arrived as a devastating surprise, breaking your heart and your spirit. Though rejection remained painful when expected, at least the hideous element of surprise was eliminated. Knowing what was coming gave you a chance to take some control, to avoid the passive victim role. To Gillian, that meant a lot. It meant everything.

So she'd broken up with Dev before he could break up with her, and she hadn't looked back. Not until now.

Now unleashed and unbidden, a hundred images tumbled through her mind, all images of Devlin Brennan. Dr. Swoon, Mark called him. Cool, good-looking Dev was definitely a man to swoon over. He had thick, dark brown hair and deep blue eyes framed by dark lashes and brows. Gillian pictured him smiling, frowning, looking thoughtful. Looking amorous. His face was more than merely handsome, his slightly irregular nose and full generous mouth made it interesting, as well.

She remembered the sound of his laugh, the way he closed his eyes when he was about to kiss her. How he looked when he stepped out of the shower, water sluicing over his hard, muscular body. At thirty-one, he still had the wiry athletic build of the track star and swimmer he'd been throughout his high school and college years.

Gillian swallowed dryly as the video in her mind continued to play, featuring Dev as the leading man. He was extremely intelligent, but he tended to downplay it. Though he'd never mentioned the facts himself, others had told her that Devlin Brennan had graduated near the top of his medical school class and was now winning rave reviews as a senior orthopedic resident at the medical center. He had a laconic sense of humor and a gift for making friends. His smooth sexuality was a natural draw to women, guaranteeing him anyone he wanted. For a brief time he'd wanted Gillian...

"Mama, mama!" Ashley squealed, and Carmen carried her over to Gillian who took the baby on her lap.

"I think Mama is the only word you know, isn't that right, cutie pie?" Mark playfully asked Ashley.

"She's only eleven months old and she makes lots of sounds and knows the meanings of some other words," Carmen chided, coming to Ashley's defense. "You can't expect her to recite the Gettysburg Address."

"Carmen, honey, I don't expect *anyone* to recite the Gettysburg Address," said Mark.

"'Fourscore and seven years ago...'" Carmen promptly launched into a complete recitation. Gillian and Mark applauded when she finished.

Carmen bowed. "I had to memorize it in sixth grade or lose recess privileges. Since recess was the only part of school I liked, I learned it fast."

"I can sing the entire score of 'My Fair Lady,' 'The King and I' and 'Camelot,' just to name a few," boasted Mark. "Shall I?"

"You wouldn't dare!" shrieked Carmen.

Gillian laughed, caressing Ashley's thick dark brown hair, so like Devlin's in color and texture. She gazed into the baby's gorgeous blue eyes, which were alert and bright and framed by dark lashes and well-shaped brows. Just like Dev's.

Ashley was a pretty baby who would grow into a strikingly attractive woman, her good looks her father's legacy to the daughter he would never know. From the moment she'd realized she was pregnant, just a week after engineering her preemptive breakup with Devlin, Gillian had been convinced secrecy was her only option.

But now—

A knock sounded at the door, abruptly ending their laughter.

"What if it's *him?*" whispered Mark.

"We'll deal with it," Gillian said firmly.

She started to the door, Ashley in her arms. "We can't sit in here cowering every time there is a knock at the door."

Brave words, but her heartbeat was hammering in her ears. When she opened the door to see Dev, his brother-in-law, and a beautiful young brunette standing between them, her pulses speeded into overdrive.

"Hi." Devlin smiled at her.

Gillian immediately recognized his social smile, the one he bestowed on the public at large. Having once been the recipient of his private, intimate smiles, she could tell the difference and felt oddly cheated by this impersonal one.

"We're taking a break and going out for a late lunch," said Dev. "Would you like to join us?"

"You're all invited," Cade said heartily, his gaze sweeping the room. "My treat."

Gillian cast a questioning glance at Devlin.

"My brother-in-law is a real neighborly sort of guy," Dev drawled. "Even toward *my* neighbors."

"I'm Kylie Austin, Devlin's sister." The young woman spoke up, smiling at Gillian. "Your baby is adorable."

"Thank you." Gillian studied Kylie. Her resemblance to little Ashley was startling. The same coloring, the same delicate features, plus the distinctive dark Brennan hair and blue eyes. It wasn't hard to imagine Ashley looking like her aunt Kylie when she was all grown up. "It's nice to meet you," Gillian said politely. "And thanks for the invitation, but we've already eaten."

"Is there anything you need?" Cade persisted. "From the store for the baby?"

Gillian looked at him, feeling a sickening wave of anxiety churn within her as she observed Cade staring fixedly at Ashley. It was as if he knew! But he couldn't be aware of her baby's relationship to Devlin Brennan, she silently argued. Dev himself didn't know.

"We don't need anything." Gillian knew she sounded nervous and tried to cover it by smiling widely. "But thank you for asking. I appreciate neighborliness." Her face felt as if it might crack, her smile was so wide. "Uh, goodbye."

She started to close the door. To her relief, Kylie and Cade started to walk toward the elevator. But not Devlin.

"Gillian." He angled his way to stand in the doorjamb.

"What?" She hadn't meant to snap, but that's how it came out.

"I feel I should explain." Devlin smiled wryly. "My brother-in-law is one of those take-charge types who feels compelled to take charge of whoever he happens to be around. When he sees a young woman with a child, he feels he should offer them food or something, I guess." He shrugged.

"You want to make it clear that this invitation wasn't your idea? Duly noted." His insouciance vexed her, though she knew she should be feeling relieved. Whatever Cade Austin's suspicions, Dev clearly had none. Gillian sucked in her cheeks. "I don't need anything from you or your brother-in-law."

She started to close the door, despite Devlin's solid presence there. Perversely, he didn't move, not even when the edge of the door was touching him.

"I'm trying to close this door," Gillian said crossly.

"I noticed." Dev crossed his arms and relaxed against the frame, as if oblivious to the door pressing against him. "I wonder how determined you are. Will you give up and wait for me to leave? Or are you going to try to slam the door shut with me in it?"

"Gillian is not a violent person," Mark piped up. "Never fear, she won't close you in the door."

Devlin seemed to notice Mark for the first time. "And you are?"

"Hoping you'll leave, Dr. Brennan," Mark replied sarcastically.

"You're keeping your sister and brother-in-law waiting." Gillian heaved an impatient sigh. "And you're keeping us from…from—"

"Listening to the score of 'My Fair Lady,'" Carmen called. "So get lost, Devlin. Now!"

"Sorry for interrupting." Devlin looked down at Gillian, who assiduously avoided his eyes. But the baby grinned at him and flexed her little fingers.

"Are you trying to wave goodbye, little lady?" Impulsively, Dev offered her his finger and she closed her small fist around it. "Can you say 'bye-bye'?"

"Ashley makes lots of sounds and knows the meanings of some words but the only one she actually seems to say in context is Mama," Mark said, sauntering over to join them at the door. "Not that she's stupid or anything, but she's not even a year old and you can't expect her to recite the Gettysburg Address, now can you?" He subjected Devlin to a scorching once-over, his gaze lingering on certain strategic areas.

"No, indeed," agreed Devlin hastily, his eyes widening. "Well, see you around, I guess." He disengaged his finger from Ashley who was trying to carry it to her mouth to sample.

"Say bye-bye to your new neighbor, Ashley," cooed Mark.

"Ba," said Ashley.

"Not bad." Devlin patted her tiny arm. "Close enough to 'bye. Keep practicing, Ashley, you'll get it."

He left, and Gillian quickly slammed the door shut. The sound reverberated throughout the hall.

"I think Dreamy Doctor Devlin was afraid I had designs on him." Mark was scornful. "He is hot, I'll grant you that, but I would never fall for the rat who abandoned my pregnant sister!"

"He didn't abandon me," Gillian came immediately to Dev's defense. "He didn't even know I was pregnant."

"And now he's living right across the hall from his own secret child!" Carmen moaned. "I can't believe it. It's a coincidence that only happens in a soap opera, but somehow it's happened to you, Gilly."

"And after all you did to keep Ashley a secret from him, it's a coincidence that strikes me as a particularly unfair twist of fate," said Mark.

"Nothing new there," Carmen said trenchantly. "Since when has fate been anything but unfair to the likes of us?"

"*I* think we've been incredibly lucky," Gillian countered, carrying Ashley to the toy-filled playpen by the window. She set the baby in it, handing her a bright scarlet teddy bear. "We all ended up at the Sinsel foster home, didn't we? That was a fantastic stroke of luck. We found each other there and became like a real family—probably *better* than a real family because they can't choose their relatives, but we did when we chose each other."

"Oh, no! Not her Pollyanna routine again." Mark groaned. "Carmen, stop her, please, I'm starting to feel queasy."

Gillian smiled at his dramatics. "You know I'm right."

"I know you're optimistic to the point of dementia at times," Mark retorted. "Is it any wonder why we got a divorce?"

The three of them laughed, and little Ashley watched them, chiming in with her own merry squeal.

"We're lucky to have each other," Carmen conceded. "But

having Devlin Brennan living so close to Ashley is like that fairy tale where the uninvited wicked fairy crashes the party. Something bad is sure to result. That brother-in-law of his already has me spooked. The way he was staring at the baby, the way he asked if you needed anything..." Her voice trailed off. "It was like he was ready to accept you as a family responsibility. As if he knows the truth about Devlin and Ashley, Gilly."

"There is no way he could know a thing," Gillian insisted, refusing to listen to her own anxiety expressed aloud.

"Unless he's psychic." Carmen's dark eyes grew round. "What if he is?"

"What if he isn't, but happens to be very familiar with Devlin Brennan's past history?" Mark speculated. "Suppose Ashley isn't the first little Brennan crawling around unacknowledged by her daddy? Maybe the handsome doctor is a walking sperm bank with kids by different women all over the place. Those children could be instantly recognizable to the brother-in-law because he knows to look for them."

"A multitude of Brennan spawns! Sounds like something out of that movie *Village of the Damned,* where all the kids looked alike." Carmen shuddered. "Of course, they were aliens, but still!"

"I can see it's time for me to reel you both back from the tangents you've gone off on." Gillian rolled her eyes heavenward. "I'm absolutely certain that Cade Austin is not psychic and I'm equally sure that Devlin Brennan hasn't populated the world with his look-alike offspring. In fact, nobody suspects anything except you two, whose imaginations have always been way too active."

"You hope," Mark said darkly.

Gillian shot him a quelling glance. "I'm going to move out of here as soon as I can find another place. But while I'm in this apartment, I refuse to live in a state of panic wondering what Devlin Brennan or his brother-in-law might or might not know. The truth is, neither of them know or care anything about Ashley or me."

"Dadadadada," Ashley sang as she tossed her toys around the playpen.

"She said 'Dada,'" Carmen gasped. "It's like she knows we're talking about her father!"

"Carmen, if you say Ashley is psychic I'll confiscate your deck of tarot cards *and* your palm-reading instruction book." Gillian was stern. "You're starting to take that paranormal stuff way too seriously."

"I'm sure the baby is just babbling," Mark said tactfully. "It's not as if she knows any word for daddy. Or what a daddy is, let alone who he is."

"Join the club, Ashley. Daddies fall into the category of unsolved mysteries for all of us." Carmen looked glum.

Ashley pulled herself to her feet by hanging on to the bars of the playpen and threw the red bear over the side. "Dada," she pronounced forcefully.

"Bear," Gillian corrected, handing her the toy.

"Gilly, you said you haven't seen Devlin since you broke up with him." A worried-looking Carmen was unable to let the topic drop. "Suppose seeing you again starts him thinking and he starts counting backward. Suppose he notices that Ashley looks just like his sister, not to mention himself. I bet our little Ash is a dead ringer for their baby pictures."

"I honestly think the brother-in-law has already realized that," added Mark.

"I honestly don't," Gillian was quick to refute. "Anyway, Devlin Brennan is too interested in having a good time with all his friends and admirers to give Ashley or me a single thought."

"You hope again," Mark muttered under his breath.

Gillian heard him. "I *know* he won't," she said firmly.

TWO

Gillian was wrong.

Devlin did think about her, especially when he was alone in his apartment, right across the hall from hers. His mind would drift from the plot of "I Dream of Jeannie" or "Three's Company" or whatever rerun was airing on TV to ponder why Gillian had ended their relationship so abruptly, so irrevocably, all those months ago.

He acknowledged that he had done his part to keep the split irrevocable. After Gillian told him it was all over between them—offering only a maddeningly ambiguous "this isn't working out" as the reason why—he hadn't said a word or done a thing to make her change her mind. He hadn't called her or attempted to see her.

Was that what she'd expected him to do? To go crawling to her, begging to be allowed back in her life? The prospect appalled him, and he rejected it now as he had then. But suppose he had made one phone call to her in the days following their breakup? Just one. A single phone call hardly constituted crawling or begging. Twenty months later, Devlin finally conceded that point.

He frowned, remembering the night she'd called it quits. After dropping her bombshell, Gillian had gone home, leaving him alone to absorb the shock. And what a shock it was... For the first time in his charmed, blessed, golden life he'd been dumped!

Compounding his woe was his lack of anyone to share it. He didn't consider confiding anything about the breakup to any member of his social circle. Why bother when he could easily predict their responses?

The attitude of the jaundiced nonromantics in the group would be a cavalier "so what?" The others would proclaim that it was about time he felt the sting of rejection, that everybody else in the world had been dumped at one time or another and now, *finally*, it was Devlin Brennan's turn.

He could have told his sister. Kylie definitely would've provided sympathy, but she might have expected him to cry on her shoulder while she offered words of solace and advice. That was too ghastly to contemplate. He was the big brother, ever cool, ever confident, and he wasn't about to relinquish his own image of himself.

So he'd opted for silence, answering the occasional question about Gillian Bailey with a nonchalant, "Haven't seen her for a while." Everybody who knew Devlin Brennan knew what that meant—he had moved on to another woman. Details weren't requested or supplied.

"For every man who breaks hearts, there is a woman who is his match," declared Holly Casale, his friend since their early med school days, who was currently completing her residency in psychiatry here at the hospital. Devlin did not appreciate her diagnosis or prophecy or whatever that cryptic observation of hers was supposed to be.

He didn't consider himself a heartbreaker; he simply wasn't ready to settle down, a point he made to any woman who tried to assume otherwise. He was honest and up-front about his commitment to staying uncommitted, which was hardly characteristic of those deceptive smoothies who *deserved* the title of heartbreaker.

As for Gillian breaking his heart, that premise was laughable. His heart hadn't even been bruised by her rejection, Dev assured himself. He'd set out to prove that being dumped wasn't the trauma all those sad songs and movies and books proclaimed it to be.

He forgot all about Gillian Bailey. He continued with his life, which was full and busy with his fourth-year residency in orthopedics, a specialty that continually fascinated him, with his many friends and with various women who provided him with sex whenever he wanted it.

Funny how he hadn't wanted it lately.

That was because he was taking a hiatus from sex, Devlin reminded himself. He'd seen some therapist-guru on a talk show who extolled periods of chastity as time to recharge energy and creativity. Dev didn't run that particular theory by Holly, but decided that his body had chosen to be chaste for a while.

Didn't he feel more energetic and creative?

Seated in front of his television set, Devlin proceeded to channel-surf through eighty-six channels, pointing his remote like a divining rod. Nothing caught his interest, and his thoughts drifted back to Gillian.

He allowed himself to admit that in spite of his busy, full life he hadn't *completely* forgotten about her. He'd given her an occasional thought during the past twenty months. When he had learned about Gillian's marriage, only a couple weeks after their breakup, he had been stunned. It stood to reason that she must have been dating her future husband all the while she'd been with him. Or maybe her three-month fling with him had been a rebound romance for her, something to pass the time until the groom-elect came through with a wedding ring.

Either notion rankled.

Dev vaguely recalled getting drunk with some of his buddies around that time and referring to Gillian as a "two-timing slut." The memory, dim as it was, now made him cringe because it implied that her quickie marriage bothered him, and of course, it had not. He'd had a good laugh when Holly Casale told him that he was "in denial" and ought to acknowledge his repressed feelings.

Repressed? Him? Devlin had found the "shrink jargon" hilarious and told Holly so. As a would-be Freudian, she'd shaken her head silently and tried to look inscrutable.

His thoughts circled back to Gillian. Who was now divorced. Obviously she'd shed her husband with the same hasty ease she had acquired him. And now she was a single mother with a baby girl.

The baby, little Ashley. He wasn't the type to go ga-ga over babies, but she was very cute. Cade, his brother-in-law, had certainly been captivated by that baby. He'd mentioned her several times over their weekend visit and yesterday, too, when Kylie had called to get an old friend's address.

Dev had kidded Kylie that Cade's interest in the baby across the hall was indicative of his desire to become a daddy, that she was going to find herself pregnant sooner rather than later. Kylie countered that Cade's interest in the neighbor child stemmed from his concern for his younger sister, currently in the middle of a bitter divorce and solely responsible for her baby. According to Kylie, Cade possessed a kind of global sense of elder brother responsibility for the children of struggling single mothers.

Devlin guessed it made sense, Cade being Cade and all.

Truth to tell, it was something of a relief to know that his brother-in-law was hyperresponsible. That was exactly the kind of husband every brother wanted for his kid sister. If Kylie were pregnant, there was no question that Cade would take care of her, would stick with her and their child. Unlike Gillian's husband, who'd been quick to split after the baby was born.

Undoubtedly that creep hadn't been much help during her pregnancy, either, Devlin concluded, and remembered the one and only time he had seen Gillian pregnant.

He'd spotted her during a rare chance encounter in the hospital cafeteria. It had been late in her pregnancy and her tiny frame seemed ready to topple forward from the bulk of her swollen abdomen. Dev had cracked to the gang at his lunch table that she looked like an overinflated balloon and probably would've made another witticism or two except he caught Holly Casale observing him with her most annoying psychoanalytic stare. So he'd lapsed into silence and purposefully directed his gaze away from the very pregnant Gillian.

Had it been Holly or someone else who'd informed him when Gillian had given birth? He had merely shrugged his indifference. What was he supposed to do, go visit her on the maternity floor with a bunch of mylar balloons? He hadn't, of course. She was married and a mother and lived her life in another universe from his.

And now it seemed their separate worlds had intersected, thanks to the random assignments made by the housing department. It was weird but entirely coincidental, a bit of computer-generated idiocy. He and Gillian could've—should've—shared a laugh about it except she had been inexplicably hostile upon learning they were neighbors.

And they hadn't seen each other since that day. Out of sight, out of mind, Dev reminded himself. It was more than a cliché, it was downright good advice.

He turned his attention back to the TV set, bypassing all the current reality based dramas and sitcoms for a black and white rerun from the early sixties. "The Dick Van Dyke Show." Relaxing, he settled back to enjoy a half hour of vicarious living in a far more simple era.

In the apartment across the hall from him, Ashley Joy Morrow wouldn't stop crying. Gillian knew the baby was teething, and she had done everything recommended in the infant and child care manual to soothe her. But nothing had worked and finally, in desperation, she called her foster mother, Dolly Sinsel, in Detroit.

"Do you think there could be something really wrong with her, Mom?" Gillian asked anxiously. "Should I take her to the emergency room?"

"She's not hot, not cold, not wet, not pulling at her ear, not throwing up, her nose isn't stuffy, her stomach isn't hard, her muscles aren't rigid," Dolly Sinsel recited the lack of non-symptoms that Gillian had relayed to her. "That baby isn't sick, Gillian. Sounds to me like she's just overexcited or overtired. Put her in her crib with a bottle of juice, close the bedroom door, and then you sit down and turn on some music or the TV."

"You mean, just ignore her? Keep her in there alone and crying?" Gillian shivered, remembering how it felt to be small and scared and all alone. "Ashley has never cried much and never like this. She—"

"She is exerting her independence. Babies need to cry to exercise their lungs," Dolly said calmly. "Now put Ashley in the crib and make yourself a nice cup of tea, honey. You two need to unwind away from each."

Gillian attempted to follow the advice. After all, who knew kids better than Dolly Sinsel, who'd raised four children of her own and taken in hundreds of foster children down through the years? Gillian had lived with the Sinsels from the age of twelve until her graduation from high school and had never seen her foster parents fazed by anything. Or anyone. Not even the most hardcore adolescent veterans of the foster care system.

Gillian still marveled at Mom and Dad Sinsel's unshakable aplomb as they dealt again and again with the young fire-setters, the kid thieves and liars, the screamers and marauders who'd been placed under their roof by the State of Michigan. The Sinsels were impervious to upset and insult, and while Gillian was able to emulate their attitude in her career as a medical social worker, she couldn't muster such calm in dealing with Ashley. When Ashley was upset, so was her mother; when Ashley was happy or excited or fearful, her mommy was, too.

"Grandma Dolly says you'd rather be alone," Gillian told Ashley as she carried the howling baby into the small bedroom filled with toys and baby furniture and bright posters of cartoon figures on the wall.

She put Ashley into her crib with its cheery Winnie the Pooh sheets and handed her a bottle of apple juice. Shrieking her displeasure, Ashley pulled herself to her feet and threw the bottle out of the crib. Distressed, Gillian put it back in, then quickly left the room, closing the door behind her.

While Ashley's roars of infantile fury echoed in her head, Gillian turned on her TV set. Nothing claimed her interest, not even the hurricane currently being tracked in the Caribbean by the Weather Channel. She decided to forego the suggested cup of tea. Her stomach was in knots and her throat felt too tight to swallow. The baby's cries continued unabated, sounding less angry and more and more piteous.

Gillian looked bleakly at her watch. Only six and a half minutes had elasped but it felt like an eternity. Poor little Ashley, exiled to her crib. Gillian wondered if she felt unwanted, alone in the dark world without anyone who cared.

It was a horrible feeling that Gillian knew all too well. To imagine Ashley having to experience such despair was unbearable. She rose to her feet and fairly flew into the nursery. With all due respect to Dolly Sinsel, isolating the baby felt all wrong.

After all, it wasn't as if Ashley had tried to burn down the house or stone a neighbor's dog; she didn't need a stint in solitary confinement as punishment. Ashley was cutting a tooth and she was uncomfortable. Why shouldn't she cry?

Gillian arrived at the cribside just as Ashley succeeded in pulling the rubber nipple off the top of her bottle and turning it upside down, emptying the juice. The baby was so shocked by her sudden soaking, she stopped crying and looked up at her mother with astonished blue eyes.

"Oh, Ashley, you're all wet and so is the bed!" Gillian was dismayed.

Ashley was furious that she'd been doused. She began to howl again.

"It's all right, sweetheart." Gillian picked her up and cuddled her. "I'll put you in nice dry jammies and then I'll change the sheet."

She sponged the sticky juice from the baby, then dried and dressed her in fresh, aqua cotton footed pajamas. And discovered that there were no more clean crib sheets. The other six were in the laundry basket waiting to be taken to the washer and dryer in the basement of the building.

"I'm sorry, Ash. I didn't realize how low we were on crib sheets and we've been so busy after work, I haven't gotten around to doing the laundry," Gillian lamented aloud.

Ashley babbled a few syllables in response. Gillian was so relieved that the baby had stopped crying, she felt almost giddy. "We'll go next door and ask Shelly or Heather if they'll stay with you while I go downstairs to do a load of laundry now, okay? You like Shelly and Heather, they're operating room nurses at the hospital, and they gave you some ice cream the other day, remember?"

She carried Ashley into the hall and walked to the apartment on their left, talking to her daughter all the while. Gillian knocked long and loud before she conceded that neither Shelly nor Heather was there.

Gillian sighed. She'd hoped to avoid having to tote Ashley and the laundry basket down to the basement laundry room but with no one to watch the baby, she had no other choice. She wasn't about to leave Ashley alone in the apartment and she hadn't met any other neighbors yet... Her eyes flicked to the apartment door across the hall from her own, Devlin Brennan's door. Assistance from that quarter was not an option. She would never ask *him* to watch her baby, not even for a moment.

And then the door opened and Devlin stepped into the hall.

Gillian froze. It was as if her thoughts had conjured him up! She stood stock-still, clutching Ashley, and staring at him. He was wearing a faded Detroit Lions T-shirt and jeans, simple and common enough clothes but the way they showcased his male attributes—his muscular arms and broad chest, his long lean thighs and flat belly—evoked a reaction within Gillian that was neither simple nor common. His face was darkened by the shadow of a beard, reminding Gillian of how sexy he looked in the morning when he awakened, unshaven and aroused.

She scowled at the renegade memory. This was no time to recall anything about her three-month lapse of sanity that had characterized her affair with Devlin Brennan.

Her dour expression did not go unnoticed. "I bet the bubonic plague got a less hostile welcome," Dev said dryly.

"I, uh, I was just seeing if Shelly and Heather are home." Gillian started toward her apartment. His mere presence threatened her.

"Neither one is there. They're both working till midnight for the next few weeks. I saw their names on the OR schedule," he added.

"Oh."

"I heard knocking out here." Devlin felt obliged to explain his appearance. She was looking at him as if he were a serial killer closing in on his latest target—which happened to be her. "Anything I can do?"

Gillian shook her head no. She was almost to her door....

Devlin crossed the hall to block her entry, positioning himself in the frame the same way he'd done on the day he had moved into the building. But that time, at least, she'd been inside with Carmen and Mark as allies. Now Mark was back in L.A., Carmen was in Detroit, and here she was, stuck in the hall with no buffers against Devlin's intimidating presence.

"No friends around as backup this time, huh?" He arched his dark brows.

Gillian was disconcerted that their thoughts were so similar. It was almost as alarming as being trapped with him like this, face-to-face with their child in her arms.

"I've been thinking about those friends of yours," Devlin continued. "How did they know who I was? You never introduced me to them and I know I hadn't met them before."

Gillian said nothing.

"Did you tell them about me?" Devlin pressed.

He looked quite pleased by the possibility that she'd been discussing him with others. Such egotism deserved to be quashed! "I told them that some jerk I used to date had moved in across the hall," she said with asperity. "When you showed up at the door, they drew their own conclusions. And they're more than friends, they're my family," she added proudly.

"Your family?"

"You find it so hard to believe that I could have a family?" Gillian was instantly, angrily on the defensive.

"No, of course not, but—"

"But you visually stereotyped Carmen and Mark and decided that we don't fit together genetically. Well, so what? We can't all be whitebread chromosonal clones, like you and your sister."

And Ashley. Gillian gulped. Why had she ever introduced the potentially explosive topic of genetics and family? Being in Devlin Brennan's presence seemed to scramble her wits and remove the usual barrier of caution between her thoughts and words. All the more reason why she must avoid him. "*Move,* Devlin. I have things I have to do and—"

"Are you all adopted or something?" Devlin studied her with an intensity that unnerved her.

She looked away from him, focusing on Ashley, who was gnawing on her tiny fist. "We were unadoptable but we did share a foster home together for a number of years." *Stop staring at me,* she silently ordered.

If he received her telepathic command, he did not obey it. He continued to gaze thoughtfully at her. "Thinking back on it, you never mentioned your family while we were seeing each other. Not a word. I don't even know the names of—"

"There are too many names to name," Gillian said flippantly. "At one time or another I was probably a foster sister to everybody who passed through Family Services in Detroit."

"But how did you end up in foster care? What happened to your—"

"Devlin, these questions are pointless. And too late," she couldn't resist adding.

"Maybe I should've asked them before," he conceded. "And maybe you should've volunteered some information, Gillian."

"Maybe I sensed that learning my family history wasn't exactly a priority of yours," Gillian retorted defensively. Telling her family history was never a priority of hers; she was ashamed of it. "As I remember, you wanted to do other things than talk."

"True, but we sure spent plenty of time talking anyway." Devlin smiled slightly. "I told you about my folks and my sister and all the places we lived, among other things. For that first month we were together, I sometimes wondered if we were ever going to do anything but talk."

"I know, I know. You expected sex on the first date and I held out for a whole month. Well, if you were so bored, you shouldn't have called me back."

"I didn't say I was bored, did I? I liked talking with you. You're the only other person I've ever met who knows as much about TV shows as I do. The only other person I've ever met who's seen every single episode of 'Lancelot Link, Secret Chimp' and remembers all the plots. Or at least the only one who'll own up to it."

"Well, you're the only other person I've ever met who knows all the words to every song in the five volume set of TV theme songs," countered Gillian. "You actually used to ask to hear it. Most people beg for mercy if I try to play it."

"I ended up buying my own five volume set," Dev confessed wryly. "I missed listening to yours when you took it back."

"I bet your TV theme songs aren't kept anywhere near your ultracool CD collection with all the right titles. After all, you like to pretend you're such a blues fan."

"I *am* a blues fan!" insisted Devlin.

"Sure you are." Gillian arched her brows. "And I'm Lancelot Link, Secret Chimp's secretary."

"Everybody but you pays homage to the blues, Gillian. The blues are universally cool. You are the first and only person I've ever known who says they're dull and dreary."

"Which they are. I like to listen to cheerful, peppy music."

"Cheerful, peppy music is insipid." Devlin grinned. They'd had this pseudo-argument many times before.

"You're saying that the 'Brady Bunch' theme is insipid?" Gillian feigned shock. "That's blasphemy!"

He held up his hands in mock surrender. "Guilty as charged."

They both laughed. Ashley regarded them curiously and said something that sounded like "Glx."

Devlin smiled at the baby. "Are you offering an opinion, Ashley? What does 'glx' mean?"

Gillian stared from the child to the man, and apprehension shivered through her. *What in the world was she doing, laughing it up with Devlin Brennan, her daughter's father?* Who had no idea that he was her daughter's father!

And she fully intended to keep it that way. She'd known from the moment that the stick in the home pregnancy kit had changed colors that she was going to have and to raise her baby alone. Mark and Carmen and the others might tease her about being an optimist, but Gillian knew that she was actually a realist.

Which was why she'd chosen not to involve anyone else in her pregnancy and Ashley's existence, except her beloved "fosters" who'd already proven themselves to be loyal and trustworthy. She knew they wouldn't hurt her, and she was equally certain that Devlin Brennan would. So she hadn't given him that chance. Nor would she.

Ashley started to bounce in Gillian's arms, leaning toward Devlin. He interpreted the baby's movements as a bid to go to him and held out his arms, ready to take her.

Gillian was not about to hand over the baby to the man who'd fathered her. She pulled back, tightening her arms protectively around her child. "Good night, Devlin."

Her voice, her expression, was cold enough to freeze fire. Devlin stared at her, baffled by her abrupt shift in mood, from laughing to glaring. From accessible to icily remote. He placed a hand on Gillian's shoulder. She was rigid with tension.

Their eyes met. "Why?" he asked quietly.

A flash flood of fear surged through her. *What had she given away? He couldn't have figured out the truth about Ashley, could he?* "W-what do you mean?"

"Why did you break up with me?" He amazed himself by asking the question he'd vowed never to ask her.

Her panic dissipated. There was nothing to worry about, his question was all about ego. His own sizable one. "Like you care." Gillian laughed coldly.

"Maybe I'm curious. After all, you never gave me much of a reason why." Even to himself, he sounded frustrated and accusing, but he couldn't stop now. "Until that night, you never even gave a hint that you were unhappy or—dissatisfied. Right out of the blue, you said 'things aren't working out' and you left me."

"You really expected a detailed in-depth analysis?" Gillian

mocked. "Is that what you do every time you break up with some-one, Dev?"

Devlin thought of all the relationships he had ended down through the years. There had never been a detailed in-depth analysis exploring the whys and wherefores of breaking up, not even one. His modus operandi was simply to never call the woman again and to avoid returning her calls. His rejectees eventually got the hint—it was over. It was up to them to figure out why, if they wanted to.

Now he was the one who had been rejected for no discernible reason.

What goes around, comes around, he recalled his late grand-mother Brennan warning in hushed ominous tones. It seemed old Grandma had been on to something.

"Point taken," he murmured. "Just one question before we close this discussion for good. Why are you so angry with me, Gillian?"

Gillian flinched. "How can you even ask me that?" she blurted.

"Because I don't know. You broke up with me because you wanted to, so why should you be mad at me? Unless you're bitter toward all men since your divorce?"

Gillian stared at him, wondering what to say. Far from being embittered by her divorce, she tended to forget all about it, just as she tended to forget she had ever been married. Certainly she and Mark had never lived together as man and wife. He'd never even visited her during those months they had been legally wed because round trips to and from Los Angeles were beyond both their budg-ets. Mark had saved his money to afford plane fare to see Ashley as a newborn. No, she could never view Mark as either her husband or her ex-husband. He was her sweet, loyal, foster brother and always would be.

But Devlin had asked a logical, valid question, one that required a response to allay suspicion. Luckily, he'd also supplied her with the answer.

"Yes, I guess I am bitter toward all men since my divorce," she echoed nervously. "I, uh, hadn't realized it until now. I wasn't even aware I was acting that way."

"Well, trust me, you are. I take it the divorce wasn't your idea?"

"I don't want to talk about it."

"I can respect that. I have an aunt and uncle who were divorced years ago and they still take every opportunity to regale anyone who will listen with all the details.''

"I'll never do that," Gillian pledged. Never had a promise been so easy to make.

"Do you share joint custody of the baby?" Devlin asked.

"No!" Gillian quickly turned aside, as if to shield her child from him. "Ashley is mine! No more questions," she added sternly.

"Okay." He moved away from the door but seemed reluctant to leave. "Now that we've ascertained that your hostility isn't personal, can I offer whatever help you needed from Shelly and Heather?"

Devlin looked from little Ashley to her vigilant, wide-eyed mother. "You did need something, didn't you? And don't automatically say no," he added. "I don't think you and the baby were paying a social call at this hour, were you?"

Gillian stole a glance at him. She couldn't fathom why, but it seemed that he wasn't about to be fobbed off. And since he now believed that *her hostility toward him wasn't personal,* she really ought to foster that delusion. Making him suspicious of her could be disastrous. Hesitantly, reluctantly, she explained her laundry dilemma.

"It's just as well the girls weren't here to stay with the baby. You shouldn't go down to the laundry room alone at night, Gillian." Devlin frowned. "The security in the building is too lax to ensure safety."

Gillian had to smile at that misplaced concern. "Compared to some of the places I've lived in, this place is as secure as a fortress. But if...if you want to do something, you could carry my laundry basket downstairs," she dared add. Asking him for anything was difficult for her, but since he'd insisted on offering aid she might as well take him up on it.

"Why don't I do the crib sheets while you stay in your apartment with the baby?" Devlin suggested instead. "Don't look so shocked. I mastered the use of washers and dryers years ago from sheer necessity."

He could tell that she didn't want to accept any help at all from him. Though she kept her face poker-straight, her eyes were expressive, revealing her internal struggle. Gillian needed his assistance, and she hated that she did. She desperately wanted to say no—but the baby had to have clean, dry crib sheets.

Her maternal instincts won out. "Okay, you can do the crib sheets," Gillian said grudgingly.

"Thank you, gracious lady," quipped Devlin. "Doing laundry for you is both a privilege and a dream come true."

Gillian fought a smile because she knew he was trying to make her smile and she didn't want to grant him even that small victory. "I'll get you some quarters," she said repressively.

Devlin told her not to bother, that he could afford to feed the machines with his own quarters, but Gillian was insistent. She did not want to be beholden to him in any way, not even for a few quarters.

Ninety minutes later Dev carried the seven freshly laundered crib sheets to Gillian's apartment. Inside, he could hear the baby howling at the top of her lungs and when Gillian opened the door, she looked tired and frazzled and on the verge of tears herself. She held the flush-faced, shrieking Ashley in her arms.

"I don't know what's wrong with her," Gillian blurted, too desperate and worried to exert her usual control. "I know she's getting a tooth—see, right here, her top left incisor—but she never had trouble when her four front teeth came in."

"Incisors can be tough to cut." Devlin recalled that fact from a long-ago child development class during his med school pediatric rotation. He rubbed his finger over the swollen bud in the baby's mouth. Ashley tried to chomp down on his finger. "Have you tried rubbing ice on her gum?"

"Yes. My foster mother suggested whiskey, but I didn't have any so I tried some of Carmen's cold beer. Nothing's given her any relief."

Devlin frowned thoughtfully. "Why don't I get my bag? I'd like to check her ears."

"She hasn't been tugging at her ears and her nose isn't stuffy," Gillian replied quickly. "And she doesn't feel feverish."

"Ear infections in babies can be tricky. Sometimes they don't touch their ears or even seem congested. If Ashley has a fever, it's only a slight one, a degree or two, but I'd still like to check..." He placed his hand on the baby's head. Her dark curls were damp from perspiration. "I'll go get my bag."

He was back with his black medical bag before Gillian could protest. Not that she would have, not now. She wanted her child to be seen by a doctor, even if that doctor happened to be Devlin Brennan.

They sat together on the sofa, Ashley on Gillian's lap, while Devlin checked the baby's temperature with a thermometer that he slipped under her arm.

Gillian was trembling as she watched. "I didn't think she was sick. I—I just thought she was fussy because of her tooth." Tears stung her eyes. "Does she have a fever?"

"A low-grade one. One hundred point two." Devlin replaced the thermometer and took out an instrument to look in her ear. "I'm looking for bunny rabbits, Ashley," he said as he turned on the light and cupped her head with his hand. "If I remember correctly, that's standard pediatric lingo during ear exams," he added dryly to Gillian.

"Her pediatrician says that same thing." Gillian swallowed. "Except sometimes she'll say puppy dogs."

"Has Ashley had many ear infections?"

"A few.

Devlin nodded. "Okay. Let's take a look at her ears." He was Dr. Brennan now— "Any puppy dogs hiding in here, Ashley?"—resorting to standard pediatric lingo as he looked inside the baby's ear.

Ashley screamed and wriggled and tried to get away. "Oh, yeah." Devlin took one more look as the baby continued to struggle. "The tympanic membrane is erythematous, all right."

"What does that mean?" Gillian cried, horrified.

"Her ear is red," Devlin translated, his smile slightly sheepish. "Sorry, I didn't mean to sound like an alarmist."

"Poor Ashley! She's sick and she's been in pain and I...I—" Gillian broke off in a sob. "She seemed fine when I picked her up at the day care center this afternoon. She started crying after dinner and...and Mom said she was just exercising her lungs."

Devlin smiled. "Those Doctor Moms have some interesting theories. Look, Gillian, you can't blame yourself. Little kids get sick fast, and this isn't serious yet. I'll write a prescription for amoxicillin—she doesn't have a penicillin allergy, does she?"

"Not that I know of."

"I'll give her something for the fever and pain, too, so she can get some sleep. So you both can get some sleep," he amended.

"Make an appointment with your pediatrician for a follow-up visit, okay?"

Gillian redressed Ashley in her aqua footed pajamas. The baby clung to her, sniffling and casting an occasional glare at Devlin as he delved into his bag for his prescription pad.

"If looks could kill, I'd be on life support with the transplant team ready to claim my organs," he remarked, catching one of Ashley's particularly baleful glowers. "One of the main reasons why I hated my stint in pediatrics was that I didn't like being universally loathed by all those sick little kids who screamed when they saw a white coat coming."

Gillian paced the room with Ashley in her arms. "The medicine." She caught her lower lip between her teeth. "I—I'll have to take Ashley with me to pick it up at the drugstore."

Devlin stood up. "I think that's as close as you'll come to asking me to go get it for you, isn't it?"

She didn't meet his eyes. He was right, of course. She couldn't bring herself to ask him, though she wanted him, *needed* him, to do it.

Dev heaved an exasperated sigh. "Consider it done, Gillian."

He strode from the apartment and was back within half an hour with a bag from the hospital pharmacy. Ashley did not like the bubblegum-thick liquid medicine and promptly spit it out when her mother gave it to her.

"Time for me to show off one of the little tricks a warhorse of a pediatric nurse once showed me. Try this." Devlin held Ashley's small jaws open and funneled the medicine down her throat. He was nimble and swift, and the startled baby swallowed the dose before she could erupt in a howl of protest.

"You're really good at that." Gillian was impressed by his dexterity.

"Ashley was co-operating, weren't you, sugar?" He patted the baby's belly. Ashley eyed him suspiciously, then turned to her mother for comfort. Devlin watched Gillian cuddle the child close. "If you think she hated the amoxicillin, just wait till we try to get the ear drops into her. No self-respecting kid likes drops of any kind."

Ashley proved herself to be a self-respecting kid by attempting to ward off the ear drops, turning her head from side to side and flailing her arms and legs while shrieking her protests. But it was two adults against one small, albeit enraged baby, and her parents prevailed.

After another dose of liquid medicine for pain and fever, Ashley was more than ready to let Gillian rock her while she sucked on a bottle of juice. The rocking chair was in the living room—the baby's bedroom was too small to accommodate it—and while Gillian gave Ashley her bottle, Devlin sprawled on the sofa and observed them.

He was reluctant to leave and Gillian was too preoccupied with the baby to remember to tell him to get lost.

"You mentioned a day care center," he said, finally breaking the long silence. "Is it the one in the hospital for employees' kids?"

Gillian nodded, her eyes never leaving Ashley's face. The baby's eyelids were finally drooping and she seemed on the verge of falling asleep. "It's a good place." She spoke in a low voice, so as not to disturb Ashley. "She's been going there since she was a month old."

"You were on maternity leave till then?"

She nodded again. "I used my paid vacation time for the first two weeks and the rest was unpaid maternity leave. Then I had to go back to work." Gillian stared into space, looking weary and dispirited. "Our foster mother is dead set against day care centers. She thinks I should hire a sitter to stay home with the baby, but I can't afford it. When Mom hears that Ashley is sick, she'll blame the center. She calls them CDCs—Centers for Disease and Contagion."

"Hmm, a wordplay on the Center for Disease Control. Not a bad one, either," Devlin said lightly.

Gillian shot him a look. "It's wordplay I don't like to hear, not even as a joke. Not when my baby is spending eight hours a day there."

"You have nothing to worry about. The hospital day care center is fully accredited. I know plenty of people on staff whose kids go there. But if I may offer you a little advice, Gillian? Don't tell your mom that Ashley is sick. Spare yourself the CDC puns. What you don't need right now is an extended guilt trip."

"Mom Sinsel isn't like that," Gillian protested. "But...maybe I won't tell her about Ashley's ear infection just yet."

"No use worrying the dear lady," Devlin said dryly.

Gillian looked up, a smile curving the corners of her mouth. Her eyes met his. And held. Her heart seemed to jump into her throat and then plunge deep into the pit of her stomach. Was she imagining it? Or was Devlin Brennan looking at her as if...as if—

Her internal gyrations picked up speed. The brooding focus of his gaze, the intensity in his deep blue eyes, were unmistakably sexual. Gillian knew that look well. He'd directed it toward her before, countless times during those three fateful months they'd been together.

Rather than attempting to conceal his desire, he was allowing her to read it in his eyes, on his face. Involuntarily, her gaze fell to his lap and she saw the hard bulge straining against the well-worn denim of his jeans. He was making no attempt to conceal that visible evidence from her, either.

Before she could suppress it, Gillian felt her own immediate response deep within the feminine center of her. It was so intense it bordered on pain, but it was a sweet pain, a tantalizing erotic combination of pleasure and searing ache. Gillian gulped for breath.

In a swift sensually explicit flashback, she felt the passion that had burned between them surface once again. It had been fierce and honest and real. With Devlin, she'd experienced the kind of enthralling lovemaking that only results from a mutual combination of trust and desire.

A definite first for her. She had trusted him and wanted him and fallen deeply in love with him, dropping her guard and her vigilance as never before. And for a while, it had worked. She'd been blissfully happy—emotionally, sexually, and every other way there was to be happy.

Physically, they had been in total accord, from the desire that flared hot and deep between them to the sweet afterglow of mutual satisfaction. But there had been more than good sex between them. They'd had fun together out of bed, too, talking and laughing and teasing each other. Devlin's hours as an orthopedic resident were grueling and they'd spent much of his time off in his apartment where he could relax and unwind. Gillian had been content just to be with him, to lie beside him while he was sleeping, to be there when he awakened, hard and hungry and wanting her.

Wanting *sex,* she amended quickly. Any woman would have served his purpose; she simply happened to be the one who was there during those three months. Afterward, Devlin had no trouble finding others to take her place in his bed and in his life.

Gillian had heard all about her successors. Though the hospital's social work department was located in another wing from the orthopedic unit, the grapevine was extremely efficient, reaching all areas. Hospital gossip seemed to travel faster than the speed of sound, especially gossip about certain attractive, eligible bachelors.

Gillian remembered that time. The pain of wanting Devlin and not having him had been intense, but she had coped. She was accustomed to coping with pain—at least it was a familiar state. Happiness wasn't, not really. Her foster sister, Carmen Salazar, had said it best when she'd once confided, "Being happy scares the hell out of me."

Gillian understood all too well. As hard as she'd worked to overcome her troubled past, there were some lessons that were too deeply ingrained to be erased in only three months, however wonderful. Being wary of happiness, fearing its loss while waiting for it to be snatched away were only a few.

"You look scared to death." Devlin's eyes narrowed as he continued to watch her intently. "Are you still worried about the baby—or is it something else altogether?"

Agitated, Gillian began to rock the chair faster. She'd never credited Devlin with much emotional insight and he openly scoffed at what he deemed "those touchy-feely-guys-who-cry," but suddenly he seemed far too perceptive.

She resolutely withdrew, blocking the memories and fighting her need for him. Years of practice made her adept at emotional shutdowns.

"I'll put Ashley in her crib now. Thank you for all your help, Devlin." Gillian stood up, careful not to awaken the sleeping infant. "I'm sorry we intruded on your off-duty hours with a medical problem. I can manage now."

"No need for me to stick around, huh? In other words, *take off*."

She flushed. "If I sounded rude and ungrateful, I apologize."

"Can you make your tone any more impersonal, Gillian?" Devlin didn't move from his position on the sofa. "I'm half expecting you to offer to write me a check for making a house call."

Gillian's temper flared. "Exactly what do you want me to say and how am I expected to say it, Dev?" she whispered crossly.

"Put the baby to bed and we'll talk about it."

"We have nothing to say to each other, Devlin."

"Don't we?"

"No!" It was hard to sound forceful while whispering. She was at a definite disadvantage, trying not to disturb the baby while attempting to send Devlin on his way. It was imperative that she get him out of here before he could act on those impulsive amatory urges he'd suddenly developed. Because if she were to respond to him...

She glanced down at Ashley, sleeping peacefully in her arms. For her child's sake, for her own sake, she had to keep Devlin Brennan away. She would play the role of nasty bitch, if she had to. A man like Dev, with women falling all over him, would have no use for a woman who didn't treat him like a god.

"When I come back into this room, I expect you to be gone," Gillian said coldly, all signs of appreciation and friendliness eradicated from her tone, from her expression.

She carried Ashley into her bedroom and laid the baby in her crib, staying there for a long time watching the child sleep. When she finally returned to the living room, it was empty. Devlin had gone.

Well, she'd figured that Devlin Brennan would accept nothing less than one hundred percent adoration in return for his golden presence. A man like him wouldn't waste his time with the cranky mother of a sick baby. Not even if that baby was his own.

"Good!" Gillian said aloud. She had driven him away, just as she'd intended. The peculiar ache in her chest was the result of fatigue and worry about Ashley, not sadness. She was not sad because Devlin had left her.

She switched on her TV set, searching for something to watch.

And bolted upright in her seat as a nattily dressed chimp appeared on the screen. Seconds later, her phone rang.

"You'll never guess what's on." Devlin's voice sounded over the line.

"I just saw him. A face from the past, Lancelot Link." Gillian couldn't help but chuckle. "I instantly thought of you."

"I'll take that as a compliment." There was a smile in his voice.

The easy moment's camaraderie turned awkward. Devlin cleared his throat. "Ashley didn't wake up when you put her in her crib?"

"No, she's out like a light."

"She should have another dose of the antibiotic in six hours, even if that means waking her to give it," Devlin was all professional physician now. "She can also have the pain and fever meds at that time, if she needs them."

"I'll set my alarm." Gillian drew a deep breath. "Thanks again, Dev."

"No problem."

They hung up, his nonchalant response ringing in her ears. Why did everybody say "no problem" instead of "you're welcome" these days? she mused. "No problem" seemed so detached, so casual…and there, she'd just answered her own question about the popular usage. Everyone knew that detached and casual was preferable to even minimal involvement.

Not that she had any reason to complain, Gillian conceded. She wanted Devlin Brennan to remain detached and casual toward her. God forbid he should ever get close enough to put together the obvious clues of Ashley's parentage.

For just a few moments Gillian allowed herself to imagine that scene. Having once been an unwanted, unexpected child herself, she had no trouble predicting the outcome. Devlin would be beyond furious to learn he had a child. She shivered, remembering her own birth father—Craig Saylor's—rage when his daughter Gillian had arrived, an unsolicited surprise, on his doorstep at the age of twelve.

Even worse than her father's anger at her existence had been his complete rejection. He'd made it unmistakably clear he didn't care that he had a twelve-year-old daughter who needed him. Craig Saylor didn't want her and refused to have anything to do with her. As far as he was concerned, it was the state of Michigan that was stuck with Gillian Bailey until she turned eighteen, not him.

That particular memory had long ago lost the power to hurt her, but the experience of seeing Ashley roundly rejected by the man who'd fathered her was one Gillian knew she couldn't bear. She loved her child too much to have her devalued as anybody's unwanted mistake.

Restlessly, Gillian wandered back into Ashley's bedroom and leaned over the crib. The baby was deeply asleep, lying on her back, her tiny fingers balled into fists. History was not going to repeat itself, Gillian promised her daughter—and herself, as well. Ashley Joy Morrow had a mother who loved her, who wanted her and would always be there for her.

Gillian stroked Ashley's dark curls. She'd loved her child from the moment the nurse in the delivery room had placed the newborn infant in her arms. Maybe even before. She smiled, remembering Ashley's gymnastics while in the womb. She had cared about the baby then, of course, but when she'd gazed at that innocent little face, maternal instinct became something stronger. Her love was also an act of will, a vow to nurture Ashley and to keep her safe always.

She'd done that for eleven months without any help from Devlin Brennan and she would continue to do so. Gillian blinked back the sudden tears that burned in her eyes.

"You're a smart girl, Gillian," she remembered Dolly Sinsel telling her many times over the years. "You don't go chasing after what you can't have. You know *what* to want, and you make sure that it's something you are able to get."

But wanting Devlin Brennan hadn't been smart. She couldn't have him. After three months she had sensed him tiring of her, had felt his waning interest, and couldn't bear the agony of waiting to hear him say he didn't want her anymore. So she'd taken matters into her own hands and ended the unbearable suspense.

"This isn't working out," she'd said one night, silently praying that he would disagree, that he would protest the breakup and convince her he wanted to be with her.

But he hadn't. He'd let her go and never contacted her again, proving that she had been right to end it when she did. Not once after her pregnancy had been confirmed had she ever considered telling him about the baby. Why would she? Devlin didn't want her and he wouldn't want their child.

Gillian sighed softly. She'd spent the past twenty months trying to convince herself she didn't want him anymore, either. After all, she was smart enough not to chase after what was unattainable. She'd learned early that people like her got what they wanted only if no one else wanted it or if it was reasonably easy to obtain.

Being loved by Devlin Brennan was none of those things, not for her. It was a delusion of grandeur that she was not crazy enough to believe. The naive and hopeful twelve-year-old Gillian had dreamed of her father welcoming her into his home and into his life after she'd found him, but the grown-up Gillian entertained no similar illusions about Devlin or anyone else.

Three

"**P**sychiatry is on the phone, raving," Marthea Franklin announced, sticking her head into Gillian's tiny office. "And take a guess who's name is up on the docket to take the next case."

Gillian put aside the file she was reading. "Suppose I were to guess that either you or Sally are next up? Any chance of that happening?"

"Wishful thinking, girl." Marthea laughed. "This one is all yours. The shrink nurse is on line four and she isn't happy."

Gillian suppressed a groan. "Psychiatry is never happy when they call us. If their own social workers aren't involved, it can mean only one thing—they have a patient on their unit who they want transferred to a medical floor."

"And you know how the medical floors *love* having psychiatric patients. Not!" Marthea exclaimed gleefully. "I can practically hear the shrieking when you arrange for the transfer. Or is that the shrieking of the psych unit when you *don't* arrange a transfer that I'm hearing?"

"Somebody will be mad at us, no matter what is decided," Gillian acknowledged, sighing. "How come these floor transfers always get kicked over to us? Why doesn't the admitting office— or some other, *any* other department—handle it?''

"They don't want to be accused of playing favorites or taking sides. We're looked on as totally neutral ground.'' Marthea shook her head. ''And basically, who cares if we get caught in the cross-fire? We're supposed to be accustomed to taking verbal abuse from all sides.''

"One of the perks of social work,'' Gillian said dryly. She hit the button for line four.

"We are not equipped to handle orthopedic patients here,'' the head nurse roared in her ear. ''This patient must be transferred to Ortho immediately!''

"How did you happen to get an orthopedic patient?'' Gillian was curious.

"We have the ER to thank, they sent him up last night.'' The nurse calmed down a little. ''The patient is a college student who was in a car accident last night and has a broken pelvis, a broken leg, and two broken arms, the left with multiple fractures. He's in traction and needs the kind of total physical care that we don't provide on our unit. Our patients are supposed to be ambulatory and fully mobile, not confined to bed. You know that.''

"Mmm,'' Gillian murmured noncommittally. The staff on the psychiatric units wanted to treat patients hospitalized strictly for emotional problems. She was also quite familiar with the rebuttal she would soon be getting from Orthopedics—that their staff could not adequately care for a mentally ill patient who should be lodged on one of the psychiatric wards. She saw both sides, which prob-ably did make her a neutral party, though the service that ended up with this hapless patient would undoubtedly accuse her of fa-voritism or idiocy or both.

"Any particular reason why ER chose to send this patient to you instead of sending him to Ortho in the first place?'' Gillian asked, going for full disclosure.

There was a momentary silence. ''The patient is a diagnosed bipolar who has been hospitalized on our ward two previous times,'' the nurse said glumly. ''He hasn't been taking his medi-cation and is currently, uh, acutely psychotic. According to his friends at the fraternity house, he hasn't slept for days. He's in the midst of a manic episode, a pretty severe one, unfortunately.''

"Ortho won't be pleased," Gillian warned. "I'll see what I can do but I'm not making any promises."

"You have to get him out of here," the nurse insisted. "He belongs on Ortho."

"No way!" the orthopedic nurse said the moment Gillian identified herself. "We've already heard all about that patient. He's in the throes of mania, singing at the top of his lungs, swearing and shouting and totally out of it. His broken bones are incidental. We can't have him on this floor, he'll disturb all the other patients, and our staff is already stretched too thin to keep a constant eye on him. He's right where he belongs—in Psych."

"Psych insists he belongs on Ortho," Gillian noted pointedly. "They say they're not equipped to care for this patient who requires—"

"What they really mean is that they don't want to take care of him," the orthopedic nurse snapped.

Gillian did not comment, not wanting to be dragged into a bout of interprofessional warfare. The next step was to arrange a meeting with the resident doctors from both services. Since the patient was being treated for orthopedic and psychiatric problems, he would be assigned a first year resident from each discipline.

As she'd expected, the lunchtime meeting was useless. The first year residents assigned to the patient each echoed the head nurses from their particular units. One insisted on a transfer, the other vehemently opposed it. Gillian knew the next step was to take the problem to the senior residents of each service who were assigned to supervise the junior residents' patient care.

She wrote down the names of those two doctors and stared at them so long and so hard that her handwriting began to dance before her eyes. Senior resident from Ortho, Devlin Brennan. From Psych, Holly Casale.

It struck her that maybe Mark and Carmen were right after all, that maybe she was subject to unfair twists of fate. Because what else could explain the grim coincidence of having to deal with both Devlin *and* Holly Casale, whom Gillian knew was the love of his life.

She'd met Holly a few times when she had been with Devlin and immediately picked up on the special relationship between them. The way Holly looked at Dev, the way he looked at her, the warmth and genuine affection between them—Gillian had been acutely aware of every nuance. Dev talked about Holly a lot, probably more than he realized. And every word he said about her confirmed Gillian's belief that Holly Casale was his true love, even if he hadn't quite admitted it to himself yet. According to Devlin, he and Holly shared a long history that had begun with an alphabetical grouping in their first year of medical school, and their close friendship continued to the present.

Friendship! As if a man like Devlin would limit himself to mere friendship with a woman like Holly Casale. Gillian conjured up a visual image of Holly, who was everything she was not: tall and willowy, dark-haired, beautiful and brilliant, from a successful, classy family. Worst of all, Holly was in love with Dev. Gillian had drawn that conclusion the first time she was introduced to the other woman. The more she'd watched the two *friends* together, the more firmly her belief had been substantiated. It was only a matter of time before both Holly and Devlin ditched the friendship ruse, admitted their true feelings for each other, and then acted upon them.

And who could blame them? Holly Casale was perfect for Devlin Brennan, just as he was perfect for her. Gillian Bailey, descended from the poster family for white trash, with a case history that read like a bad made-for-cable-TV movie script, was not in their league. Not even close. Three months into her relationship with Dev, Gillian had faced those facts and given up. One lesson she'd learned well was that it was useless to fight the inevitable. She knew when to hold and when to fold, so she'd ceded Devlin to Holly.

She still vividly remembered that particular night twenty endless months ago, when Holly called Devlin to ask him to accompany her to a family wedding in upscale Grosse Point. Gillian had been lying naked beside him in bed and had listened while he joked and teased Holly about her family and the wedding, about using him for a "faux date." She'd heard him switch to a more serious tone as they discussed various medical cases, then turn nostalgic as they traded where-are-they-now news about mutual acquaintances. The conversation had lasted nearly an hour and covered a range of topics while Gillian lay there and forced herself to face reality.

She'd been living in a fool's paradise for three months and it was time to move out. Devlin belonged with Holly, who loved him and who fit in his world, just as he fit into hers. Gillian could picture the two of them mingling at that upper class wedding, she could see Dev and Holly as bride and groom at their own elegant wedding, but she couldn't begin to imagine herself even setting foot in exclusive Grosse Point.

That same night, after the lengthy phone call had ended and Gillian reached her irrevocable decision, she had passionately made love with Devlin knowing it would be for the last time.

The next day she'd told him "things weren't working out" and ended their relationship...much to Dev's relief, of that she was certain. Ever since, she'd been braced for the news of a Devlin Brennan-Holly Casale love affair. Instead she'd heard about Dev with a succession of leggy, busty, allegedly dumb blondes. What was with Holly, anyway? Gillian sometimes wondered. Why didn't the lovely lady doctor claim Devlin for her own?

As for Dev, if he wanted to waste his time with women who weren't worthy of him, it was too bad he wasn't still with her, Gillian mused wryly. She wasn't much, but she was certainly a sight better than those interchangeable borderline babes of his that she kept hearing jokes about.

Whatever, she now had the unenviable task of sitting down with both Devlin and Holly to discuss a patient that neither of their respective staffs wanted. The meeting was supposed to be an informal one, scheduled at five o'clock in a conference room in the social work department, a site presumably chosen for its neutrality.

Gillian glanced anxiously at her watch. Her workday was supposed to end at five, and right now she should be heading to the day care center to pick up Ashley. A pang of longing shimmered through her. She wanted to hold Ashley, to see her wide baby grin and sparkling blue eyes.

She checked her watch against the big clock on the wall. The center closed promptly at six. This meeting would have to be over before then.

But first, it had to start. By five-fifteen, neither doctor had arrived and Gillian was pacing the small room fighting the urge to fling furniture out the window. Jeff, one of the foster kids at the Sinsels, had had a penchant for doing that. Whenever his fury and frustrations flared to flashpoint, chairs and tables and anything else he could heave would come flying out the windows of the room he happened to be in. For the first time, Gillian found his actions understandable rather than terrifying.

When Devlin and Holly strolled into the conference room seven minutes later, laughing and talking and carrying cups of coffee, Gillian's fingers closed over the top of a wooden chair. It would be far more satisfying to fling the chair at their heads instead of out the window....

Of course, she did no such thing. She was too controlled to ever lose control like that. Gillian studied the two of them, both in their starched white lab coats, both tall and striking, exuding confidence and class.

"This meeting will last fifteen minutes and not a second more," she announced icily, sitting down on the chair she'd longed to hurl. "Please give me whatever information you think I need before I can render the proper decision about where the patient, Evan Weil, should be placed."

Devlin and Holly exchanged glances. "Hello to you, too, Gillian," Dev drawled.

"Time's ticking, Dr. Brennan." Gillian tapped the face of her watch.

"Gillian, we are so sorry to be late," Holly exclaimed. "We both got trapped in meetings that ran longer than expected and—"

"The line at the cafeteria must have been longer than expected, too," Gillian cut in caustically, eyeing the cups in their hands. She could've used a bolstering jolt of caffeine herself, but she'd declined to go to the cafeteria for coffee because she *hadn't wanted to be late for this meeting.* Her stormy blue eyes conveyed her thoughts so effectively that both Devlin and Holly shifted guiltily in their seats.

"I never knew you could be so intimidating, Gillian," Dev remarked, striving for a light note.

Gillian knew she could be ferocious, but she'd never shown him that side of her. "Why can't Evan Weil remain on the psychiatric unit, Dr. Casale?" she asked pointedly, ignoring Devlin.

Holly Casale outlined all the reasons why a patient in traction with numerous fractures could not be properly cared for on the psychiatric unit, psychotic though he may be. She said the same things the others on her staff had said except she was so gracious and pleasant, Gillian felt her ire slowly begin to fade.

Until Devlin stoked it all over again. "How's Ashley?" he asked when Holly finished speaking.

Gillian felt fury surge through her, bringing a hot rush of color to her neck and cheeks. Devlin clearly hadn't given the baby a thought when he'd scheduled this meeting for five o'clock and then shown up twenty-two minutes late. And now he had the nerve to ask about Ashley, as if her existence had suddenly reoccurred to him. Or was he merely using the baby as a polite conversation gambit? Gillian burned, angry at his thoughtlessness and even angrier with herself for the disappointment she felt in his offhand attitude.

It was her own fault. Every evening for the past week, since diagnosing Ashley's ear infection, Devlin had knocked on their apartment door to inquire about her progress. When he asked to see the baby it seemed churlish to refuse, so against her better judgment, Gillian let him in to check Ashley's ear. Every night for an entire week.

Somehow, the visits grew longer; last night he'd stayed almost an hour. His conversation focused mostly on what a bright, beautiful, marvelous child Ashley was and Gillian found it impossible not to respond. She loved talking about her baby, she was terribly proud of her. It was exhilarating to see someone else appreciate how very special Ashley was. Dev certainly seemed to.

Feeling at ease with him, inevitably, she and Devlin would end up talking about TV shows and laughing at their arcane knowledge of the subject. Dev had always been fun to talk to—they were both masters of the art of superficial conversation and Gillian hadn't felt threatened by his presence or the possibility of him probing deeper.

Spending any time at all with him had been a mistake, Gillian acknowledged. Because now she felt let down and it was all her own fault for expecting Dev to—

To what? What did she expect of him? Gillian gulped back the lump in her throat. She didn't expect anything from anyone, she reminded herself.

"Ashley is still in the day care center because I've been here, waiting for you two—" she almost added *yangos* but restrained the impulse "—to arrive," she said tersely. "Now will you please get on with this, so I can get out of here and take my child home?"

"You're supposed to leave your office at five!" Holly cried. "We shouldn't have scheduled a meeting that caused you to work overtime and make you late picking up the baby."

Gillian raised her brows. Holly wasn't telling her anything she didn't already know. Still, the psychiatric resident appeared so appalled by the careless scheduling, that Gillian bit back the snotty retort she would've liked to deliver.

Tightening her lips into a straight line, she turned her pale blue eyes on Devlin. "Since Evan Weil is in traction and also has two broken arms, the left one with two pins in it, why doesn't he belong on Orthopedics, Devlin?"

"I could point out that the Weil kid is out of his head on a manic high." Dev met and held her gaze. "But since all of us already know that, I won't." He shrugged. "Have him transferred to our floor. I'll write an order saying he should be there, that his orthopedic problems supercede his psychosis."

Gillian's eyes widened. "You will? Really?"

This was it? No arguments, no dragged-out, deadlocked meeting, no seeking still another meeting with a higher authority, the lordly attending physicians, who would consider her a bothersome pest? By writing an order for the transfer, Devlin was even sparing her the necessity of making the unilaterally unpopular decision. After all, a doctor's order was like God's will in this place.

Gillian watched Dev write the order for Evan Weil to be transferred from Psychiatry to Orthopedics, effective immediately. His handwriting was as illegible as every other physician's but his hand was big and strong, his fingers long and deft as he held the pen. A tiny erotic ripple shuddered through her at the sight, and she quickly looked away.

"I trust your people will still follow the boy while he's on our floor? Regulate his medication, continue psychotherapy?" Devlin asked Holly.

Holly nodded her head. "Of course. Thanks, Dev."

"Yes. Thank you." Gillian slumped in her chair as tension slowly abated from her body. "What a relief! I wish all the transfers were resolved this easily."

"Been through some nasty turf wars, huh?" Dev smiled at her.

"To put it mildly, especially between Medicine and Psych over Alzheimer's patients." Gillian flinched at the awful memories of those fights. She always identified with the unwelcome patients, who needed a place yet didn't seem to fit in anywhere. The people who nobody wanted. For most of her life, she'd been in that same situation, though lucky for her, she hadn't also been sick while in need.

"I'll take this to the admitting office right now," Gillian said resolutely, gathering up her things and heading to the door. "Thank you both," she added, suddenly regretting her earlier hostile demeanor. She wondered if she should apologize, then decided against wasting another second in that room. She wanted to get her baby without further delay.

"We shouldn't have stopped for coffee," Holly said to Devlin after Gillian was gone. "She was really mad at us for being late and I don't blame her."

"She's a redhead with the implied temper." Devlin stared at the door where Gillian had exited. "But usually she gets distant—cold, not fiery—when she is angry."

"She is very pretty." Holly watched him closely. "So petite and feminine. Smart and effective at her job, too, from what I've been told. Everybody who works with her likes her. Gillian Bailey is a definite departure from your usual tacky taste in women, Dev."

"Don't go there, Holly," Devlin warned. "She's divorced, with a kid, you know. Her marriage barely lasted long enough for the ink on the license to dry."

"So I heard. There was something extremely weird about that so-called marriage of hers," Holly said. "I also know you can't take your eyes off her when you're in a room with her."

"Of course I can," snapped Dev.

"Can you? Well, then you don't *want* to take your eyes off her because when she's around, you watch her the way a dieter looks at a hot-fudge sundae he desperately craves but—"

"Shut up, Hol."

"But can't have," Holly finished anyway. "Why don't you just tell her how you feel about her, Dev?"

"There is nothing to tell, Holly. Now go shrink someone else's head. I don't have time for this, I have a date tonight."

"Just because you refuse to talk about your feelings doesn't mean that you don't have them," Holly persisted.

"Oh, that's profound, Holly. Are you quoting Jung or Adler? Or maybe a greeting card?"

"I remember how much you hated our psychiatry rotation back in med school. The only part that interested you at all was the new psychotropic drugs that are being developed and provide a biochemical view of mental illness."

"It's still the only part that interests me. I don't think any patient can be cured of anything by merely talking about it. All in all, I'd rather be operating."

"Spoken like a true surgeon. But being emotionally reticent has cost you, Dev. It cost you Gillian. If you'd hadn't been set on playing it cool, if you'd been honest and told her how you really felt about her, chances are she wouldn't have ended your relationship. And don't give me that bunk about *showing* her how you felt about her in bed."

"And now you're Dear Abby," Dev mocked. "What about that acclaimed cliché 'actions speak louder than words,' Hol?"

"There is certainly some truth to it, but Gillian is a woman who needs the words as much as the actions. Probably even more, considering her background."

"What do you know about her background?" Devlin scowled. "For that matter, how do you know there was something weird about her marriage? What are you doing, moonlighting as a private investigator? Holly Casale, M.D., P.I. What a concept! Do you think we could sell it as a network series?"

Holly folded her arms and gave him a leveling look. "One of our psych social workers is best friends with one of the social workers in Gillian's office. One day we had a long talk over coffee about Gillian Bailey. That's how I know about her and if you want more information—"

"Do me a favor and stick to your head cases, okay, Holly? Gotta go!" Devlin fled from the conference room and Holly's irritating theories and intrusive advice.

Gillian hurried down the brightly painted corridor leading to the hospital's in-house day care center, eager to pick up Ashley and go home.

"Tina, I'm so sorry I'm late," she apologized to the child care worker the moment she set foot inside the center.

Tina was busy trying to keep the two-year-old Petersen twins from biting her and each other, but she glanced up to reply, "You're not late, honey, we're open till six, remember?"

Gillian nodded, but ten-to-six felt late, much too late for her little Ashley to still be here. She looked around for Ashley, who wasn't in sight. No doubt she'd been placed in a playpen in one of the other rooms for her own protection—the Petersen twins were carnivorous, always trying to chomp on somebody—but the thought of her child being alone and out of sight bothered her greatly.

"Hey, Ashley, here's Mommy." The sound of Devlin's voice halted her in her tracks.

Gillian blinked at the sight of him walking toward her, Ashley in his arms. She felt her jaw drop. "I— You— What—" She'd been reduced to total incoherence!

"Dr. Brennan is here visiting Ashley," Tina called from the front playroom, somewhat after the fact.

"Mama!" Ashley crowed with delight and tried to jump from Dev's arms into Gillian's.

"I, uh, knew you'd be stopping by here." Devlin handed Ashley to her. "I thought I'd catch you and..." He drew a deep breath. "Ask you for a ride back to the apartment building."

Gillian was absorbed in playing one of Ashley's favorite little games that involved a combination of peekaboo and tickling kisses. She paused to glance at him. "You need a ride?" It sounded bogus, yet it must be true because why else would he be here?

"Yeah, I need a ride. My car died in the parking garage. I already called for a tow to the nearest body shop." Devlin watched Gillian and Ashley, and wondered if he'd ever spun such a lame excuse. Not within recent memory. Even in high school, he'd managed to be more creative.

His car was in excellent working order and parked in the garage, but on impulse, he'd gone in the opposite direction and ended up here. After identifying himself to the kindly, overworked Tina, he had been allowed to take Ashley from the playpen where she'd been standing up, holding on to the bars and peering out. The baby greeted him with a huge grin, then lost her grip and sat down hard. But she hadn't cried, she'd crowed happily and extended her little arms to him.

"Ashley seemed overjoyed to see me," Devlin remarked, walking alongside Gillian as they left the center. "Or maybe it was the prospect of being sprung from that pen that thrilled her," he added drolly. "Do you want me to carry her? You look pretty well weighted down."

Gillian held Ashley on her right hip and carried an enormous diaper bag slung over her left shoulder. He'd taken week-long vacations with a smaller bag.

Gillian tightened her arms around the child. "You can take this if you really want to carry something." She thrust the rainbow-colored diaper bag at him.

He accepted it, pondering the weight. Ten pounds? Twenty? What was in this thing?

"Everything squared away with Admitting concerning the Weil kid?" Dev asked as they trotted along. He was feeling ignored. Gillian was talking to the baby who babbled back in her own language while he'd been relegated to the role of silent pack mule.

"Yes, Evan Weil will be transferred to Ortho sometime this evening," she replied crisply.

"Glad I won't be around for that."

"I'm sure you'll hear plenty tomorrow," Gillian predicted.

They rounded a corner and headed toward the elevators leading to the floors reserved for employee parking. Holly was standing in front of the elevator door, impatiently pressing the call button.

"Hello again." Holly's dark eyes swept over Devlin, Gillian and the baby, lingering on the diaper bag dangling on Dev's shoulder. "Gillian, your little girl is precious. She has the most beautiful eyes! And I love that little yellow and blue plaid romper suit she's wearing."

Gillian reflexively thanked her for the compliments while watching the two doctors exchange glances. She was instantly attuned to the tension between them. "Dev, you can catch a ride with Holly since she's leaving now, too," Gillian said quickly. She wasn't going to be thrust into the third point of any triangle, not even for a few minutes.

"Where's your car, Dev?" asked Holly. "I saw you drive it in this morning."

Dev shook his head. This was going from stupid to ridiculous. No wonder he'd never bothered with romantic strategies before! "My car isn't, uh, operational at this point in time," he said dryly.

Holly laughed. "I see."

He was certain that she really did, especially when she added, "Sorry, Dev. I can't give you a lift anywhere. I'm not leaving yet, I'm just going to get something from my car." Holly smiled at Gillian. "Looks like you're stuck with him."

Gillian was acting as if he really were a pesky bore she'd gotten stuck with, Dev observed irritably as he followed her to her car, a white Chevy compact. Male pride told him to stomp off and drive his perfectly fine car home. Gillian certainly wouldn't mind, she'd already tried to pawn him off on Holly.

He really ought to leave and seek the company of those women who wanted him—there were lots that did, he reminded himself. The problem was, he didn't want any of them. And why was that? Devlin frowned thoughtfully. It wasn't as if his body's virile responses weren't in excellent working order. In fact, just standing here, looking at Gillian bend over as she placed the baby in the back seat, was making him hot and hard with arousal.

He stared at the way her straight gray skirt pulled tightly over her bottom as she bent over, outlining the rounded curves. Her ribbed gray-and-white-striped cotton shirt slid a little above the waistband of her skirt, exposing a small band of tender flesh. Devlin felt an overwhelming urge to kiss her there, to run his tongue along the sensitive skin, to cup her buttocks with his hands and sensuously knead before slipping the skirt over her hips. Then he would take off her little cotton shirt and turn her around to face him....

He experienced an erotic flashback as the memory of Gillian naked, her body soft and rounded, her skin a silky pink and white as she lay beneath him, as she cuddled against him, unfolded before his mind's eye.

He felt his face flush. How long had it been since the mere sight of a woman—and a fully dressed one at that—made him tremble with urgency? He took a wild guess at the answer. About twenty months, maybe? He remembered the last night he and Gillian had spent together. After dinner he'd quickly undressed her and made love to her. For the last time. Of course, he hadn't known it was the last time, not then. But the next day, she'd dropped him cold.

He took a deep breath. *Something weird about her so-called marriage. If you'd been honest and told her how you really felt about her, chances are she wouldn't have ended your relationship... A woman who needs the words as much as the actions.* Holly's observations swirled through his head as his body throbbed and ached with acute sensual hunger.

An expression of decision and determination crossed his face.

While Gillian buckled Ashley in her car seat, which resembled some space-age contraption, he slid behind the wheel, adjusting the seat to his much greater height.

Gillian hadn't realized what he was doing until she'd finished securing Ashley in the baby seat and moved to get into the car herself. On the already occupied driver's side.

"I want to drive," she announced, staring at her keys in his hand. Obviously he had removed them from the lock while she'd been occupied with the baby.

Devlin shook his head. "Sorry, honey. When I'm in a car with a woman, I'm the driver."

"Is that some kind of commandment in the macho creed?" She folded her arms in front of her chest. "Well, I don't ascribe to it. I'm driving, Devlin."

"Wrong. Since I have the keys, I'm doing the driving." Grinning up at her from behind the wheel, he jangled the keys as bait.

She guessed that he expected her to make a lunge for them. Gillian resisted the impulse. She would not be lured into a losing contest. Her head held high, she walked around the car and climbed into the passenger seat beside him.

"You give up too easily," Dev remarked as he watched her meticulously adjust and fasten her seat belt.

"I learned a long time ago that the bigger and stronger person is going to win any battle that depends on size and strength."

"So you sharpened your wits and decided you would win other kinds of battles by other means?"

"I try to avoid battles whenever possible," Gillian said succinctly. "Since you insist on driving, please start the car. Ashley is hungry for her dinner and—"

"What are you having?" Devlin asked, casting a quick glance at the back seat. Ashley was sucking her thumb and she smiled at him around it. Warmth rippled through him. She was the cutest little kid.

His gaze returned to Gillian, and the glow of warmth was abruptly transformed into a dizzying heat. Already a sensual heaviness suffused his loins, now his erection felt as solid as stone. Swallowing hard, he tried to keep his train of thought from being totally derailed. "For, uh, dinner."

"I'm not sure," Gillian murmured breathlessly. She felt his gaze on her as tangible as a touch. Her lips tingled, then the points of her breasts tightened under his hot blue eyes. His breathing was deep and heavy, and when she happened to glance at his lap...

Gillian actually blushed. What if he were to reach for her and pull her into his arms? It looked like he might do exactly that. He was turned toward her, leaning closer, his gaze urgent and intense. A tremor of sheer anticipation quivered through her.

She told herself that she was relieved when Dev fastened his seat belt and started the car instead. After a long day at work, the last thing she wanted or needed was to be groped in the hospital parking lot with her baby in the back seat.

Her baby, who also happened to be his. Her heart slammed painfully against her rib cage.

"As long as you don't have any particular meal planned, why don't we stop somewhere and get something to eat?" Devlin invited as he steered the car along the narrow exit ramp.

"Oh, no, I— No, we—"

"TGIFriday's? The China Palace? Vincenzio's?" he rattled off some suggestions. "If you don't make a choice, I will, Gillian."

"I choose to go home. Immediately."

"That isn't an option, Gillian."

Fury ripped through her. The realization that there was more than a little sexual frustration surging through her only heightened her ire. "The hell it isn't!"

"The hell it is." Dev laughed, and her anger soared into the stratosphere.

"You can't...can't commandeer my car and take us where I don't want to go!"

"Watch me."

He drove on and Gillian stewed in silence. Short of leaping from the car and calling the police to charge him with carjacking and kidnapping, there really wasn't anything she could do to keep him from pulling into the parking lot of a TGIFriday's restaurant.

"It's dinnertime, princess," he announced to Ashley. He reached around to free her from the car seat. Despite its complex appearance, getting the baby out proved to be surprisingly simple. Carefully, he lifted Ashley into the front with Gillian and himself. Ashley made a grab for the key ring swinging from the ignition.

"Come on, Gillian, let's go." Holding the baby in one arm, he opened the door a crack.

"Why are you doing this, Devlin?" Gillian reached for Ashley. The baby ignored her, too busy investigating the unfamiliar roughness of Devlin's five o'clock shadow with her tiny hands. The little traitor!

"You mean, why am I going to have dinner?" Devlin arched

his brows. "Because I'm hungry. I spent the morning in the operating room doing knee replacements, grabbed a cheese sandwich around one, and spent the afternoon working on an especially tricky lumbar fusion. I want something to eat, preferably a thick juicy steak. What about you?"

Gillian heaved an exasperated sigh. "You know what I mean! Why are you being so...so..."

"Masterful?" he suggested.

"I was going to say overbearing. Or intractable. Or...or obnoxious."

"Ouch. I definitely prefer masterful, but I'll settle for persistent." He caught Ashley's little hand—she was attempting to thrust her tiny fingers into his nostrils—and kissed the sweaty baby palm. "The kid is trying to rearrange my features. She must think I'm Mr. Potato Head or something. Let's find her a worthy diversion inside the restaurant."

He got out of the car, carrying Ashley, and headed around to the other side. It occurred to Gillian that he was going to open her door for her, an unprecedented move.

"Holly has given me so many lectures on archaic sexist conduct that I've abandoned what my mother taught me about How A Well Mannered Man Treats A Lady," Gillian remembered him saying with a laugh, whenever he failed to perform such small courtesies as opening doors, offering to carry packages, or letting her enter or exit before him.

Yet within the past week, he'd done the baby's laundry, carried the diaper bag and was now intent on opening her car door for her. It was freaky. Carmen would probably claim he was possessed by some demon of politeness.

Preposterous, of course, but the little niceties, the special attention he was bestowing on her, were dangerous in themselves, causing her to lower her guard, to make her think that he— Gillian didn't even let herself complete the thought. Quickly, she flung the door open herself, before he could reach it.

"I really resent this, Devlin," she said crossly, scurrying to keep up with him as he headed toward the entrance of the restaurant. Since he was carrying Ashley, she really had no choice but to go along, Gillian reassured herself.

His long-legged stride took him farther and faster, and when he noticed, he paused, then slowed his pace to match hers. Another first. In the past he'd usually zipped along at his own speed, and if she happened to be a city block behind him, so be it.

He slipped his arm around her, cupping her shoulder with his long fingers. Stroking her. Gillian shivered and tried to ignore him. Soon tendrils of heat were uncurling deep within her. Desperately she tried to shrug his hand off her, but he held firm, refusing to be dislodged.

"I don't get it, Devlin." She stared up at him, her pale blue eyes cloudy with confusion. "Is this some kind of game?"

"No games, Gillian. I just want to have dinner with you."

The characteristic note of irony or mockery was missing from his voice. Gillian gulped. "This isn't at all like you, Dev. You were never—pushy like this. You used to be able to take no for an answer. In fact, it didn't seem to matter whether the answer was yes or no. You didn't really care one way or another."

"That's what you think, hmm?"

"That's what I know." She lifted her hand and removed his from her shoulder. He allowed it to drop to his side.

"That's what you've guessed. What is more important to you, Gillian? Words or actions? Or do you need both?"

"What I need are my daughter and my car keys so I can drive home. You can stay here and eat. Call one of your many friends or admirers to come join you."

"I take it you don't include yourself in that number? You're neither a friend nor an admirer of mine?"

They reached the door and stopped in front of it. "You don't care what I think of you, Dev," she informed him tautly.

"That's what you think, hmm?" he repeated wryly. "Go on, Gillian, that's your cue to say your line. We could have a circular argument to last all through dinner, if you want."

"I don't want to—"

"Good, I don't, either." He hooked his fingers into the waistband of her skirt. "Let's go inside."

The touch of his fingers against the bare skin of her waist sent shock waves of sheer sensation jolting through her. And his grip was so firm that she had no choice but to go with him, propelled along in his possessive hold.

Four

"**I** was taught an invaluable lesson tonight," Devlin drawled as he knelt beside the bathtub where Gillian was bathing an exuberant, energetic Ashley. "Never give a baby a bowl filled with salad. Especially one smothered with ranch dressing."

"If I may interject a comment?" Gillian poured a dollop of shampoo on Ashley's thick curls and worked up a lather.

"Please do."

"Duh!"

"You think my hard-learned lesson was that obvious, hmm?" Devlin laughed. "How was I to know that Ashley prefers throwing food to eating it? And that she has a penchant for rubbing salad dressing in her hair?"

"I was in the rest room for all of five minutes and when I returned to the table, the salad was scattered like confetti and Ashley reeked of buttermilk and garlic." Gillian couldn't suppress a smile at the memory of the messy scene in the restaurant.

"The kid works fast," Devlin said dryly.

Gillian proceeded to pour water over the baby's head from a small plastic pail. Ashley struggled a little to escape the waterfall effect, but continued to make grabs for the fleet of colorful toy ducks that bobbed around the tub.

"I thought little kids screamed while they were getting their hair washed, but Ashley doesn't mind a bit," Dev marveled.

"She loves the water. I'm thinking about enrolling her in swimming lessons at the Y. They have a program for babies and mothers that meets for an hour a week."

"Sounds like a good plan—get kids swimming before they can develop a fear of the water. I remember how my loser cousins Brenda and Brent would howl their heads off whenever my dad and his brother, our uncle Gene, tried to get them into the pool during our visits to Port McClain."

Dev grinned in reminiscence. "Aunt Bobbie and Uncle Artie—Brent and Brenda's parents—never took them swimming and by the time they were school age, they wouldn't even get their feet wet. Naturally, their bawling inspired me to splash them at every given opportunity and to show off my own swimming and diving skills, which Dad and Uncle Gene praised to the skies."

Gillian shot him a look. "You sound like you were an insufferable show-off. My sympathies are with your cousins. Did it ever occur to you that it was smart of them to have a healthy respect for the water because they couldn't swim?"

"Ah, as ever, the social worker champions the underdog." But his tone was more affectionate than acerbic. He placed his hand on her nape and began to rub.

It was a casual gesture but Gillian felt its effects in every nerve in her body, particularly in her traitorous erogenous zones that suddenly clamored with heat and urgency. Her pulses raced as desire and arousal built with unnerving speed.

"Don't!" she ordered, shrugging her shoulders and twisting her neck in an attempt to remove that enticing hand. "Stop it, Dev." She leaned forward, concentrating on rinsing the soapy, slippery Ashley.

"Stop what?" Dev played dumb and went on caressing her neck.

He'd seen the flare of awareness in her eyes, heard the husky note in her voice and recognized the sexual tension for what it was. His body tightened in response to her nearness and to her own response to him. A pleasant heaviness suffused his loins.

Paradoxically, he felt both at peace and tremendously excited, which was certainly a strange phenomenon. How could a man feel both at the same time? Especially when he was kneeling on the bathroom floor while the baby splashed water around as merrily as she'd flung food at the restaurant an hour earlier.

"Stop trying to come on to me, Devlin," Gillian said firmly. She rose to her feet, scooping up Ashley in her arms—and escaping his lazy massage.

The baby squawked a protest at being removed from her water play. Her wet little body imprinted on the shirred bodice of Gillian's daisy print sundress. She'd donned it right after their arrival back at the apartment, while Dev kept an eye on Ashley during the quick change.

Then, instead of going home himself, he'd stuck around while Gillian played with the baby, joining them in rounds of peekaboo and looking at picture books, stacking colorful plastic rings and building blocks.

Now his eyes lingered on the rounded fullness of Gillian's breasts, outlined by the damp elastic bodice of her dress. Her nipples peaked, stimulating him even more.

"Is that what I'm doing? Trying to come on to you?" He tried to sound nonchalant. When he handed Gillian a towel to wrap around the squirming baby, his knuckles skimmed her bare arm and the contact electrified him.

"Well, isn't it?" Gillian's stern look of disapproval should've squelched any amorous impulses on the spot.

Dev half wished she'd been successful. This burst of one-sided lust was finely tuned torture. "Maybe," he admitted, and heaved a mock sigh. "Okay, yes, I confess. I was trying to come on to you, Gillian." He followed her out of the bathroom into the baby's small bedroom.

How was she supposed to answer that? Gillian felt a hot surge of color pink her cheeks. They were on dicey ground here, thanks in large measure to her own bluntness. Better to leave things unsaid and ambiguous, the way it always used to be between her and Devlin.

Or perhaps it was best to spell things out, in the most harsh unmistakable way. She drew a deep breath. "I want you to leave now, Devlin. You...you've inflicted yourself on us long enough and I'm not humoring you for another minute. Just go!"

She had no doubts that he would leave, offended by her insult.

After all, Devlin Brennan's company was highly sought after, he'd never *inflicted* his coveted presence on anyone in his life. To be accused of doing so would surely strike him as an unforgivable cut.

Instead of storming out the door, he laughed out loud.

"Maybe you didn't hear me correctly?" Her voice fairly dripped icicles.

"Or maybe I did. My sense of humor just kicked in. Isn't there something perversely comical about me gazing lustfully at you while you look at me the way one eyes a cockroach crawling on the kitchen counter?"

Gillian stared at him, nonplussed. His eyes met hers and ripples of sensual heat throbbed through her. The way he was looking at her made her feel helpless and powerful and very, very feminine. She swallowed hard, suddenly breathless.

"I'm not going anywhere, Gillian," Devlin said huskily.

Before she could panic at the determination in his voice, a wiggling impatient Ashley let out a shriek of displeasure.

Immediately she turned her full attention to her daughter. "I have to get Ashley ready for bed," she mumbled nervously.

"Do you need any help?"

Gillian shook her head. She was excruciatingly aware of Devlin watching them and tried to think of something, anything, to say to him but her mind seemed to have gone blank when it came to dealing with him. She could function effectively with Ashley, dressing her in her yellow Tweety Bird pajamas and playfully cuddling her, but she couldn't cope with Devlin's presence at all.

So she ignored him. Completely.

She acted as if he were invisible as she prepared Ashley's bottle and fed it to her as they rocked together in the big rocking chair in the living room. A sleepy Ashley reached up to touch her mother's cheek with her small fingers. Gillian looked into her baby's beautiful blue eyes and smiled tenderly at her.

Another very similar pair of blue eyes quietly observed them from the sofa. Devlin didn't try to counter Gillian's passive resistance to him, not wanting to spark a more active rebuff. A flash of male pride demanded why he was doing this, why he was staying where he was patently unwelcome, but Devlin paid no mind.

His intuitive side—which he rarely acknowledged—told him

that he was far from unwelcome, that Gillian wanted him to stay though she couldn't and wouldn't admit it, especially not to herself.

Gillian is a woman who needs the words as much as the actions. Holly's words circled 'round and 'round in his head. *If you'd been honest and told her how you really felt about her, chances are she wouldn't have ended your relationship.*

But he hadn't said the words because twenty months ago, he wasn't sure how he really felt about her. Oh, he'd known right from the start that everything had been different with Gillian Bailey. Petite, edgy redheads with a predilection for control had never been his preference, but he'd asked Gillian out the day he'd met her after a hasty introduction in the hospital snack bar.

He always hoped for sex on the first date but Gillian, nervous and defensive from the moment he picked her up for dinner, made it clear that he wasn't even going to be permitted to hold her hand that evening. Time dragged, and just when he'd decided that their first date would be their last, they hit on the subject of TV shows. Gillian wasn't ashamed to admit that she was as avid a viewer as he was. Her knowledge of TV trivia rivaled—at times even topped—his own. He was pleased to find that when she wasn't on guard, she was an entertaining conversationalist.

So he'd called her for a second date. And stuck around for an entire month of feverish good-night kisses at the door but nothing more, waiting for Gillian to want him as much as he wanted her. When she finally said yes and spent the night with him, their lovemaking had been shattering in its intensity, providing them both with boundless pleasure culminating in the bliss of mutual fulfillment. And it was like that every time they made love. Sexually, they had complemented each other perfectly.

But there had been more than great sex between Gillian and him, Devlin acknowledged wistfully, there'd been a connection he hadn't felt with any other woman. He didn't fully understand what was happening, but he had been curious and intrigued and willing to explore the bond growing between them, content to let it develop at leisure.

After all, why rush to talk about something he couldn't completely comprehend? Eventually, he'd find words to go with his actions. Though in hindsight, his actions had been as lacking as the words he'd never gotten around to saying.

The glimmer of insight disconcerted him. Thoughtful gestures, romantic surprises, small presents—none of those were part of a Devlin Brennan courtship and, true to form, he'd given none to Gillian. He wondered if he would have, eventually.

But time had run out and *eventually* wasn't to be. Out of the blue, Gillian had broken up with him, leaving him reeling with anger and confusion. And pain.

She'd hurt him, Dev admitted at last. Because he had really cared about her. He could deny it to Holly, he'd certainly denied it to himself. But sitting here, staring at Gillian with her baby, he faced the truth.

He had really cared for her and maybe, possibly, Dev hedged carefully, he still did. Twenty months ago he'd let her walk away without even token resistance from him because he wasn't used to fighting for what he wanted. He'd never had to, not when everything he wanted had always come so easily to him.

Was he willing to fight for her now? Devlin stared at Gillian with the fierce concentration he'd applied when studying his copy of *Gray's Anatomy* in med school. He wanted to go to bed with her again, he allowed that much. But Gillian had given him no clear signal what he could expect. Too many wrong moves on his part, and he might end up alienating her permanently.

He tried to put aside the flood of sensual memories washing over him. He wished he knew her better, then he could more correctly gauge her reactions. The irony of the situation wasn't lost on him. They'd made love, been intimate, yet so much of Gillian remained unknown to him.

Considering her background, Holly had said. The cryptic reference had been gnawing at him. Considering he knew next to nothing about Gillian's background, it seemed a good place to start.

"What did you mean, you and your foster sister and brother were unadoptable?"

His voice broke the silent stillness in the room.

Gillian felt her nerves tighten with anxiety. She forced herself to relax when her tension was communicated to the baby, causing Ashley's big blue eyes to snap open. She rocked the chair, her tone soft and soothing, until her child's eyelids drifted closed again.

Gillian raised her eyes to Devlin's and found him waiting expectantly for her answer. It seemed that he expected to pick up the threads of last week's conversation in the hall as if no time had intervened.

"Why do you want to know?" she countered. One of her least favorite subjects was how and why she'd ended up a ward of the state.

"I'm curious."

"Well, you know what they say about curiosity," she said dampeningly.

"About the cat getting killed?" He smiled. "Nonapplicable, Gillian." He leaned forward, his eyes gleaming with curiosity, despite the metaphorical cat's fate.

Gillian frowned. She didn't want him asking a lot of questions that might enable him to draw an informed conclusion. But her past status was unrelated to his paternity and if she pacified his irrelevent questions, he might not ask the important ones.

"By the time any of us were eligible for adoption—you know, after the state finally and irrevocably severed parental rights—we were too old for anyone to want us. Too old and too awful," she added, smiling grimly. "I wouldn't have adopted any of us, either. God bless the Sinsels for letting us live with them as foster kids. They deserve medals equivalent to battlefield bravery."

"What did you do that was so awful?"

"Oh, you name it. One of us did it, at some time or another." She stood up, the sound-asleep baby in her arms. "I'm putting Ashley in her crib now, Dev. Time for you to go home."

"I'd rather stay here."

"Too bad. You're leaving."

"Don't want to hang out with me, huh?"

"No, I want some time to myself." She started toward the bedroom, expecting to hear the front door open and close as Devlin departed. When she heard no sounds of movement, she turned around to see him still seated on the sofa.

"What do you usually do when you're here by yourself, after the baby is in bed for the night?" he asked, ignoring her glare.

"I relax and enjoy the peace and quiet. I give thanks that I'm not—not being stalked by some pest who lives across the hall."

"That's the first time I've ever been called a stalker. Or a pest, for that matter. You're tough, Gillian." But he didn't take offense, he seemed totally impervious to her insults.

She made one final attempt to reason with him. "Dev, you're still in your shirt and tie and white coat from work. You need to change clothes, to go check your mail and your answering machine."

"I wouldn't mind putting on something more comfortable and I ought to check my mailbox," he conceded. "Want me to get your mail, too?"

"No, thank you. I'll get it myself, later." Satisfied that she'd successfully diverted and dispatched him, Gillian left to put Ashley in her crib.

With some trepidation, she returned to the living room a few minutes later but Devlin was no longer there. Gillian reminded herself how glad she was as she turned on her television set. It took some channel-surfing before she finally happened on a classic episode of "The Munsters."

She was getting caught up in the antics on screen when her front door opened.

Gillian gasped when Devlin strolled nonchalantly into her apartment. He wore a pair of old loose-fitting khaki trousers and a well-washed blue polo shirt that somehow matched the color of his eyes.

"I took your advice and changed clothes," he announced cheerfully. He'd taken something else, too. Her keys. He seemed to be making a practice of it. He held her key ring in his hand as he walked toward her.

"Here's your mail. Now you won't have to go down to the foyer for it." Devlin handed her a packet of envelopes as he sat down beside her on the sofa. "Anything interesting? Mine was all junk."

"Devlin—"

"'The Munsters.'" He eyed the TV screen, then sprawled in the middle of the sofa to watch. "Oh, this is the one where Lurch is—"

"What part of 'go home' don't you understand, Devlin?" She dropped her mail on the small end table without glancing at any of it.

"What part of 'I'm not leaving you' don't you understand, Gillian?" Moving swiftly and with inexorable precision, he fastened his hands around her hips to pull her down onto his lap.

"I'm not going anywhere, baby," he said, his voice husky and thick as he pressed her close to him.

Gillian felt his radiant masculine heat and desire, forceful and sharp, tear through her. Her heartbeat thundered in a dizzying accompaniment.

"I'm staying, Gillian." Dev's voice seemed to come from another dimension. "And you want me to stay."

Hesitantly, she raised her eyes to his. They were glazed with desire and she knew her own eyes must hold that same glow.

"Don't you?" Dev whispered. He caught her hand and pressed her palm to his lips. "Say it, Gillian. Say you want me as much as I want you."

She felt passion and sensuality unfurl within her, urging her to surrender to this elemental hunger he aroused. Gillian ached with the temptation to lose herself in the fiery heat of desire, the way she'd done with him before. Only with Devlin had she ever let down her guard enough to be free from the rigid demands and controls she placed on herself. With him, she'd been released from the pain and fear of loving and losing—at least for a little while.

But there had been a high price to pay for that rapturous respite. Though she didn't regret their child's existence—she wouldn't have missed having Ashley for anything—she dreaded the abiding pain and confusion her relationship with Devlin had brought, the crushing burden of loss and grief when he was gone. Now he was here again, making her feel things again...

"Dev, I—I admit I'm tempted but I—oh!" Gillian broke off abruptly, her breath catching in a gasping sigh as his big hand covered her breast.

She could feel the strength and the heat of it burn through the material of her dress, searing her like a brand. A bolt of sensual electricity jolted through her as his fingers found her nipple that was already tight and straining against the cloth.

Dev heard only the aching need in her voice. His senses were filled with her, the supple softness of her skin, her unique feminine scent. He hungered for the taste of her, wanting her mouth with an urgency and desperation he'd never experienced before.

"Yes, baby," he whispered, his lips brushing hers. "Yes."

The intensity of that brief, light touch rocked them both. Gillian's mind spun away and reflexively she closed her eyes as his mouth caressed hers, gently at first, his lips nibbling at hers until she moaned softly and pressed closer, seeking more.

Her lips parted in silent invitation, and his mouth opened hotly over hers, hard and hungry and demanding. Gillian's arms tightened around his neck and her fingers combed caressively through his hair. His tongue thrust into her mouth and she rubbed it with hers, kissing him back, deeply, fiercely, matching his passion with her own.

They kissed and kissed as if starved for each other, as if making up for twenty long months apart. Devlin ran his hands over her soft curves, feeling the mature fullness of her breasts, the hollow of her waist and roundness of her hips.

Gillian wriggled sensuously under his evocative caresses, letting herself feel without thinking, responding to him while making her own demands. She wound herself around him, clinging to him in surrender that was as irresistible and seductive as the passion burning torridly between them.

Devlin's breathing grew ragged. His usual self-control, which had always permitted him to carefully choreograph his moves while mastering his passion, was obliterated, making his surrender as total as hers.

Slowly, he laid her back on the sofa, pressing her against the upholstered cushions with his weight. He slid one hand under the hem of her dress, gliding his palm along the smooth bare warmth of her thigh.

A shudder of desire racked her body. She was overwhelmed by the touch and the taste and the feel of him. She hadn't been held, hadn't been kissed or touched since she'd left him and now she was powerless to stop her voluptuous responses to him. She felt his virile arousal against her and automatically parted her legs to better accommodate that bold pressure. He moved his thigh between hers and she arched against him, trying to soothe the feverish ache deep inside her.

She was dizzy with anticipation. Devlin knew exactly how and where to touch her, he knew her body intimately. He'd been the one to awaken her to passion, who had schooled her in the pleasures of sexual excitement and arousal, finally bringing her to deep satisfying fulfillment.

And now it was happening again. Gillian felt as wild as the sensations rippling through her. She and Devlin would be intimately joined as one, giving and taking and sharing pleasure, making love. She was so in love with him...

She whimpered as his hand smoothed over the silky material of her panties, pausing to squeeze the soft roundness of her derriere. One long finger slipped between her legs, feeling the sensuous heat and moisture gathered there. Flames of fire scorched through her. She wanted him so much she felt delirious from the force of it.

"Oh, Dev." She sighed breathlessly, clinging to him. "Please, now..."

"Not here, honey. This is too important for a quickie on the couch." Devlin's voice was thick and deep as he withdrew his hand from under her skirt and sat up, taking her with him. "Let's go to bed."

He rose quickly to his feet, sweeping her high against his chest as easily as Gillian lifted Ashley.

Ashley, their child. Alarm bells instantly sounded in Gillian's head. Ashley Joy, her much loved, accidentally conceived baby, who Devlin didn't know was his. Because he didn't want to know? The question had long plagued her.

There had been clues, had Devlin bothered to pursue them. He had seen her pregnant at least once—Gillian well remembered that glacial encounter of theirs in the hospital cafeteria—but he'd never questioned the timing of her pregnancy or the date of Ashley's birth. And not once during the past week while spending time with his daughter had he noted her resemblance to himself, and particularly to his sister Kylie.

Maybe he was in denial. And what about her? Was she in love or in need? Did she have to cloak her sexual urges with pretty fantasies of being deeply in love?

Gillian flinched. Never had a reality check been as well-timed as this one, but that didn't mean she had to like it.

"Put me down, Dev," she said wearily. "This is as far as it goes. And it's a whole lot farther than we should have gone."

"Gillian—"

"Put me down right now, Devlin."

He continued to hold her, nibbling softly on the curve of her neck. "Baby, you don't mean—"

"I hope you don't intend to turn into one of those cheesebags who insist that when a woman says no she really means yes."

Gillian eyed him warily. She began to struggle but didn't have to escalate her efforts, for Devlin set her on her feet.

"See, I haven't turned into a cheesebag," he said gruffly, then dropped back onto the couch. His whole body was one throbbing, roaring ache and merely standing up required too much exertion.

Gillian stared blindly at the TV screen. The laugh track seemed to be echoing in her head. Her legs were shaky and her whole body pulsed with unslaked desire. She guessed that Devlin felt much the same way. "Thank you," she murmured.

"For what?" he snapped.

"For not—you know—trying to force me."

"I've never had to force myself on any woman and I never will, Gillian. I'd just like to know what happened." He rubbed his temples with his fingers. "You were with me all the way and then—boom! You lowered it."

"I—I wasn't thinking straight."

"I agree, you weren't, especially not when you told me to stop."

She groaned. "That's not what I meant, Dev." Her whole body was still tingling from the sensual magic of his touch and the feel of his hard muscles seemed to be imprinted along the length of her. She squeezed her thighs together, trying to ease the ache, painfully aware of the liquid emptiness there.

"Why don't you tell me what you mean, Gillian." He held out his hand to her. "Come here, sweetheart."

Instead, she backed away, staring at him as if he were a creature conjured up in a botched lab experiment. She'd been expecting anger and accusations and was ready to confront that. His unexpected display of understanding—not to mention calling her *sweetheart!*—floored her.

Gillian sank into the chair across from the sofa. "I'll tell you straight up, Devlin, so there can be no more, um, misunderstandings." She took a deep breath. "I'm never having sex again."

Dev bolted upright in his seat. "What?"

"I guess I should amend that to 'I'm not having sex unless I'm married' but the chances of me getting married are zilch so..." Her voice trailed off and she shrugged.

He gaped at her, his blue eyes wide. "Gillian, what are you—"

"I've been listening to Dr. Leah on the radio," Gillian cut in earnestly. "And she says that sex is wrong except in a committed, caring, legal relationship—that would be marriage. Dr. Leah is right, too. If only I'd listened to her before we—'' She clasped her hand over her mouth, shocked by what she'd almost given away.

But Devlin didn't notice; he was too stunned by the first half of her statement. ''You listen to a shrink on the *radio?* And you take the advice from such a program seriously?''

''Very seriously. Dr. Leah says things that need to be said. Things I need to hear.''

''Good God, Gillian, if you must talk with a shrink, at least do it personally. Face-to-face. Make an appointment with Holly. She's supposed to be very good at what she does.''

''I'm sure she is,'' Gillian said flatly. Confide to Holly— who loved Devlin—that she'd given birth to Dev's child? A chill shuddered through her. ''But Dr. Leah has been very helpful to me.''

''By telling you never to have sex again.'' Devlin was incredulous. ''And you actually go along with that?''

''I'll have sex when I'm married and not until,'' Gillian insisted. ''That's responsible behavior and don't try to talk me into behaving irresponsibly, because you can't. And I won't, not ever again.''

''Making love with someone you care about is not irresponsible, Gillian.''

''In other words, 'If it feels good, do it.' Wasn't that the motto on buttons and T-shirts in the sixties? People confused a catchphrase for words to live by.''

''Then the seventies came along and replaced it with 'Have a nice day,''' Devlin interjected dryly. ''And in the eighties, it was 'Don't worry, be happy.' Definitely words to live by.''

''The eighties also gave us 'Just say no,''' Gillian reminded him.

''Which brings us to the nineties. Doesn't 'Just do it' strike a chord with you?''

She smiled a little. ''How about 'Been there, done that, got the T-shirt'?''

''A brand-new cliché. But frankly speaking, your new slogan—which would be, what? 'Hold out for a ring'—doesn't have much chance of mass appeal, Gillian.''

''Then it's a good thing I'm not in marketing, isn't it?'' She picked up her mail and shuffled through it. ''Dev, remember when

I asked you to leave? Well, I'm asking again and this time, I really, *really* mean it.''

Devlin said nothing.

Gillian cast a quick, covert glance at him. "I know you're mad at me but—"

"I'm not mad at you." True, his body was wired with sexual tension and frustration prickled at every nerve, but he wasn't angry. He couldn't define the strange mixture of emotions welling up within him but anger wasn't one of them. "Did you expect me to tear around the room like a wild stallion whose studly instincts had been thwarted?"

She blushed. "I...sent you the wrong signals and you acted on them. You have a right to be furious."

"It would certainly make it a lot easier to evict me if I were ranting and raving, wouldn't it? But here I sit, polite and nonthreatening, and you're wondering how on earth you're ever going to get rid of me."

"How on earth am I ever going to get rid of you, Dev?" She threw up her hands, half joking, half serious.

Before he could reply, the telephone rang. Gillian hurried to the small kitchen to answer it, relief coursing through her. At this time of the evening, chances were good that it was Carmen or Suzy or one of her other foster sisters calling. Dev would hardly hang around while she talked on the phone, especially if the conversation was a long one filled with sisterly trivia. He would flee from sheer boredom.

To her astonishment, the female voice on the other line asked for Devlin. "It's for you." She held out the phone.

Devlin looked sheepish. "I left your number on my answering machine."

"Because you thought you'd be spending the night here?" She glowered at him, wondering which was worse, his confidence or his unmitigated gall. Maybe they were the same thing.

"You can reach him at—" Gillian began, but he snatched the receiver from her before she could direct the other woman to call Devlin Brennan at his own place, not hers.

"Brenda?" Gillian heard him say.

The name instantly clicked with her. He'd mentioned a cousin Brenda a short while ago, one he described as a "loser." From his less-than-pleased tone of voice, it seemed quite possible that very cousin was now on the other end of the line.

"Calm down, Brenda. I can't understand a word you're saying," he ordered on a note of unconcealed exasperation. He caught Gillian's eye and made a gun with his thumb and forefinger, holding it to his head, leaving no doubt that this phone call was already maddening.

She flashed him an evil smile and sauntered back into the living room. "The Munsters" had ended, but she found a vintage "Welcome Back, Kotter" episode to watch.

Forty-five minutes later, Devlin staggered out of the kitchen. "That was my cousin Brenda."

"The one who couldn't swim? The one who cried while you enjoyed flaunting your superior pool skills?"

"We were children then, Gillian," he growled. "But I certainly wasn't expecting to hear from her now. I haven't seen much of Brenda over the years, and even when we happened to be together, like at a funeral or a wedding, we hardly spoke. We have nothing in common and very little to say to each other."

"Well, I guess you made up for lost time with that phone call." Gillian's lips quirked.

"That phone call was the longest conversation I've ever had with her! Or with anyone, for that matter. I don't like being tied up on the phone, I'll take E-mail any day."

"But E-mail is so less personal."

"My point exactly. Especially when dealing with Brenda."

"From what you've said, you and your cousin haven't been very close in the past. Does Brenda hope to change that?" Gillian asked sweetly, needling him and enjoying it.

"Brenda's a lunatic! She is planning to bring her kid here to the hospital and intends to stay with me!"

Gillian's widened with concern. "Is her child sick?"

But Devlin didn't hear her, he was pacing the floor like a manic lion. "I have a one-bedroom apartment, Gillian. One bedroom! Where am I going to put Brenda and her twelve-year-old kid? The place is too small for *one* person and I'm supposed to board guests?"

"What's the matter with Brenda's child? Devlin, sit down and calm down!" Gillian added sternly.

He came to an immediate halt. "You sound like me trying to

get through to Brenda." Dev grimaced wryly. "See, I'm already getting crazy and they haven't even arrived. What in the world am I going to do with Brenda and Starr Lynn?"

"Starr Lynn is the sick child?" Gillian guessed.

"She's Brenda's daughter, but she isn't sick." Devlin walked over to the sofa and sat down beside Gillian. "Starr Lynn is an aspiring ice skater. According to my sister, the kid has had some success. She's the regional novice champion, whatever that is."

"The novice level of figure skating is the competitive rank below juniors, which is just one step from the top, the senior ladies' division," Gillian said knowledgeably. "That's the big time, where the stars who go to the World Championships and the Olympics come from—you know, like Kristi Yamaguchi and Peggy Fleming." She shrugged when he stared questioningly at her. "I like to watch ice skating on TV, so I know a lot about it."

"Then maybe you can relate to Brenda and Starr Lynn. I don't watch ice skating at all, not even during the Olympics. There's something about men in sequined suits that makes me uneasy."

"You're of the if-men-are-on-ice-skates-they'd-better-have-a-hockey-stick mentality? How predictably yango!"

"What?"

"A yango is—" she paused, smiling. "I wish Mark was here to describe all the fine points that constitute yango-hood. Or is it yango-icity? He has an encyclopedic knowledge of the subject."

"That would be Mark, your foster brother, the one who was here the day I moved in?" Devlin was adept at putting names with faces, when he chose to be.

"Yes, Mark Morrow. He lives in L.A. He's working as a waiter but he's really an actor. He's very talented and I just know he'll get his big break soon."

"Wanting to be an actor sounds about as realistic as wanting to be an Olympic ice skater," scoffed Dev.

"Some people have dreams that go beyond our own prosaic goals, Devlin. They shouldn't be mocked for them."

"I never considered being an orthopedic surgeon to be a prosaic goal." Dev looked sulky.

"All right, orthopedic surgeons are exempt from being prosaic." Gillian was patronizing. She leaned forward, resting her elbows on her knees. "Getting back to your little cousin Starr Lynn... What's wrong with her?"

"Understand that this is third-hand information, from various doctors to Brenda to me," he cautioned.

"I'm not investigating a malpractice suit, I just asked a question."

Devlin chuckled. "Color me paranoid. Talking to my cousin takes its toll." He grew serious. "Apparently, Starr Lynn has a stress fracture in her right leg and some damage to the ligaments and cartilage in her right knee. An orthopedic specialist at the medical center in Columbus, Ohio, told her to take at least a year off from skating and concentrate on physical therapy exercises to heal and strengthen her leg. Another doctor suggested arthroscopic surgery for her knee, which would require a minimum six-month recovery, and yet another says to give up skating altogether because of the danger of permanent damage to her leg. Brenda doesn't like what she hears from any of them. She's decided to come to Michigan and get another opinion."

"Yours."

"Mine," Devlin affirmed darkly. "Never mind that I'm still a resident, and she already has professional advice from three orthopedic specialists, all with experience in sports injuries. Brenda will leave no stone unturned trying to hear what she wants to hear."

"Which would be that Starr Lynn can keep on skating with no time off and no problems," Gillian surmised. "What does Starr Lynn want?"

"Good question. Brenda went on and on about the kid's talent and potential. Said that her mother—that would be my aunt Bobbie—refinanced her house to help pay skating expenses. It's a sure bet that both Starr Lynn's mother and grandmother are rabid for Olympic gold and all the money and fame that go with it."

"What about Starr Lynn's father? Doesn't he have a say?"

"Her father has never been in the picture. Brenda had the kid at seventeen, and the guy was already history." Devlin's eyebrows narrowed and he looked squarely at Gillian. "Like that husband of yours, I guess. Except Brenda never married her baby's father."

Neither did I. The thought resounded so loudly in Gillian's head that she feared Devlin might hear. She stood up, suddenly too edgy and tense to remain still. It was imperative to keep the focus away from her and Ashley—and Ashley's father, who had never been in the picture, either. Until now. Gillian gulped.

"I feel sorry for your cousins. Obviously, Starr Lynn does have talent or she wouldn't have gotten as far as she has. It must be awfully hard for her and her mother to have to face the fact that her career could be over before it's even really begun."

"Twelve-year-olds shouldn't have careers. And mothers shouldn't live their lives through their children. Like it or not, Starr Lynn's injuries have to be dealt with and treated, no matter how it affects her skating. Brenda and Starr Lynn need to hear those facts and I intend to make sure they listen."

"At least try to be tactful, Dev. It'll be a crushing blow for them both if their dream really is over. They'll need understanding, not a lecture from you."

"I guess that's true." Devlin nodded thoughtfully. "Maybe I should arrange to have Brenda and Starr Lynn talk to Holly. Handling big emotional scenes is her bailiwick. Holly is especially interested in working with adolescent girls, and Brenda could provide an interesting war story to share at future American Psychiatric Association conventions." He grinned.

Holly, again. Gillian saw the warmth in his eyes as he spoke of his true love and felt a sickening, hollow ache in her chest. Once again she reminded herself to never forget where Devlin's heart really lay. Foolishly she'd managed to do exactly that during those passion-drugged moments earlier, and she berated herself for her stupidity.

"I think you should go call Holly right now, Devlin." She wanted him gone. She'd played the deluded fool long enough tonight.

He stayed seated. "I'll call her tomorrow at her office."

"When are Brenda and Starr Lynn coming?"

Devlin sighed. "Tomorrow. They're driving up and should arrive around dinnertime."

Gillian walked to the front door and opened it. "Good night, Devlin," she said decisively.

Reluctantly, Dev decided that her point was well made. "I guess Holly does deserve some advance warning." Heaving another sigh, he headed toward the door. He paused, towering over Gillian. "Do I get a good-night kiss?"

Unexpectedly, tears burned her eyes. Why did he play these cruel games, trying to kiss her while his thoughts were all of Holly? Did she deserve such treatment because she'd encouraged him earlier on the sofa?

She wondered what answers Dr. Leah would give to those questions and imagined herself calling in for advice. The doctor would ask questions of her own in that direct no-nonsense tone and style of hers, and at the mention of Ashley, Dr. Leah would insist that it was Gillian's moral obligation to inform Devlin of his child's existence because children need two involved parents.

And if Gillian were to try to explain that it was too hard to tell him, that it was *impossible* to tell him, Dr Leah would declare with her characteristic alacrity, "Doing the right thing isn't always easy but you have to do it anyway."

Dr. Leah often said that keeping certain secrets was tantamount to telling lies. She was an ardent advocate of the truth, not even little white lies were to be tolerated.

Gillian shivered. Yes, that is exactly how the phone counseling session would go, and Dr. Leah was right, of course. If only she had the requisite courage...

She was lost in thought, but Devlin mistook her hesitation for consent. He leaned down and covered her mouth with his.

Gillian drew back as if he'd slapped her, pushed him away, and quickly slammed the door shut.

Five

Devlin stood alone in the hall, the searing image of Gillian's face imprinted on his mind's eye. *She'd looked ready to cry.* He had seen the tears shining in her light blue eyes, the pain etched on her face, her hurt unmistakable yet inexplicable.

Because he'd tried to kiss her good night? That didn't make sense, not considering those passionate kisses they'd shared earlier tonight. He trudged into his apartment, a wave of exhaustion crashing over him. He'd never been one to expend energy on the emotional front but since his path had recrossed with Gillian's, he felt like he was leading the charge. And getting nowhere. When he tried to advance, she retreated.

Frustration surged through him. Gillian Bailey was definitely a high-maintenance woman, a category he had taken care to avoid—until that fateful day he'd asked her out. Only to be unceremoniously dumped three months later!

She'd married and divorced another man and had a child, yet he was still drawn to her. Unfinished business perhaps? Maybe he had to have her again so he could get her out of his system once and for all. A dismal thought, because he'd never considered himself to be a player in such vengeful ego games. Worse, it was a game he couldn't even win because Gillian had added an impossible, ridiculous condition with which no man in his right mind would comply.

No sex unless preceded by a wedding. No marriage, no sex. A rule from a radio shrink's relationship handbook from hell.

But was he doing the logical thing, the sane thing, and distancing himself from Gillian? Oh, no, not him. Instead he was pursuing her. Actively. It was enough to make him question his own mental state. Maybe he should tune into Dr. Leah's program or write out a psychiatric consult for himself.

The gallows humor helped a little. He'd have to keep that in mind tomorrow when Brenda and her ice-skating prodigy arrived, determined to alter medical science to suit themselves.

Thinking about all the consults that he would have to set up made him lament his cousin's stubborn persistence all over again. Brenda had been adamant about coming *tomorrow* with Starr Lynn; he'd been unable to put her off for even one week. That meant he would have to ask his superiors in the orthopedic service to rearrange their schedules to squeeze in appointments with his young cousin—whose condition was already well-documented and did not qualify as an emergency.

And ultimately, the entire endeavor would turn out to be a waste of everybody's time and energy. Injuries were injuries and couldn't be wished away. Invariably, the specialists here in Michigan were going to see the same stress fracture and knee problems that their colleagues in Ohio had diagnosed, whether Brenda and Starr Lynn liked it or not. And it was a sure bet they wouldn't like hearing a repeat of the news they had already rejected.

Gillian had advised him to be tactful and understanding with his cousins. Devlin shook his head in anticipatory exasperation. She didn't know what she was asking! Professional tact was definitely required, which brought Holly and yet another consult to mind. He punched the button that speed-dialed her number.

"Let me guess. You need a ride back to the hospital to pick up your car in the parking lot," Holly said as soon as she heard his voice.

"Damn, I forgot all about my car!" Devlin groaned. "Tonight is going from bad to worse."

"Your *date* didn't work out according to plan? Poor Dev."

Devlin heaved a long-suffering sigh. "Will you give me a ride back to the hospital so I can pick up my car, Holly?"

"So now your car is operational again? Convenient how it breaks down when you need an excuse to be with Gillian. And it's miraculous how it runs again, just as soon as you want it to."

"I'm glad you're having so much fun with this, Holly."

"But you're not? What happened, Dev?"

"Never mind the details, but did you ever hear of a quack on the radio named Dr. Leah? Well, Gillian is one of her faithful disciples."

"I know the program, and the doctor isn't a quack. Actually, she's a certified psychologist with Ivy League credentials and a—"

"Spare me the accolades, Holly. Just get over here and pick me up. And be forewarned, I have a favor to ask you, a professional one."

"If you want Evan Weil transferred back to my floor, forget it," warned Holly.

"Nothing that simple. My cousin Brenda will make the Weil boy seem like an afternoon stroll along the sunny shores of Lake Dexter."

"Sounds challenging. I can hardly wait."

Fifteen minutes later Gillian heard a jaunty rhythm of knocks on Devlin's door. She sneaked a peek through the peephole in her door, and then cursed the masochistic compulsion that had caused her to look in the first place.

For standing outside Devlin's door was Holly Casale, tall, lean and gorgeous in a navy jumpsuit that showed off her long, long legs. Gillian stood behind her own door, feeling short and dumpy and inadequate, but she couldn't seem to look away. She watched as Dev opened his door to Holly.

"It's about time you got here," he scolded in a deep mock growl.

He was smiling and the affection in his tone, on his face, caused Gillian's heart to contract painfully. She crept away from the door and turned up the volume on her television set to block out any further sounds from across the hall.

Don't think, she ordered. Concentrate on "The Brady Bunch" and forget that Devlin and Holly are over there together.

But the Bradys couldn't keep her from speculating on what was happening across the hall. Sex, of course. How could Devlin resist a woman as beautiful and sexy as Holly? Why would he want to? And how could Holly not crave Devlin, who was the most fascinating, appealing, irresistible man Gillian had ever met?

Gillian touched her fingers to her lips, remembering the feel of Devlin's mouth on hers. And gulped back the sob welling in her throat. If only life could be as uncomplicated and easy to understand as on TV where everything was resolved in either thirty or sixty minutes—even less, with time out for commercial breaks.

After dinner the next day Ashley tooled around her playpen, jabbering to the toy population who resided there. A few feet away, Gillian, dressed for housework in cut-off jeans and a short pale lime T-shirt, finished the mealtime kitchen cleanup.

She tensed at the knock on her door and immediately admonished herself. She'd told Mark and Carmen that she did not intend to cower every time she heard a knock, yet here she stood, cowering. Worrying that Devlin Brennan was the one knocking. Afraid of her own weakness for a man who was willing to use her for sex, but who loved someone else.

The knock sounded again, more insistently. Gillian reminded herself that her unexpected visitor could very well be Shelly or Heather from next door. But no matter what or who, she could not continue to cower! Gillian walked resolutely to the door.

She gaped at her unexpected visitors, Devlin's cousins, Brenda and Starr Lynn Brennan, whom she recognized on sight. They didn't even have to introduce themselves, she guessed who they were because she knew they were due in town today and—well, they looked like Brennans.

Brenda's resemblance to Kylie was strong, though her black and purple spandex outfit didn't look like something elegant, classy Kylie might choose to wear, at least not outside a gym. Starr Lynn, a slim, striking young girl with huge blue eyes and a thick dark brown ponytail, could've passed for a junior edition of either Kylie or Brenda.

Or a twelve-year-old version of baby Ashley. Gillian's pulses went into overdrive.

"I'm Devlin's cousin Brenda and this is my daughter Starr Lynn," Brenda announced, and stepped inside without waiting to be asked, dragging her child along with her. "We're supposed to come over here and meet you."

Gillian looked puzzled. "Did Devlin—"

"He went out to get us a pizza for dinner," said Brenda. "That's what Starr Lynn wanted to eat and we decided to splurge on the calories tonight."

"He wanted to get away, I could tell," Starr Lynn put in. "I bet he takes his time coming back. Kylie says he's not used to having company." The girl looked directly at Gillian. "Who are you?"

"She's Cousin Devlin's neighbor, Gillian Bailey," Brenda explained. "Cade said we should introduce ourselves to her, remember?"

"Oh, yeah." Starr Lynn nodded and her ponytail bobbed up and down. "But I forget why."

"He didn't say why." Brenda stared assessingly at Gillian. "So you know Kylie and Cade and Devlin, huh? Well, now you know us, too."

"Nice to meet you," Gillian said faintly.

"Oh-hh! You have a baby!" Starr Lynn exclaimed, spotting Ashley in her playpen. She ran across the room and lifted Ashley out. "Look, Mom, isn't she cute?"

"Starr Lynn, be careful! Don't drop the baby!" Brenda called, while Gillian rushed over to the two children and hovered anxiously, just in case Starr Lynn should lose her grip. On her baby cousin!

Ashley was beaming at the older girl, delighted with her presence. She made a grab for the bright colored beads on Starr Lynn's necklace, wrapping her tiny fist around it. Starr Lynn didn't seem to mind. "What's her name?"

"Ashley."

"That's practically my most favorite name! I know two Ashleys at the skating rink and there are three more in my class at school," said Starr Lynn, shifting Ashley from one small straight hip to the other.

"It's a popular name," Gillian conceded, remembering Devlin's response. At least his young cousin was more diplomatic.

"Starr Lynn just loves babies." Brenda joined them. "She can't wait for Kylie and Cade to have one so she can baby-sit."

"I wish *you'd* have one, Mom," Starr Lynn retorted. "If you and Noah get married and have a baby, then maybe—"

"Don't start with me on that," warned Brenda. "Here, let me hold the baby." She held out her arms, reaching for Ashley.

Starr Lynn whirled around, not ready to relinquish the baby. Ashley chortled, enjoying the motion, and the twelve-year-old obligingly twirled twice more. "I want to play with her, Mom."

"Oh, okay. I need to talk to Gillian anyway. Why don't you take the baby to her room and see what she's got in there?" Brenda suggested, and Starr Lynn scampered off, Ashley in her arms.

Gillian started after them but Brenda caught and halted her as the two young cousins disappeared into Ashley's room. "I think I get it now," Brenda murmured.

"W-what?" Disconcerted, Gillian stared at Brenda's fingers manacling her wrist. She had long, sculpted primrose-red nails. "Excuse me, I'll go check on the children."

"They'll be fine. Starr Lynn is good with little kids. She even helps the younger skaters at the rink, gives them pointers and all." Brenda dropped her hand and folded her arms in front of her, staring at Gillian with undisguised curiosity. "I'm pretty sure I figured out why Cade made such a big deal about insisting that I meet you."

"I don't know why he would do that." Gillian trembled with apprehension.

"It's because of Ashley, of course." Brenda looked quite pleased with herself. "But how come you and Devlin are keeping the baby a secret from the rest of the family? Afraid his folks will freak 'cause you're not married? Uncle Wayne and Aunt Connie are pretty traditional and all that, but—"

"Oh, God!" Gillian gasped, grabbing the top of the playpen for support. "Brenda, you can't—please, don't—don't say anything about the baby to Devlin."

Brenda stared at her, perplexed. "Huh?"

"He doesn't know he's Ashley's father," Gillian blurted.

The moment the words were out, she knew she'd made a terrible mistake. She shouldn't have admitted anything, she should have laughed off Brenda's allegations and stuck with the story of her faux marriage, no matter what. But she'd been deeply shaken by the other woman's perception and exceptional bluntness and now, now...

"Wait a minute! You mean, Devlin lives across the hall from his own child and doesn't know she's his?" Brenda was incredulous. "How can that be? Cade and Kylie know and—"

"No one told Cade or Kylie anything about Ashley," Gillian interjected desperately.

"Well, then, Cade took a good look at the baby and guessed she was a Brennan, just like I did." Brenda frowned thoughtfully. "But maybe Kylie doesn't know. She didn't say anything to me about you, Cade did, when she was out of the room. He said it was imperative—that was the word he used, *imperative*—that I go to your apartment and meet you while I'm here in town." She stared into space, seemingly thinking aloud. "I thought it was because of Starr Lynn, that maybe you had skating connections or something. But it's not Starr Lynn at all, it's Ashley. Cade wanted me to see *her*."

Gillian shook her head helplessly, searching for words.

Brenda had plenty. "Cade is brilliant—and very sly. He wanted the family to know about Devlin's child but didn't want to say anything about Ashley himself. Cade is always griping about the backstabbing, gossiping Brennans, and he didn't want to seem like one. Now he can claim that I just happened to figure things out all on my own. He hopes I'll be the one to tell."

"Brenda, please don't. You see, Dev hasn't figured out anything," Gillian said softly, giving up any hope of further pretense. She sensed it best to make an ally of Brenda now.

"And Devlin and Kylie are supposed to be the smart ones in the family!" Brenda gave a derisive hoot. "Ashley looks exactly like Starr Lynn did when she was a baby. She looks just like the baby pictures of me and my sister Bridget and our cousins Kylie and Polly. Devlin had to notice!"

"I don't think he ever spent a lot of time looking at baby pictures."

"Maybe not, but what about the facts? You had sex, he can count to nine months, and the baby looks just like a Brennan. It's so obvious. How could Devlin not suspect?"

"I made sure he didn't suspect," Gillian confessed, and gave Brenda an abridged version of their breakup and her quick marriage of convenience to Mark.

"Brenda, please, please, keep our secret," she pleaded. "You're a mother yourself, and you know what—"

"Self-centered jerks men are," Brenda concluded vehemently. "Oh, yeah, I know! I mean, *most* men are jerks," she amended. "My boyfriend Noah is different, but even he doesn't understand certain things like the sacrifices a mother makes for her child. Especially a single mother."

"Brenda? Starr Lynn?" Devlin's voice sounded in the hall, amidst the sound of opening and closing doors.

"Daddy's home," cracked Brenda.

Gillian paled. "Please, Brenda!"

"Relax! I won't spill. But you'd better let him know we're over here." Brenda wandered over to the TV and sat down, letting Gillian relay their whereabouts to Devlin.

Gillian met Devlin in the hall. He was wearing the baggy, faded blue scrub suit he'd purloined from the hospital laundry for comfortable off-duty wear, and holding a steaming pizza box. He looked baffled. "I know it seems impossible to lose anybody in a one bedroom apartment but it seems to have happened. I can't find my cousins."

"They're at my place." His look of utter astonishment was comical, and Gillian couldn't suppress her smile. "They knocked on my door and introduced themselves. They, uh, were being neighborly."

"Like my brother-in-law!" Devlin was appalled. "I'd apologize, but I'm not sure what for. The town of Port McClain seems to produce citizens eerily obsessed with neighborliness." He rolled his eyes. "Or maybe it's not the town at all, maybe it's just my relatives who are strange."

Gillian refrained from comment. "I'll tell Brenda and Starr Lynn that you're back with their dinner."

He followed her to the door of her apartment while she informed her drop-in guests that dinner was about to be served across the hall. Brenda didn't glance up from the television program she was watching.

Starr Lynn, still holding the baby, appeared in the living room. "I want to stay and play with Ashley," she announced. "Can't we eat the pizza here?"

"No," Devlin said firmly. Bad enough his relatives were imposing on him, it was unfair to permit them to intrude on Gillian, too. "We'll eat in my apartment. Now."

"Then I don't want any pizza," said Starr Lynn. "You and Mom can have it. I'll be over later." She waltzed Ashley out of the room.

Brenda's eyes remained glued to the TV screen.

Devlin and Gillian looked at each other. She shrugged.

Devlin cleared his throat. "Brenda, please tell your daughter that the three of us are going over to my apartment to eat—and that we're leaving right now!"

"Starr Lynn will want Ashley to come, too," said Brenda. "She loves that baby already."

"Ashley is staying here with her mother," Dev decreed. "Come on, Brenda, get your kid and let's go!"

"Oh, lighten up, Devlin!" Brenda snapped. "Starr Lynn said she won't eat the pizza over at your place. I can't force it down her throat, you know. Why can't we just stay here and eat?"

"You can," Gillian said quickly. "I'll get some paper plates and napkins. What does everybody want to drink? I have soda, iced tea, beer—"

"Starr Lynn likes diet soda and I'll have a beer." Brenda rose to her feet. "Let me help you set up."

"This is ridiculous!" Devlin shifted the pizza box from one hand to the other, looking like he'd prefer to heave it at his cousin. "We're not imposing on Gillian for another minute. She has things to do, she has a baby to take care of. Brenda, let me make one thing perfectly clear. I will not kowtow to any child, no matter how accustomed she might be to calling the shots. If you don't tell Starr Lynn to get over to my place—where she will eat the damn pizza!—I'll carry her over there myself."

"Devlin, you're overreacting," Gillian admonished nervously. "I'm glad for the company. Ashley was, um, fussy earlier and Starr Lynn is doing a great job entertaining her. I'd like them to stay. Really."

"As long as you don't mind, Gillian," Devlin said through gritted teeth.

"She doesn't mind. You're the only one who seems to mind, Devlin," taunted Brenda. "I wonder why."

Gillian wondered if Dev's cousin was seeking some overdue revenge for those long-ago games of one-upsmanship at the Port

McClain swimming pool. It was horrifying to think that her most vital secret was now a lethal weapon possessed by Brenda Brennan. To be used in a future round of family warfare?

"The Brennan men are always trying to boss people around," Brenda said conversationally as she helped Gillian set the table. "My dad and uncle Guy aren't too good at it, but Uncle Wayne did it well for years in the Navy. And of course, there was our grandfather and Uncle Gene. Remember that pair of nasty old grouches, Devlin?"

"I have fond memories of both Grandfather Brennan and Uncle Gene, Brenda."

"Well, I don't. They were mean, and they were always yelling." Eyes flashing, Brenda turned to Gillian. "Oh, not at Devlin and Kylie, of course, not at those perfect angels."

"Kylie and I weren't perfect, but we didn't live in Port McClain and our visits there were fairly short," Dev explained to Gillian. "We weren't around long enough to get on anybody's nerves."

"Oh, really?" Brenda smiled sardonically.

Gillian decided an immediate change of subject was in order. "Let's call Starr Lynn in to eat before the pizza gets cold," she suggested brightly.

"When Devlin and Kylie and their parents used to come to town it was like the Royal Family had arrived." Brenda was still resenting every minute of those miserable past visits. "The rest of us could've dropped off the face of the earth and nobody would've noticed."

"You're exaggerating, Brenda," Devlin protested mildly.

"Devlin was the first Brennan grandchild, and he came first with them, all right." Brenda presented her case to Gillian. "Grandma used to call Devlin her little prince, but he wasn't always so princely. I remember one time Prince Devlin punched my brother so hard he broke poor Brent's nose!"

"Brent had it coming." Devlin shrugged. "He'd locked Kylie in a trunk in the attic, she could have suffocated. What's Brent doing now, Brenda? I heard from my dad that he's out on parole again."

"Yes. And the terms were that Brent had to leave town and the State of Ohio."

"I see the fine hand of Cade Austin in that deal." Devlin grinned.

"No doubt. Brent moved to Phoenix and got a job there. He seems to be doing okay." Brenda sighed. "We miss him, but it's for the best, I guess."

"Except for the unfortunate citizens of Phoenix," drawled Devlin.

"It can be helpful for a person to make a fresh start in a new area." Gillian was tactful.

Devlin sat down at the table and helped himself to a piece of pizza. "Gillian is a social worker, ever optimistic about fresh starts no matter how long the odds."

"Which probably explains a lot about her relationship with you," muttered Brenda.

Gillian flinched. She could not allow herself to become the battleground in yet another round of Brennan hostilities. "Starr Lynn, the pizza is ready!" she called.

Nibbling on a slice of pizza, Starr Lynn chattered about upcoming skating competitions, rattling off the strengths and weaknesses of other skaters, but not mentioning her own injuries. Devlin and Brenda listened and ate in silence. Gillian watched Ashley, who was insistent upon practicing her new walking skills.

Still unsteady on her feet, the baby took a few wobbly steps, then landed on her bottom on the floor. Gillian tried to be nonchalant about her daughter's tumble. All the baby books advised staying calm and murmuring something like, "Uh-oh," in a cheerful tone.

Starr Lynn, having read no such manuals, immediately rushed over to pick up Ashley and shower her with sympathy. But Ashley was in no mood to be coddled. She wanted to walk, and she wriggled and struggled to be free, finally emitting a yowl of protest.

"The baby doesn't want to be held, Starr Lynn," said Brenda.

"Put her down," ordered Devlin.

"But she might fall again." Starr Lynn was worried. "It hurts to fall."

"Falling on the carpet isn't like taking a fall on the ice," explained Gillian. "And look how short Ashley is! She doesn't have very far to go to get to the ground, does she?"

"She's so little and cute." Smiling, Starr Lynn set Ashley on her feet.

The baby toddled off, tumbling again after a few steps. She immediately pulled herself back up to try again.

"That's exactly how you were when you were learning to walk, Starr Lynn," Brenda said fondly. "No matter how many times you went down, you got right back up and started again. You were the same way with your skating."

"Maybe Ashley will be a skater like me!" Starr Lynn exclaimed. "I can give her some lessons while she's really little, and when she's four she can start training with my coach."

"Four years old isn't really little?" Devlin arched his dark brows. "Since when?"

"Four isn't too early to start training seriously if you want to get anywhere these days," Starr Lynn said earnestly.

"That is probably one of the most alarming statements I've ever heard." Devlin frowned his disapproval. "Start strenuous training for a competitive sport at the ripe old age of four? Why? So by age twelve, the young athlete will be faced with stress fractures, torn ligaments, and lifelong knee problems that could ultimately affect mobility? And I don't mean skating, I mean the ability to *walk* without pain."

"If you're talking about Starr Lynn..." Brenda began defensively.

"Of course I'm talking about her," Devlin cut in. "I've looked over her medical records you brought along, Brenda, and I set up appointments with two of our top orthopedic specialists for tomorrow, but I can tell you now, they're going to say—"

"I don't care what they say, I'm going to skate!" Starr Lynn threw down her half-eaten pizza crust and jumped to her feet. "I'm the regional novice champion and I'm not going to lose my momentum. After all these years, I'm finally getting noticed! I'm going to take the tests to qualify for the junior level and I'm going to pass them. Next year, I'll be skating at nationals as a junior, and I'm going to win there, too. *Nobody* is going to stop me, especially not some stupid doctors who don't know anything about me or about skating!"

"All the coaches say that Starr Lynn has the attitude and determination of a true champion." Brenda gazed with awe at her daughter. "She insists on practicing and competing, even if she's sick or hurt or tired."

"I'm a winner," Starr Lynn announced. "As long as I'm skating, I don't get sick or tired or hurt."

"That's not a winning attitude, that's denial," Devlin said sharply. "Being able to accept the truth is as vitally important as training is to any athlete, Starr Lynn. And the truth is that you cannot continue to skate unless your stress fracture heals and your knee has been—"

"I'm not having any operation!" Starr Lynn shouted. "It'll take too much time to come back from it. And I'm not going to sit around and miss the competition next month. I'm going to skate and I'm going to win."

"You're going to cause permanent damage to your knee and your leg unless you take the necessary time off and get the proper treatment," argued Devlin. "And we're going to make sure that you get the right care, whether you want to or not."

"I don't like you, I wish we weren't here!" Starr Lynn cried. "Let's go home right now, Mom." She stormed toward the door and flung it open.

"Uh, Starr Lynn, honey, we can't leave tonight," Brenda hedged, rising to her feet. "It's too late for another long drive."

"Okay, tomorrow then," Starr Lynn called from the hall. "But I don't want to stay in his stupid apartment. Let's get our stuff and go to a hotel and drive home in the morning."

"Tomorrow you're going to the hospital for your appointments with two of our busiest orthopedic surgeons," Devlin sternly called to her. "They agreed to work you into their schedules as a personal favor to me, and you're damn well going to show up."

"No!" Starr Lynn shrieked. Several doors opened along the corridor.

"What's going on?" someone called from down the hall.

"Mind your own business," the twelve-year-old ordered the onlookers, and her proclamation was followed by doors slamming up and down the hall. Glowering, Starr Lynn leaned against the door to Devlin's apartment, her arms crossed defensively in front of her chest.

"First a temper tantrum, then she insults the neighbors." Devlin scowled his disgust. "Brenda, will you please control your daughter!"

Brenda moved slowly across the room. "It was a mistake to come here. Cade said you could help and I hoped he was right, but you're as negative as those other doctors in Columbus. We'll check into a hotel tonight and leave for home tomorrow."

"No, you won't!" Devlin snapped. "Do you know how much trouble it was to get those consults on a single day's notice? Starr Lynn is going to the hospital tomorrow and she is going to follow the medical advice she is given. It's for her own good, Brenda. Starr Lynn is just a child, and it's up to you to take care of her, to look after her best interests. For god's sake, you're the parent—act like one!"

"You're telling *me* to act like a parent?" Brenda practically spit out the words.

Gillian's heart leaped into her throat. She watched the outraged Brenda glare at Devlin, saw her turn her head and look at little Ashley who was cruising along the length of the sofa, babbling happily. She could almost read the other woman's mind.

"Brenda, don't," Gillian pleaded.

But Brenda didn't look at her. Perhaps she didn't even hear her.

"You're the biggest self-righteous hypocrite I've ever met, Devlin Brennan," Brenda cried, her dark blue eyes boring into her cousin with laserlike intensity. "You have some nerve lecturing me about acting like a parent when I've spent the past twelve years taking care of my child. And I've taken good care of her, too. I'd do anything for my daughter, I'd give her anything."

"Then help her face the truth about her injuries and the need for treatment, Brenda," Devlin said quietly. "Living in a state of denial isn't going to—"

"*I'm* not the one living in a state of denial," Brenda cut in, her voice rising with each word. "You are! Shame on you, pretending that Ashley isn't your child. Why don't you take your own advice, Devlin? Face the truth and act like a parent to your own daughter."

Six

For a few long, tense moments, Brenda's words seemed to reverberate throughout the room. Gillian felt them pounding into her skull. She forgot to breathe, she thought her heart actually stopped beating.

"Rats! I'm not too good at keeping quiet about things. I bet Cade knew exactly what would happen when he sent me over here." This time Brenda sounded more disgruntled than outraged.

"Mama!" Ashley exclaimed gleefully, and all eyes were drawn to the baby who was proudly displaying her walking and talking skills.

Gillian and Devlin didn't move, didn't make a sound.

Brenda turned to Gillian. "I know I promised not to tell, but I didn't, really," she insisted. "I don't believe that Devlin didn't already know. He knew, he was just pretending not to. You know, like...like denial. I'm sure that's what Cade thought, too, and he wanted me to end the whole stupid charade."

Numbly, Gillian listened to Brenda justify her betrayal by pinning it on Devlin himself. She rushed over to Ashley and scooped her up in her arms. She clutched her child, rocking back and forth in reflexive maternal rhythm, trying to derive courage and comfort from the small, warm body.

Ashley, however, was in no mood to be held. She wriggled and arched her back in an attempt to win her freedom.

"Gillian." Devlin's voice seemed to fill the room. He said her name, nothing else.

Just the sound of it pained Gillian. She kept her gaze averted from him, focusing on Ashley, trying to interest her in a thick cardboard picture book. Ashley gummed the corner of the book, but when Gillian tried to hand it to her, she tossed it to the ground with a reproving, "Ba-ba-ba-ba!"

"She's got attitude, just like Starr Lynn," Brenda remarked admiringly.

Devlin glanced from Brenda to Gillian, who finally gave up trying to cuddle Ashley and set the baby on her feet. Ashley smiled in triumph and took a few steps before sitting down hard. He watched her grasp a chair and determinedly pull herself back up.

He felt as if he were in a waking dream, a kind of weird fugue state. He stared at the baby while Brenda's words ran through his head like the soundtrack to a movie. *Ashley...your child...your own daughter...* Could it possibly be true?

Nobody said anything. Only the low drone of the TV broke the silence.

"Do you want Starr Lynn and me to keep Ashley while you two go someplace to talk?" Brenda prompted at last. "I mean, you must have lots to talk about right now."

"No," Gillian said quickly, her voice shaking. "I just want everybody to go and leave us alone."

"You want us to disappear and pretend this didn't happen?" Devlin found his voice. The haze of shock was beginning to lift, and he felt anger stab him like shards of glass. "No way, Gillian. Brenda has made this—allegation and I demand to know if..." He paused to swallow hard. "If there is any truth in it."

"Why would I make it up?" Brenda shrugged. "You know it's true, Devlin."

"I know that Gillian was married when she gave birth to Ashley," Devlin said tightly. He had to address his cousin because Gillian refused to look in his direction. He could hardly bring himself to look at her, either. His eyes flicked over her, then darted away to again focus lingeringly on Ashley. His child?

He waited to be struck with some kind of elemental paternal bolt that would suddenly turn him into this baby's loving daddy. Wouldn't that happen if he really were her father? Wouldn't he feel it on some primordial level? But all he felt as he gazed at the little girl was confusion mixed with a sickening anger.

What if it were true?

Gillian ran the tip of her tongue over her dry lips. What should she say? What could she say? She was too distraught to speak so she remained silent, watching Ashley take some steps and fall and get back up to walk again.

Brenda heaved a sigh. Clearly she was losing patience with the couple, and if neither of them had anything to say—well, she did. "Gillian's marriage was a fake," she informed Devlin, breaking yet another confidence. "Did you actually think she went right from you to another guy and got pregnant within a week or something? Jeez, Devlin, that's real *princely* of you!"

Devlin felt winded, as if Brenda had kick-boxed him directly in the solar plexus. Guiltily, he darted another glance at Gillian whose face was flushed a hot scarlet. She did not take her eyes off Ashley who seemed cheerfully oblivious to the tension surrounding her.

"Well, just in case you want to know, Daddy..." Brenda's voice was laced with scorn. And a certain enjoyment. She didn't bother to conceal either one. "Gillian got a friend to marry her when she knew she was pregnant so the baby wouldn't be born illegitimate, but it wasn't really a marriage, if you know what I mean."

"No, Brenda." A muscle twitched in his jaw. "No, I don't know what you mean."

"Gillian never even slept with that Mark guy, not before or after," Brenda said blithely. "He might've been her husband for a little while, but he's not Ashley's father."

"Mark," Devlin echoed. Gillian's former husband was named Mark? The fact registered at the same instant he recalled her telling him Ashley's name, on that first day they'd remet in the hall. *Ashley Joy Morrow.* It resounded in his head, clear as a digital recording.

"Mark Morrow." Devlin rubbed his temples, frowning

fiercely. He looked up at the same moment that Gillian did, and their gazes collided with almost tangible force. He was truly staggered. "Mark Morrow is your foster brother, the one who was here the day I moved in. The one who is gay."

"Foster brother? And he's gay?" Brenda's eyes widened. "Wow, it really was a fake marriage!"

"Is it true, Gillian?" Devlin rasped. As if suddenly breaking the invisible bonds that had kept him motionless and in check, he surged across the room and grabbed her. "My God, is this whole wild story true?" When she instinctively started to struggle, he dug his fingers into her shoulders and gave her a hard shake. "Answer me, dammit!"

Quick as a flash, Brenda raced to the phone. "I'm calling the police if you hit her, Devlin!"

Stunned, he dropped his hands to his sides and stepped back. Gillian moved away just as quickly in the opposite direction. Advance, retreat. The words joined the cacophony already jangling in his head.

"The police?" Devlin gaped at his cousin in disbelief. "Have you lost you mind? Put down the phone, Brenda. I have never hit—"

"You did, too! You broke Brent's nose!" Brenda still clutched the telephone receiver.

"I was going to say, I've never hit a *woman*. And I certainly don't intend to start now." He heaved a heavy sigh. "Gillian, come with me. Brenda is right about one thing and that is, we have to talk. Without an audience."

Devlin glanced over at his cousin who had replaced the receiver but was still regarding him warily. "Brenda, will you please take care of the baby while Gillian and I talk privately?" His tone was measured and cool, which seemed to reassure Brenda.

She nodded her head, and for a silent moment they all looked at Ashley, who was off on yet another walking expedition.

But Gillian saw the glitter in Dev's eyes, the taut set of his jaw, the tension in his muscular frame as he strove to appear calm and at ease. For some reason, his iron control alarmed her more than his earlier burst of emotion.

"There really isn't anything to say," she said slowly. Her voice seemed to be coming from far away, as if she were talking in a tin can, her words echoing in her ears. "Nothing has to change, things can stay just like they are. After all, this...this situation isn't anybody else's business, not Brenda's or Cade's or...or even Dr. Leah's."

Gillian offered a mental apology to the doctor whom she knew would vehemently disagree with her intention to keep Ashley's father out of Ashley's life.

"A child is not a *situation!*" Devlin exclaimed hotly.

He sounded exactly like Dr. Leah about to embark on a tear. That annoyed Gillian. Greatly. Dr. Leah could lecture her over the air waves but not Devlin Brennan, not any place or any time. She felt something building inside her, something strange and powerful that grew stronger with every word he spoke. Silently, Gillian willed Devlin to be quiet.

"If you think I can simply forget what's been said tonight, that I can just forget about being told that I'm a father..." Devlin did not pick up on her telepathic request. He kept on talking. And talking. "If you think such a thing, then you don't know very much about me, lady!"

"And you don't know anything at all about me!" Gillian blurted, surprising herself by the wildness in her tone. She wanted to sound calm and rational, to gain control of the situation by maintaining her cool.

But the words kept pouring out of her. "You thought I was a tramp who hopped from bed to bed, from man to man. When you saw me in the cafeteria and I was pregnant, you never bothered to ask me when the baby was due! You didn't care about me or the possibility of being a father, you didn't want the responsibility for either of us."

She was vaguely aware of tears flowing down her cheeks but it didn't dawn on her that she was crying until her voice broke on a sob. But she railed on, unable to stop herself.

"Even after you spent time with Ashley, you never noticed how much she looks like you, and apparently like every other Brennan, too. Your brother-in-law and your cousin took one look at Ashley and knew she was yours. Right away, they knew! But you... You never even asked when her birthday was! Because you didn't want to know she was yours!"

"That isn't true!" Devlin said tersely, and Gillian hated him for staying in control. He was in full command of himself and ultimately, of her, because she'd totally lost it.

"Ashley is my cousin?" Starr Lynn's eager young voice broke into Gillian's awareness. "Oh, cool!"

Gillian trembled, mortified to realize that sometime during her diatribe, the youngster had come back into the apartment. A twelve-year-old shouldn't have to witness adult turmoil; she knew from personal experience how disturbing that could be.

Starr Lynn, however, seemed unscathed by the confession. She was in the midst of lifting Ashley into the playpen and then climbing in, too. Gillian watched her daughter hand the bright red teddy bear to the older girl, watched Starr Lynn make the bear do a silly dance that made Ashley laugh.

It occurred to Gillian that Ashley was surrounded by family—her mother, her father and two of her cousins. *Ashley's family!* Gillian felt an awful choking sensation and tried to fight it.

"I—I'd like to get some air," she managed to say. "Brenda, if you'll watch Ashley for a little while..."

"Of course," Brenda assured her. "We'll be glad to."

Gillian rushed from the apartment. She would walk around the block a few times. Brenda would take good care of Ashley, she had no worries on that score.

"Gillian!" Devlin's voice sounded authoritatively from behind. She tossed a quick glance over her shoulder and saw him walking down the hall. Toward her. Panic gripped her in earnest. He couldn't possibly think that she wanted him to come with her! Or maybe he didn't care if she did or didn't. He was following her anyway.

She had to get away to pull herself together, she needed time alone. But Devlin didn't go away, he didn't stop. He kept calling her name, kept coming after her, as relentless as *The Terminator.* Her mind splintered and acting on pure instinct, she began to run.

She'd originally intended to go down the stairs; she usually avoided the lumbering, inefficient and increasingly temperamental elevator. But since the stairwell involved making a left turn and the elevator was a straight shot ahead, she went for it.

By some miracle, the car was standing open and she raced into it and frantically pressed the button for the ground floor. And pressed it again and again, along with the buttons for every floor below.

"Are we going up or down?" Devlin entered the elevator and stood directly in front of her, blocking her escape.

"I don't care where you're going!" Gillian raised her arms and pushed at his chest. "But you're not coming with me. I'm getting as far away from you as possible." She gave another hard shove.

Devlin didn't budge. It was like trying to dislodge a boulder with toothpicks.

"Not a chance, baby. I'm not letting you out of my sight." He covered her hands with his and held them against his chest, holding her in place.

"Let me go, Devlin." Her fingers balled into fists. Her breathlessness was making her weaker than usual. If only she had a paper bag to breathe into!

When the elevator doors banged shut and the car began its creaky descent, Devlin released her hands. Gillian scurried to the other side of the car.

"Trailing after me is only going to make things worse." She tried to inject the necessary venom into her warning to make it a threat.

"Things can't get any worse," he said flatly.

Mere seconds after he spoke, the elevator lurched to a violent stop and the light in the top of the car was snuffed out, plunging them into pitch blackness.

"Oh, no!" Gillian gave a startled cry.

"Anybody who's ever watched ten minutes of TV knows that saying a line like 'Things can't get worse' is challenging fate." Devlin heaved an exasperated sigh. "Well, getting trapped in a stalled elevator definitely qualifies as worse."

"Don't you dare be glib!" Gillian felt a white-hot streak of fury bolster her as forcefully as a shot of adrenaline. Anger usually displaced anxiety, and it worked this time, too, as air whooshed into her lungs, energizing her. "This isn't a TV show."

"I'm not being glib. It's just that the scene back there with Brenda played like bad melodrama in a canceled series. One that's not even going to be rerun on cable."

"And that's not being glib?" Gillian was outraged. "We're talking about our child."

"Yes, we are. Finally."

She shrank against the elevator wall, suddenly grateful for the darkness so total that she couldn't even see her hand when she lifted it in front of her face. "We have to get out of here."

She groped her way to the panel and pressed every button she could feel, to no avail. It came as no real surprise that the emergency phone wasn't working, either. It was turning into that kind of evening, where everything that could possibly go wrong, did. Frustrated, angry and nervous, Gillian kicked at the closed doors, though her sandals provided neither sound nor force.

"Do something!" she demanded, fighting the hysteria bubbling within her. "Pound on the door. Kick it! Just get this thing moving!"

"Are you claustrophobic?"

"I could be, if I'm stuck in here with you much longer!"

Devlin kicked the door a few times with his thick-soled shoes, then pounded on it. "Nothing," he said unnecessarily, for there was no response from anyone. He tried to pry the doors apart, pushing and pulling at the crack between them. Which remained sealed tight.

"It's like they're cemented together," Dev muttered, frustrated. "I don't think even the Incredible Hulk could force them open."

"Yes, he could," countered Gillian. "Superman could do it, too. And probably the Six Million Dollar Man."

"If that's a jab at the inadequacy of my male strength, let me remind you that it works both ways. If I were stuck in here with Wonder Woman, she'd open these doors with the flick of her pinky. Ditto, the Bionic Woman."

Being Devlin and Gillian, two ordinary mortals, they remained trapped in the dark motionless elevator car.

"Yell!" Gillian commanded impatiently. "At least let somebody know we're in here."

"Don't panic." Devlin's voice, calm and steady, was in sharp contrast to the increasingly rattled sound of hers. "Sit down on the floor and take some deep breaths."

Though it was too dark to see him, Gillian knew he was near. His body seemed to emanate a heat that radiated into her and surged fierily through her. She breathed in his scent, a unique mixture of a woodsy aftershave and disinfectant soap and virile male. Her nerves tingled.

He was too close! She scooted away to a far corner and followed his orders, sitting down and breathing deeply while Devlin yelled and pounded and kicked.

Finally someone heard and came out into the hall. "You okay?" a disembodied male voice asked through the door.

"Yes, but we're stuck," called Dev. "Please put in a call to maintenance or the super, whoever can get us out of here."

"I don't think there's anything that can be done, at least not right away," said the voice. "The electricity is out in the entire building. We don't know why. One of my neighbors left a few minutes ago to try to find out what's going on. We'll let you know something as soon as we do."

"The electricity is out everywhere in the building?" Gillian repeated, not wanting to believe it. "For how long?"

The voice didn't reply.

"He's gone," Devlin said. "Back to sit in the dark in his apartment, I guess."

Gillian's heart thumped as she pictured her own darkened apartment—and her not in it. "Ashley is—"

"She's fine," Devlin said firmly. "Brenda might be a walking, talking migraine headache but she is perfectly capable of looking after a baby for a while, and Starr Lynn will keep Ashley amused. Don't worry about her."

"I am worried, I can't help it. I'm trapped in an elevator with no electricity in the building and my baby is—"

"*Our* baby."

The bald pronouncement silenced Gillian instantly. Crouched on the floor, she leaned her forehead against her knees and tried to quell the fear and dread spasming through her.

"We're stuck in here and we can't get away from each other." Devlin's voice sounded above her. "It's time for us to have the discussion we should have had at least twenty months ago, Gillian."

"I thought you didn't believe that Ashley was yours," she said wearily, not lifting her head.

"I never said that. I didn't know the truth until tonight and now...well, I believe it."

Gillian rallied a little. "It doesn't matter to me what you believe, you are not a part of our lives and you aren't going to be."

"Like hell!" Devlin sat down beside her, so close that she was wedged between him and the corner. "Now that I know I have a child I'm damn well going to be a part of her life, a big part."

Gillian tried to move and couldn't. She was doubly trapped now, and her fighting instincts surged to the fore. "There is no—"

"I'm Ashley's father!" Devlin's voice rose. Hearing the admission from his own lips sent a new surge of shock waves through him. He was a father! Dark-haired, blue-eyed Ashley was his daughter.

He felt a peculiar stirring in his chest and wondered if it was the kindling of that primal patriarchal bond or pure and simple rage at Gillian for her deception.

"My God, Gillian, how could you do this? Why did you do it? Do you hate me so much? Did you want revenge or...or to punish me for—"

"I don't hate you. I wasn't thinking about revenge or punishment," she interrupted, astonished by his misinterpretation.

"You lied about Ashley, you went so far as to marry another man to perpetrate the fraud that I wasn't her father." He felt his fury building as he reviewed her offenses. "That is vengeful, punishing behavior, Gillian. At least own up to it."

"I—I didn't find out I was pregnant until after we'd broken up and I didn't want her to be born illegitimate. That might be considered trendy by some these days, but never by me." She was intimidated and defensive, and sounded it. Which would only makes things worse, she knew. Gillian shuddered. She'd learned years ago that a display of weakness was dangerous in the survival-of-the-strongest world.

"I did what I had to do," she finished more forcefully.

"What you did was deceptive and cruel and...and criminal! You willfully falsified a legal document, Ashley's birth certificate. You either bullied or bribed that poor chump into marrying you and then divorced him just as deliberately. For eleven months, you've kept me from my own child while you—"

"You don't understand!"

"You're right about that, I don't. But I want answers and you're going to give them to me."

She felt his arms go around her, caging her against him. "Get away from me! Don't touch me."

"I'll do whatever I want. I've decided to play by *your* rules, Gillian. You know, do whatever the hell you feel like without any thought for anybody else's feelings or rights or needs. Did you pick up that philosophy from the acclaimed Dr. Leah?"

"No!" Gillian was horrified by the slander. "Dr. Leah says it takes courage, conscience and character to do the right thing and—''

''Then you haven't been listening to her very well because your actions these past twenty months don't contain a shred of any of those things.''

Gillian felt sick. Listening to Devlin's analysis put a whole new slant on things. She thought she had taken responsibility and accepted the consequences for her actions, just like Dr. Leah advocated on her radio show. Was it possible that she had somehow misconstrued and mixed up the wise doctor's message?

''I thought I was doing the right thing,'' she whispered. ''Mark and Carmen and Suzy and Stacey and a few others, including my foster parents, agreed with me.''

''Did you ever stop to think why?'' he asked, then proceeded to supply the answer. ''Because they only heard your side, your point of view, your opinion of me—and I can guess how low that is.''

''No!'' she protested.

''What did you tell them about me, Gillian?'' he pressed. ''That I was a coldhearted snake who couldn't be trusted? That I might even harm you or the baby?''

''No, of course not. I didn't paint you as some kind of psychopath, I simply told them I was sure you wouldn't care about the baby.''

Her matter-of-fact reply enraged him. ''How could you be sure I wouldn't care about my own child?''

''Because she was my child, too, and you didn't love me and I knew it. If there is one lesson I've learned well it's that having a baby doesn't bring the mother and father closer. That's a romantic myth that has probably done more damage than any other. We broke up because you didn't love me and I had no illusions that pregnancy would—''

''Have you somehow forgotten that *you* broke up with *me* and you didn't even give a reason?'' Devlin's voice rose. ''Except to say that 'things weren't working out,' whatever that was supposed to mean.''

''It meant I knew you didn't love me and I couldn't pretend any longer. I knew that you loved Holly!''

''What?'' Devlin jumped to his feet. Gillian could sense, not see, that he had moved as far from her as was possible, given the confines of their captivity. "Holly Casale?"

"What other Holly is there?" Gillian pulled herself up and clung to the rail lining the elevator wall for support. "Except the Christmas plant," she added, striving to break the unbearable tension with a small stab at humor.

Her attempt fell flat. Even in the darkness, she knew Devlin hadn't come close to smiling.

"Holly is one of my closest friends," Dev decreed. "I care about her, I respect and admire her, but I've never even kissed her." He paused, forcing himself to take a deep breath, to stay in control.

He tried to remember if he'd ever been this furious and couldn't. Even as a kid when he'd socked his cousin Brent and broken his nose—the most violent act he had ever committed— he had been cool and calm, his actions calculated to bring about the response he wanted, Brent's confession to stashing Kylie in the trunk.

But right now he was as far from cool and calm as he'd ever been. He wanted to rant and rave, he wanted to tear open the elevator doors with his bare hands and get far away fast from Gillian Bailey.

"To use Holly as an excuse, to blame her for your own unconscionable behavior is one of the most unfair, appalling..." His voice trailed off. "This is beyond words."

"You and Holly have never kissed?" Gillian was still reeling from his amazing admission.

"That's what I said," he snapped.

Flabbergasted, Gillian tried to process the information. Did Devlin and Holly prefer to yearn chastely for each other instead of giving in to their natural desires? And then it struck her with the force of a two-by-four to the skull. Devlin and Holly were living by Dr. Leah's standards, abstaining sexually until they were united legally in marriage. They had courage, conscience and character while she, Gillian, woefully lacked all three.

But they had never even kissed, not once? That struck Gillian as a tad extreme. After all, Dr. Leah didn't ban all physical contact; she recognized the very human need for affection. Still, if kissing led to intercourse, which was what had happened to Gil-

lian with Dev, maybe superior higher-love couples like Devlin
and Holly were wise to avoid it.

Gillian pondered her newly found insights. Though it was
warm in the elevator, a chill shook her and she shivered. She felt
cold, demoralized and discouraged. Was it possible for someone
like her to ever get it right?

And then suddenly, without warning, the elevator began to
move. Not at its usual sluggish pace, but so fast it was as though
it had been injected with a dose of high-powered rocket fuel.
Except instead of shooting upward like a rocket, the car descended like a high-speed roller coaster plunging down a ra-
vine-steep drop.

Time seemed to be suspended during the free fall. Gillian heard
screaming and vaguely realized she was the one doing it. The
sound heightened the primitive terror of falling in the darkness.

When the car finally impacted, it did so with force, hurling
both Gillian and Devlin to the floor. The screaming stopped, and
there was utter silence in the dark interior of the car.

Gillian opened her eyes. At least, she thought she did, for nothing changed whether her lids were opened or closed. There was
only the frightening, unrelenting blackness.

"Gillian? Are you all right?" Devlin's voice shattered the eerie
stillness.

Gillian lay still, sprawled on the floor. She couldn't see— or
could she? She couldn't breathe—or maybe she was simply
winded from the fall? The uncertainty unnerved her, and coupled
with the shock of the precipitous drop, unleashed the emotions
that she'd been trying so hard to suppress. She burst into tears.

Devlin crawled to her side. "Gillian, are you hurt?"

The concern in his voice only made her cry harder. She'd had
nightmares like this, where she was trapped in the dark, terrified
and alone, except this time she wasn't alone. She was with someone who hated her...

She'd lived that nightmare, too. She had to get away but when
she tried to get up, she couldn't. Gillian inhaled on a gasp of
horror. In her befuddled state, it took a few moments to register
that the reason she wasn't moving was because Devlin was holding her down.

"Sweetie, lie still and tell me what hurts." Devlin's hands
moved carefully, thoroughly, over her body, gently flexing each

arm, each leg, examining her neck, her torso, for injuries. He didn't allow her to get up, though she was struggling to do exactly that.

"Devlin," Gillian murmured raspily.

"Yes, honey, I'm here. You don't have any broken bones but if you're in pain—"

"I can't feel any pain. I can't see anything, either. It's so dark." She sobbed convulsively, the deluge of tears choking her. "We crashed, just like Grandmother and Granddaddy's car did. What if we're dead, just like they were after their crash? It's so dark. Maybe we are dead and we don't even know it yet. Maybe we're ghosts like in *Topper*. How long does it take to know that you're dead? How long before—"

"Gillian, stop it!" Devlin commanded. He slipped his hands under her arms and lifted her to a sitting position. "You're getting hysterical."

"Who wouldn't? We don't know if we're dead or not. How can you be so calm when any minute now we might end up in drawers at the morgue?"

"We're not dead!" Devlin stood, pulling her to her feet along with him.

She swayed dizzily, her body shaking so violently that her knees buckled. Devlin propped her against the wall and pinned her there with his body.

She was vaguely aware that his weight was supporting her, that if he weren't holding her up, she would slide to the floor like a floppy rag doll. Or a dead body?

Devlin seemed to read her mind. "If you were dead your body would be lifeless, Gillian. You'd be cold and stiff." His voice, deep and low, sounded in her ear as his hands traveled over her. "And you're not cold. You're warm. Oh, God, Gillian, you're so warm. So soft."

A small whimper escaped from her throat. She was still trembling but her hysteria had subsided. She'd stopped crying, though she was racked by intermittent sobs.

"If we were dead, we'd feel nothing." Devlin was breathing heavily.

She quivered. Oh, yes, she definitely could feel him feeling her, his hands big and warm and strong as they moved over the curves of her body. His breath fanned her neck, and his lips nibbled on the sensitive skin there. He leaned even closer, his legs entangling with hers, and she felt the virile burgeoning of his sex.

"I can feel your softness, I can feel your warmth." He slid his hands under her T-shirt and cupped her breasts. Round and firm, they filled his palms, and he squeezed them gently, his thumbs skimming over the hard tips of her nipples that were already jutting against the thin fabric of her bra.

Gillian moaned softly.

"And you can feel this." He took her hand in his and placed it over his enormous erection that strained against the loose material of his cotton scrub pants.

Her fingers fitted herself around him. The full, hard, formidable length of him pulsed in her grip. Her eyes tightly closed—or maybe they were open, the total blackness rendered such confusing details irrelevant. Gillian conformed her palm to his shape. He felt strong and male, he felt like Devlin, the only man she'd ever loved.

"I want you so much, Gillian," he whispered urgently. His lips feathered her jawline, then blazed a trail of stinging little kisses along the sensitive curve of her neck. "Oh, baby, so very much."

Gillian felt a surge of wild joy sweep through her. She and Devlin were alive and they were together. In the hazy aftermath of hysteria and fear, that basic and profound reality was the only thing that mattered.

He said he wanted her, and she ached with the sweet pain of wanting him, too. Gillian slowly uncurled her fingers from that virile vital part of him, turning the release into a seductive caress. She moved her hand upward and tugged at the drawstring of his scrub pants, slipping her thumb inside to trace the circular hollow of his navel.

He sucked in his breath on a gasp of need. Gillian smiled in the darkness. It felt good to know that he wanted her, to feel the incontrovertible physical evidence, to hear it. She slid her hands over his muscled chest, up to his shoulders. Locking her arms around his neck, she provocatively arched her body into his.

"Oh, God, Gillian, it's been so long." Dev groaned the words. "I have to have you. Please, sweetheart, let me have you."

He held her tight, as if he'd never let her go.

Gillian didn't want him to. "Yes," she whispered, her voice heated and throaty with the thrilling passion spreading through her like liquid wildfire. "Oh, Dev, yes."

Seven

His mouth closed over hers and her lips parted, welcoming the thrust of his tongue. Gillian clung to him, kissing him hungrily, wildly, the way he was kissing her. She wanted his kiss, needed to be kissed like this, deep and hard and demanding.

Devlin crushed her against him, and another great shudder of desire shook his body. She moved her hips against him, acknowledging his need, encouraging it, and communicating her own.

His thigh was between hers, rocking against the vulnerable softness there, tantalizing her, pleasuring her. All control spiraled away, taking along with it her fear and guilt and self-doubts. She loved him so much and with her self-imposed restrictions removed, she was free to express her love, fueling her desire, her need for him.

His hands were on her breasts and he kneaded them gently, lovingly, until he could no longer stand the impediment of her clothing between them. He pushed up her T-shirt and unclasped the front-fastening clip of her bra. When his palms closed over her bare breasts, they both groaned with satisfaction.

Gillian needed to touch him, too, to reciprocate his caresses. She slipped her hands under the top of his scrub suit to feel the smooth skin and wiry mat of hair beneath. *I love you,* she said over and over again in her head. *I love you, I love you.*

The warm wet feel of his mouth on her nipple thrilled her. She moaned her pleasure as Devlin laved the sensitive little bud with his tongue, then closed his lips around it to sensuously suckle her.

Gillian held his head to her, her fingers threading through the springy thickness of his hair. A wave of tenderness and desire and love surged through her. She felt feminine, she felt needed and loved, similar to the way she'd felt when she had nursed Ashley, yet daringly and excitingly different. She wanted to give and give to Devlin, the man she loved, the man who had given her so much. He'd given her a child, he'd given her Ashley.

Devlin's hands moved purposefully to her waist where he opened the metal button of her jeans shorts with practiced ease. His fingers dipped lower as the zipper slowly began to slide down its track. He examined the curve of her waist, then her soft, not-so-firm-as-it-once-had-been belly. She was wearing bikini panties and he slipped his fingertips beneath the lacy band, then withdrew them quickly, teasing her a little.

Gillian uttered a small moan of protest. An almost unbearably exciting urgency sizzled through her. She wanted him to touch her intimately, she wanted to feel his hands on her bare thighs, between them...

"Oh, Devlin." Her voice echoed thickly in her ears, her yearning, her hunger unmistakable.

The sound sent Devlin higher. Knowing that Gillian's need for him matched his for her, that she wanted what he wanted, made him feel powerful and very male. Yet there was more, something new. He felt deeply bound to her.

"Dev, please," she whimpered.

"I want to please you, baby." Devlin gave a hot, sensual laugh. "And I will. I promise." He pulled down her jeans and panties in one quick movement, then placed his hand between her legs. Already, she was hot and wet and welcoming.

Gillian cried his name once more as his fingers combed through the downy triangle of hair. She clung to him as he caressed her intimately. When he eased one long finger inside, her sensitive inner muscles flexed and tightened to hold him within.

Her response jolted through him like liquid lightning. His breathing was ragged, his whole body throbbing with the need to merge with her. Reeling in a sensual daze, he felt her push the loose scrub pants over his hips, felt her small hand grip him. She knew exactly what he liked and how to do it. He couldn't stop himself from thrusting in counterpoint to her motions.

Fireworks seemed to explode in his head. "Gillian, I can't wait any longer." His voice was guttural, the words slurred. Speaking was as difficult as thinking, which he had ceased to do except on the most rudimentary level. Every fiber of his being was focused on becoming one with Gillian.

She wanted it as much as he did. "Don't wait, Devlin," she said huskily. "I don't want you to wait. I need you so much."

His mouth took hers in a deep, rapacious kiss as he lifted her hips and positioned her to receive him. He thrust into her, his penetration deep and sure and swift. Gillian gasped as her body stretched to accept him, melting to accommodate his size and strength, taking him deeper and deeper into her.

He moved, his strokes thrilling and masterful, and she loved it, reveling not only in the erotic pleasure he was giving her, but also in the marvelous feeling of fullness. Having him inside her filled an emptiness, an ache that only he had been able to relieve.

Her fingers dug into his back as she clutched him, matching his rhythm, meeting his sensual demands while making her own. His need spurred hers, and hers incited his in a wondrous, continuous cycle of giving and taking. Gillian gave herself up to him and her love for him.

Abruptly, an intense staggering release pulsated through her, and Gillian sobbed aloud, consumed with pleasure, not wanting it to end yet overwhelmed by its power. While she was still shivering with ecstasy, Devlin reached his climax, calling her name as sheer physical rapture exploded through him.

Slowly, by unspoken mutual consent, they slid to the floor still intimately joined, neither willing to break the connection. They lay there in the dark silence, emotionally and physically united in the sweet languorous afterglow.

"Maybe we did die, after all," Devlin said after a while, his voice laced with lazy humor.

"And this is hell?" Gillian murmured languidly.

He gave her a swift, playful swat on the rump, then kissed her tenderly, lingeringly. "This is heaven. Sheer heaven."

A sultry silence fell, and they lay together quietly. Only the sounds of their breathing broke the stillness.

"We never did it standing up before," Gillian murmured drowsily. She felt blissfully content and cuddled close, raising her head to kiss the curve of his neck.

"True. This is definitely a first-run episode." His mind was drifting in a pleasantly insensate haze. "Did you like it?" he remembered to ask. He was drained, utterly replete, unable—and unwilling—to move or even think.

She laughed huskily. "Take a wild guess."

"I guess yes. You liked it."

Gillian smiled at the possessive, very masculine satisfaction in his tone. "You're right, I liked it. I really, really liked it."

They both chuckled, then nibbled lightly, teasingly, on each other's lips until playfulness was no longer enough for either of them. They needed more sustained contact, deeper intimacy.

His hands moved to cup her bare bottom, his fingers splayed and caressed her as their mouths fused naturally for a deep, dizzying kiss that lasted a long, long time.

When he finally lifted his mouth, Gillian squirmed against him. Her breasts were nestled against his chest but their shirts, askew and tangled around them, were becoming an uncomfortable irritant. She wanted to be naked with him, she wanted him completely nude. The hard floor was becoming a distraction, too. She wished they were lying in a bed, not on the floor—had it been washed in recent history?—of a malfunctioning elevator.

"Devlin?" Her voice sounded more like herself. A little edgy, a little more in control. She became aware of the sticky moisture of perspiration that seemed to glue their skin together.

"Mmm, what is it, sweetie?" He was slow to answer. He sounded as if he'd been half dozing.

"It's still so dark in here. I can't even see you."

"I'm here, baby." His arms tightened possessively. "I'm not going anywhere."

Gillian bit her lip. Her mind was slowly beginning to clear. She knew that reality was dawning, and she didn't want it to, she wanted to insulate them in this surreal dreamworld.

And couldn't. "Is the electricity still off?"

"I think so. No one has come to find us and there aren't any lights."

"Then why did the elevator go down like it did?"

"Good question. Maybe the cable snapped, which might've been coincidental to the electrical outage. Or maybe not. We're lucky we weren't hurt."

He brushed his lips through her hair. She felt him flex inside her. Was he getting hard again? A thrill of sensation spun through her. She knew his stamina, and despite the fulfillment they had given each other—because of it?—she wanted him even more now than before.

From the very first, they had been sexually well matched. Devlin had often said so, marveling, while Gillian took their sexual compatibility for granted. She loved him and thought it natural that their energy and sensuality were completely in sync.

He stirred within her again. Suddenly she was acutely aware of the intimate flood of inner wetness—and what it signified.

"Oh!" She jerked frantically in a sudden attempt to disengage their bodies. "Oh, no!" Her heart gave a panicked lurch, then seemed to pound in triple time. "Devlin, we didn't use any—any p-protection." Her body was still too relaxed and replete for her to escalate to a state of full-blown hysteria, but she knew she would've, if she could've.

She felt him separate his body from hers, the slow withdrawal momentarily distracting her from her anxiety, sending tiny sensual thrills through her. Reflexively, her hips lifted and her fingers tightened around his shoulders. She wanted to keep him inside her as much as she wanted to distance herself from him, physically, emotionally, in every possible way.

Though their bodies were no longer joined, he held her close, and she sensed him watching her. She wished she could see his face. What was his expression? What was in his eyes?

"I know you're going to find this hard to believe but I didn't actually remember having...unprotected sex with you before." Devlin hesitated, almost stumbling over the incriminating phrase. "If I did, I would've at least suspected that...that Ashley was mine."

Gillian knew that under any other circumstances, she would've run from him and this conversation. But they were trapped in the dark elevator, and her body was sated with sensual lethargy. Even if she could have mustered some rage, there was nowhere to flee. So she answered honestly. "I...figured you might not have remembered because you'd never said anything the morning after our, uh, slip-ups. I mean, the *mornings* after," she corrected herself. There had been more than one such morning, more than one such night. Plenty more. "There was also the possibility that you didn't want to discuss it, that if there were any problems, they were to be all mine."

"Gillian, no, it wasn't that at all. Stupid as it seems, I didn't put the facts together till now, even though I remember those times we'd wake up in the middle of the night and... I guess I thought you were using something, the Pill or a diaphragm, maybe." He sighed. "The truth is, I didn't think about it at all."

"You have to go to a doctor for those, and I couldn't get an appointment for weeks. So I bought some of that foam stuff at the drugstore." She swallowed hard. It was peculiar, it was difficult, holding this sexual post-mortem. They had never discussed anything so frankly before, and they should have, she conceded. Perhaps it wouldn't have seemed so impossible to tell him about Ashley if they'd delved beyond the superficial.

She heard Devlin groan. "The user-failure rate with that stuff is way too high. But we already know that firsthand, don't we? Gillian, I have friends in OB-GYN, you should've told me you needed an appointment. You wouldn't have had to wait, they'd have seen you immediately."

"My mistake," she said sarcastically. "I didn't realize how completely you yangos cover for one another, from your sex life to—"

"Don't get defensive, I'm not trying to cast blame, Gillian."

"It sure sounded that way to me. I didn't deliberately set out to get pregnant, Devlin. I tried to remember to use that foam but—"

"I know," he said softly. "But I'd wake you out of a sound sleep in the middle of the night. Who could remember who was using, or not using, what?"

"We were both careless," she murmured. "But as a woman I should've taken total responsibility for myself. Carmen says I didn't know the basics. That since I waited so long to finally sleep with a man, I didn't know what she and the others had already learned back in high school."

"Gillian, tell me you aren't saying you were a...that I was your first—"

He sounded horrified, almost comically so. She might've laughed if the joke wasn't on her. "I was and you were," she said flatly.

"But why didn't you tell me at the time? Why didn't I realize it ? Gillian, you were damn good in bed and I never for one moment thought that you...that you—"

"Happened to be a new player in the game?" she supplied helpfully. "Thank you. I'll take that as a supreme compliment, coming from you, Dev. I never once considered telling you I was a virgin, Dev. I knew it would've freaked you out. And I was thrilled that you didn't guess the truth. You made it easy for me to be good in bed." She smiled slightly. "You made it so good for me it seemed as natural as...as breathing."

"I was so good I knocked up a virgin!" Devlin choked out. "Gillian, I am so sorry, for everything. Before I met you—and since—I've always been scrupulously careful. Always. So I never considered the possibility...the obvious consequences." The note of remorse in his tone was unmistakable.

Gillian felt sympathy for him stir within her. "I didn't think about consequences, either, not at the time," she admitted. "But then my period was late and Carmen bought me that pregnancy testing kit."

She sat up straight, remembering that day. She'd been terrified and had cried while Carmen hugged her and cursed men and fate and bad karma and anything else she could think to curse.

"What was it like that day?" Devlin asked thickly. "Finding out? Knowing that—"

"It's not a memory I care to dwell on." Gillian was suddenly brusque. "What's the point? I have Ashley now, and she's a beautiful, healthy baby. She's all that matters."

Her voice became even brisker, cool and bureaucratic, the tone she used on the phone when dealing with flak-catchers at the Social Security Administration. "I want to get dressed now." She tried to move away from Devlin. "We can't be caught like this when the electricity comes back on."

He held her fast. "Don't shut me out again, Gillian."

"Shut you out? I don't think I'm capable of it." She gave a bitter laugh. "I just let you nail me in an elevator, remember?"

That irked him. "I didn't *nail* you. We made love, Gillian, and it was so good—no, good doesn't even come close to describing what just happened between us. There has to be another word to—''

"How about 'stupid'? Because what we just did was impulsive and reckless and—and stupid beyond imagining.'' She began to struggle. His arms were no longer comforting, they were imprisoning. She no longer felt sexy and voluptuous, she was sticky and wet and ashamed. And possibly, in serious trouble. Again!

The full implication of what she'd done struck her with resounding force. She had just had unprotected sex with the father of her child, the man who had already proven himself to be a virile, fertile match for her!

"I can practically hear Dr. Leah's voice.'' Gillian's own voice quavered. "She would say, 'Why did you do that?' It's what she always says to people who do something so incomprehensibly idiotic and so irresponsible you can hardly believe it. And if the caller tries to give some lame excuse, she—''

"Gillian, I don't want to discuss Dr. Leah, however astute her admonitions and advice. We don't need a third party in here with us, we need to—''

"Get our clothes on.'' She tugged down her shirt, then reached under it, trying to get her bra in place. "Please, Dev!''

"Okay.'' He held up his hands, releasing her. "It's not like either of us is going anywhere. We're going to talk, Gillian. And you can start by telling me why you didn't tell me you were pregnant.''

"We were broken up and—''

"That's one of those lame excuses Dr. Leah wouldn't let you get away with.''

Gillian located her panties and quickly pulled them on, blushing at the intimacy of such an action in front of Devlin, though she knew he couldn't see. She was grateful for that.

"You said we couldn't mention Dr. Leah,'' she muttered, slipping into her shorts. Her hands were shaking so much, she fumbled with the metal buttons. It took several attempts before she secured them.

"And it's not a lame excuse. I already told you why I broke up with you. I knew you didn't love me and I knew a pregnancy wasn't going to change that. I wanted no part of a shotgun wedding. I—I'd rather have the shotgun pointed at me and the trigger pulled than have to marry an unwilling man who—''

"I'm having trouble following your logic, Gillian, especially since you went through the motions of that fake marriage with Mark Morrow."

"Mark wanted to help me out and there was no pretense of anything else between us. Neither of us trivializes illegitimacy, probably because we both were and hated that we were."

"I wouldn't want a child of mine to be born illegitimate, either, Gillian."

"But I didn't know that. I mean, it's not like we ever discussed the subject."

"And you had with Mark?"

"Of course. We lived at the Sinsels together for six years. Mark and Carmen and Suzy and Stacey and I have no secrets from each other. But it was different with you and me." She paused, frowning thoughtfully. "I'd never told you much about myself. You and I always talked about fun things, we liked to fool around and have a good time together."

A discussion of her dismal past hadn't fit within the parameters of their budding relationship—and she'd ended it before they could ever reach that point. Gillian sighed wearily. "To be honest, I never expected you would offer to marry me, Dev."

"What did you expect I would do?" His voice lowered ominously.

"I thought there was a possibility you might say it wasn't your problem because the baby wasn't yours." Gillian heard him draw an audible breath. "But mostly I thought you'd offer me money for an abortion that I didn't want to have. It just seemed to make more sense to leave you out of it."

"You really do think I'm a heartless bastard, don't you?"

"It's just that I know a little more about these things than you do. You see, my mother routinely found herself pregnant by men not interested in marriage and fatherhood. I vowed to be different from her and I was, too—until I met you." Gillian's voice shook. "Then, at the advanced age of twenty-five, I found myself unmarried and pregnant by a man who didn't love me. Seems I wasn't so different from good old mom, after all. I guess it's true what they say, that the apple doesn't fall far from the tree."

"I didn't mean to imply that you were some kind of a—"

"Tramp? God knows I never wanted to be."

"Gillian, you aren't," he said tersely.

"I'm certainly acting like one." She flinched at her own observation. "Dr Leah says you have to have the courage to face facts and the facts are, we've just had unprotected sex again. Except this time, we don't even have the excuse of being involved with each other. Because we're not."

"We seem pretty involved to me, Gillian."

She tried to interpret his tone. Sarcastic or angry? Perhaps both. She retaliated in kind. "Having a quickie in a stalled elevator is not involvement, Devlin. With your extensive romantic track record, you must know that basic fact."

She was heartsick, she was hurting. After all these years of trying to be the antithesis of Jolene Bailey, she was not only going down the same road as her mother, she seemed to be standing in her very footsteps!

Gillian held back her tears, though she felt like crying her eyes out. "Dev, if something results from...from this—"

"You mean, *somebody,* don't you?" Devlin asked archly.

She nodded her head, then realized that he couldn't see her nod of assent. "Yes. If somebody results, I'll move. Right away. Maybe I should move anyway, no matter what. I won't go to Detroit to be near Carmen or the Sinsels, I'll go much farther, maybe to Texas where Suzy and Stacey, two of my foster sisters, are living, or to California."

"To the home of the aspiring actor who is down on the official records as the father of *my* child?"

Devlin sounded strange, and Gillian wished for the hundredth time that she could see his face so she could better interpret his terse remark. Expression was key to subtext, far more valuable than tone or even the actual words.

"Yes, Mark is there," she replied carefully. "And he—"

"Gillian, if you intend to suggest another faux marriage to Mark Morrow—"

"He'll do it if it needs to be done. I know he won't let me down. Mark has a heart of gold."

"Gillian, just...just shut up!"

She jumped, startled by his vehemence. And then her temper snapped like a piece of dry kindling. "Don't yell at me! You're not going to have to get involved, I promise. I protected you the last time, and if need be, I'll do it again. But I won't put up with...with any verbal bullying from you. Do I make myself clear?"

"Obviously, I haven't made myself clear. Hell, Gillian, I feel like we're having parallel conversations—in parallel universes. You won't let me say 'shut up' to you because you consider it insulting and disrespectful—"

"It is!" she cut in hotly.

"Okay, you're right. And I apologize." He'd dropped the thundering roar, but he still sounded incredulous and exasperated. "Yet you're willing to allow me to walk away from any responsibility to you and our daughter and possibly another child, as well. Does that make any sense to you? Because it doesn't to me."

Gillian flushed. It made perfect sense to her, though she knew someone like Devlin, who'd been wanted and welcomed and loved his whole life, wouldn't get it at all. "Devlin...oh, never mind."

"If we're going to be married, it would help a lot if we took the trouble to understand each other, Gillian."

Her heart did a crazy spin, and she willed it to slow down. "But we're not going to be married."

"We're applying for a marriage license tomorrow, Gillian, and this time next week, we'll be married."

"No!"

"Yes, you will marry me," Devlin said in a calm, cool tone that was somehow scarier than his roar. "Tomorrow I intend to hire a lawyer to help me establish Ashley's paternity. We'll have blood tests, DNA, whatever is required, to prove that I am her biological father and then the legal documents will be altered to fit the true facts. I'll be declared Ashley's father and I'll support her—and you."

"That's ridiculous, Devlin! I can't marry you."

"I want to be Ashley's full-time, live-in father, but If you don't marry me, I'll file for joint custody, Gillian. I'm going to be in my daughter's life. Accept it."

"You can't take my baby away from me!" Gillian felt as if she'd been kicked in the stomach. She closed her eyes and clutched the railing, feeling faint. "Devlin, please, no, you wouldn't!"

"You really do think I'm the devil in disguise," Devlin said grimly. "I wouldn't take a baby away from its mother, Gillian. I said *joint* custody and for me that means visitation rights and a say about where Ashley lives. You couldn't simply take her and move to—well, Texas or California, unless I agreed. And I won't agree to that, Gillian. I've already missed eleven months of Ashley's life and I'm not missing any more."

"It's not right that you have any say in where I go or what I do!" she cried.

"We have a child together—maybe even two after tonight's little tryst. That means we'll always be connected, Gillian."

"And I thought vampires were the only ones that were eternally cursed!"

"I hadn't thought of it that way." He laughed mirthlessly. "We could skip the courts and the issue of joint custody if you'll marry me, Gillian. You may as well. I'll be seeing Ashley regularly and if you'll be honest with yourself, you know that we'll end up making love again before too long. It's inevitable, under the circumstances."

"The circumstances being that I'm a sleazy, easy lay and you're irresistible?"

"No. You're irresistible and I'm the sleazy, easy lay," he drawled.

"Don't you dare be flippant!"

"I promise not to be flippant if you'll be honest with me. Tell me why you're afraid to marry me, Gillian."

"I'm not afraid!"

"Uh-oh, I feel an attack of glibness coming on." Moving fast as quicksilver, he pulled her into his arms and held her close. "I feel something else coming on, too."

Gillian gasped in surprise as his mouth opened over hers in a hard, possessive kiss. She was instantly transported into a dizzying vortex of passion, and all thoughts of distancing and detaching herself from him eddied away. It was impossible; she loved him too much.

The kiss went on and on, until he finally lifted his lips from hers. Dazed and breathless, she leaned against him, holding on tight.

"Say yes to me, Gillian."

The raspy huskiness in his voice was a potent source of arousal in itself. His big, warm hands slid under her shirt, and began a leisurely massage along her spine. When he reached her bra, he stopped, his fingers gliding over the material, and she could almost hear him making the decision to unclasp it, to remove that offending barrier. Worse, she wanted him to. Badly.

She took a deep breath, trying to clear her head. "We can't, Devlin. Not here, not again."

"I mean, say yes to my proposal." He kissed her neck. "Tell me that you'll marry me."

"Devlin." The protest she'd intended sounded instead like a passion-drugged sigh.

His lips toyed with hers, eliciting sensations that made her shiver. And throb. And ache for him all over again. "Say you will, Gillian."

His voice echoed in her ears. Not being able to see anything seemed to heighten her other senses, intensifying her response to him. They were the only two people in this very private world, and everything that had seemed so obvious before was not so clear-cut anymore. "Are...are you sure you want me to?"

"Yes," he said firmly. His voice held none of the dreamy confusion resonating in Gillian's tones. His course of action was perfectly clear to him. She was the mother of his child. He should've already married her, he would have if she had chosen to let him in on her little secret, he assured himself.

He was a father! The realization stunned him all over again.

Holding Gillian in his arms, he slid one hand around to press his palm against the flat softness of her belly, wondering how it had felt when his child had moved and kicked within her womb. He remembered that time he'd seen her in the advanced stages of her pregnancy, how swollen she'd looked, burgeoning with a new life. She'd been carrying his baby!

And he hadn't bothered to ask her a single question. He had leaped to a conclusion that even his cousin Brenda, not knowing Gillian, had rejected in an instant. Why had he so easily accepted that the child she carried was another man's? Why had he let himself believe in her bogus marriage?

They were more self-recriminations than questions, and they haunted him. Would there ever come a time when they wouldn't? But now he knew the truth and had a chance to right the wrongs, to take responsibility and assume command.

Strange how his father's voice was playing at full volume inside his head. *Take responsibility, assume command!* Captain Wayne Brennan's words to live by. Professionally, Devlin had always followed that wise paternal advice, though he'd stayed single and free by avoiding the responsibility of romantic commitments. Or so he'd thought. Gillian Bailey and a little girl named Ashley Joy had proved him wrong. Toward them, he'd been shirking and irresponsible.

But it wasn't totally his fault. Devlin felt a niggling resentment creep through him. Gillian had broken up with him and done it with such cool precision that he hadn't thought to question her feelings. And then she'd convinced the golden-hearted Mark to marry her, further blurring the facts.

In his world, people didn't live according to soap opera scripts and Gillian's actions—the lies, the cover marriage and divorce, the secret baby—could've been lifted from "Days of Our Lives," the show that half his dorm used to watch during their college years.

"Dev?" Gillian placed her hand over his and seemingly automatically, their fingers linked. "You...don't have to go through with it, you know. Don't worry, I won't hold you to your proposal, if that's what it is."

"That's what it is, Gillian. And I am going through with it." Anger continued to build within him. Take responsibility, assume command. He was not going to let her keep him from doing the right thing!

"You sound so grim and determined." Gillian was wry and wistful. "Like somebody on his way to the dentist for a root canal."

"I'll follow up with a more romantic proposal—flowers and champagne, the whole bit if you'd like—when we're not trapped in this elevator, Gillian," he replied tautly.

Gillian stirred uneasily and pulled away from him. Forget the dentist, he was beginning to sound like someone about to face execution. "Look, Dev, I know what it's like to be foisted onto someone and I know how it feels to have somebody you don't want just dropped into your life. I grew up that way and I don't care to repeat it as an adult, not even for a short while. I certainly don't want Ashley to be anybody's unwanted burden."

"She won't be. Come back here, Gillian."

He felt her withdrawal on a visceral level the moment she had moved out of his reach. His anger immediately dissipated, leaving only the need to have her close. He decided he was truly becoming a basket case. Maybe Holly would give him a discount for her psychiatric services.

"Do you think we'll use up all the air in here before we're rescued?" Gillian asked instead, staying where she was and sounding more than a little desperate.

He moved slowly, trying to locate her. It was maddening not being able to see; he was really sick of it. "We won't suffocate. There must be air vents somewhere in this car or we would already be unconscious."

"I just want to get out of here!"

Devlin cleared his throat. "Why were you in foster care?"

"If you're making conversation to pass the time, I'd rather talk about 'Taxi' reruns. Or 'The Bob Newhart Show,' the first one, where he's married to Emily. Either are a lot more entertaining than The Gillian Bailey Story. If it were a TV pilot, it would've been scrapped right after filming."

"You don't always have to entertain me, Gillian."

"Oh, you'd prefer that I bore you to death?"

"You know, for the first time I'm finally seeing how deftly you evade any attempts to get close to you." It came as something of a revelation to him. "I always considered myself to be a champion of keeping things on a superficial level but you're definitely my equal, Gillian."

"Well, since neither of us wants to be close to the other, getting married would definitely be a demented move on both our parts."

"Now who's being glib? Come on, answer the question and get it over with. I'm going to keep asking till you do."

"You don't want to hear, it's the stuff of trashy talk shows. The kind where the audience boos the dysfunctional losers."

"Okay, consider me warned. Now get on with it."

Gillian heaved a long-suffering sigh. "My mother, Jolene, was sixteen when I was born. She dumped me on her parents while she came and went with her various boyfriends. My grandparents were kind to me but they were old and tired—they'd unexpectedly had Jolene when they were almost fifty. She was their only child and she'd been a hellion from Day One. So the last thing they wanted or needed was a little kid around. I tried not to be any trouble because I knew how much I needed them. But I lost them anyway. When I was seven, Grandmother and Granddaddy were killed in a car accident, and I went to live with Jolene and her revolving-door lovers for a couple miserable years till she decided she didn't want me around at all.''

"Gillian, I—''

"No sympathetic response is required.'' She cut him right off. "It was a long time ago and I'm only talking about it because you demanded to know why I was in foster care.''

"It must have been tough,'' Devlin interjected, determined to offer that sympathetic response she didn't require.

"It wasn't great. When you're placed in foster care because your own mother won't take care of you, it's like you're nothing but garbage, put out because nobody wants you.'' She sounded bored, as if she were reciting the plot of a too-often-viewed movie that she hadn't particularly liked the first time. "We used to envy the delinquent kids who got taken away by the courts for some crime they did. At least that didn't mean their parents didn't want them. There was nobody in the system lower than us—the throwaways, we were called.''

Devlin winced at the phrase. "Put the blame on the one who deserves it, Gillian. Your mother. It wasn't your fault you were in the system.''

"As a kid I felt it was. I think all kids feel that way. You know, if only I'd been better, maybe if I'd been cuter or smarter, maybe Mom would've wanted me. She kept my half-brother with her and—''

"Your half-brother?'' He found it odd that she'd spoken easily of foster brothers and sisters but hadn't mentioned a blood sibling till now.

"Jolene had me, my half-brother Jody, who is six years younger, and two other babies I never saw, who she gave up for adoption. Actually, I think Jolene sold those babies to some shady adoption lawyer because she had a wad of cash after each pregnancy. There was another baby boy who was born prematurely and died in the hospital a few months before Jolene turned me over to the court and waived her parental rights. Maybe she's had other children since, I don't know. I haven't seen her or Jody since I was ten. I have no idea where they are.''

"Do you want to know?'' Devlin asked curiously.

"Not where Jolene is. I...wouldn't mind seeing Jody again.

I've always wondered if she ended up dumping him in some other state. I know they left Michigan years ago. End of story.''

"Not quite. You were nine years old when you went into foster care. What happened to you then?''

"The usual. When I was twelve I finally ended up with the Sinsels and stayed, but in the years before, I was transferred from one foster home to another. A few of those places were bad, some were okay, and one was the world's worst.'' She kept her voice cool and steady. It mattered to her that she didn't sound downtrodden or swamped with self-pity.

"You were an unwanted child and don't want to be an unwanted wife.'' Viewed from her perspective, he guessed that her actions did follow a certain depressing logic. "That's why you're so nervous about marrying me now. And why you didn't tell me about Ashley.''

"If you say so, Doctor,'' she said dryly. "Keep on sharpening those analyzing skills and maybe Dr. Leah will let you fill in as guest host someday.''

If she'd intended to divert him, she failed. "Gillian, there is no connection between being placed in foster care and marrying me.''

He was filled with sorrow and anger on her behalf—and something that felt strangely like fear. Despite Holly's gibes, he hadn't slept through his entire psychiatric rotation in medical school. He'd retained enough to see a direct correlation between a childhood filled with rejection and pain and the emotional damage that could ensue.

Every muscle in his body tensed. He didn't want to devote the time or energy required to tending an emotionally needy woman; he didn't want a head-case marriage filled with problems and strife. Whenever he'd imagined himself married—true, it wasn't often—he pictured the kind of stable, easy companionship his parents shared. He didn't mind working hard at the hospital...but working hard at marriage? Now there was an alarming, exhausting concept.

"There is a big connection, Dev, and we both know it.'' Gillian's voice sliced through his reverie. "You feel that marrying me is your civic duty, like serving on a jury or something. Let's face it, you never thought your wife would be someone like me and I certainly never expected to marry anybody like you. It's sort of a fractured version of *Cinderella* except she came from a much better background than mine."

The fact that she'd practically homed in on his thoughts irked him. Was he that shallow, that transparent, *even in the dark?* "Well, I'm no prince, no matter what Brenda claims that our grandmother said," Devlin rasped through his teeth.

"Someone like Holly Casale is the obvious match for you," Gillian continued with what he considered annoying surety. "Holly herself is the natural—"

"Stop dragging Holly into this. She's like a sister to me. Marrying her would be almost incestuous. But you wouldn't consider that a deterrent, would you? You did marry your foster brother," he added snidely.

"But Holly isn't your sister," Gillian observed. "I've seen the two of you together, Dev. You have—*chemistry!* Your relationship is nothing like the totally platonic, asexual bond I share with Mark."

"Oh, change the channel, Gillian," snapped Devlin. "I'm tired of this program."

"The fact that you can't even discuss your relationship with Holly without getting defensive proves—"

"Nothing except that you've overdosed on Dr. Leah and her psychobabble," Devlin finished for her.

Gillian was certain he was glaring at her. She was definitely glaring at him. It was odd, glaring unseen into utter blackness. Something of a wasted effort.

And then, just when she couldn't stand the dark silence another minute, a voice sounded from outside the elevator. "Everybody okay in there?"

"Yes." Gillian pressed herself against the doors, shouting through them. "Please get us out."

It didn't take very long for three maintenance men to pry open the doors with crowbars. Gillian stumbled out first, squinting against the beams from their flashlights.

"This must be how a bat feels if it leaves its cave before dark," she murmured, averting her eyes from the almost painful brightness of the light.

Devlin stood behind her and placed both his hands on her shoulders. "Is the electricity still off?" He could tell they were in the basement but the overhead lights weren't on.

"A dead tree branch downed a power line just up the street," one of the men explained. "The power is out for blocks. Should be restored in a few more hours."

"I'm just glad to be out of there!" Gillian's relief was heartfelt. "Thank you so much for helping us."

"Yeah, thanks," said Devlin. Did she have to sound *so* happy to be released? When he thought of that passionate interlude they'd shared, he was ready to get back in the elevator to be trapped with her even longer. Still, things being how they were between them, he knew they would make love again, and very soon.

But would they have to be re-entombed together before she confided in him again?

"Glad to help. Don't know what happened to cause the elevator to fall, but I hope it wasn't too bad, having to wait so long." Their rescuer was solicitous.

"It wasn't bad at all. The time flew by and we're fine." Devlin kneaded Gillian's shoulders and hung on to her when she tried to shrug him off. "Let's go home, honey."

They started up the stairwell together while the trio of workers went their own way in the basement.

Gillian made another attempt to get away from Devlin. And didn't succeed. He kept his arm locked around her as they walked side-by-side up the flights of stairs.

"Let's go home?" She tried mocking him. "That sounds like a sappy closing line from the last scene in an episode of 'Lassie.'"

"By home, I meant your apartment." Devlin didn't rise to the bait. He cast out his own. "It makes sense for me to move in with you and Ashley since you have two bedrooms. In fact, I'll stay with you tonight, and Brenda and Starr Lynn can have my place to themselves."

"In fact, you won't stay with me." Her heart was pounding and not from the exertion of climbing stairs.

"In fact, I will."

"I want you to keep away from us, Devlin," she said crossly. "I—I don't need you!"

"Good. Because I'm not the kind of man who needs to be needed. I don't want to be needed. I guess that makes us the perfect match, doesn't it?"

"Only in a contest for the perfect match from hell."

They argued the whole way to her door. Brenda let them in.

"The baby's fine. We put her to bed, and she went down without a peep. I called Kylie and Cade," Brenda added. Her smile looked downright devilish in the candlelight glow. Gillian owned many candles, and it appeared that Brenda had found and lit every single one.

Devlin scowled at his cousin. "You shouldn't have called them, Brenda."

"W-what did they say?" Gillian stammered.

"Well, Cade suspected about the baby all along, just like I thought," Brenda said smugly. "He said he guessed the truth from his first glimpse of her and from the weird way Devlin was acting around Gillian that day."

"I wasn't acting weird that day!" Dev protested.

"And then Cade spouted all his usual complaints," continued Brenda, "about how the Brennans are exasperating and infuriating and were probably put on this earth just to drive him crazy, until Kylie told him to knock it off. But she was shocked, Devlin. Just shocked!" Brenda was just gleeful. "Kylie couldn't believe her big brother would do such a thing. Wait till your folks find out! You're supposed to call her the minute you get in, which would be right now."

"I'll call Kylie tomorrow," growled Devlin. "Meanwhile, you and Starr Lynn can go over to my place now, Brenda. I'm staying here tonight."

Brenda nodded her agreement. "I also called Noah Wykcoff. He's the man I've been seeing, you know, Cade's best friend, the number two guy at BrenCo. Noah is driving up tomorrow. He said Starr Lynn absolutely has to see those doctors at the hospital. I...think I know he's right."

While the cousins were talking, Gillian slipped into Ashley's room where the baby was sound asleep in her crib. Shadowy light from the candle on the dresser formed odd flickering patterns on the ceiling. Gillian laid her hand on the baby's head and gently stroked her dark curls. She loved Ashley so much. Imagining herself parted from her child was too awful to even contemplate.

Visitation rights. The ominous phrase suddenly sprang to mind. If Devlin demanded them—and he'd practically promised that he would—did that mean Ashley would be away from her overnight?

For an entire weekend? It was hard enough being separated from her baby eight hours a day during the work week. She couldn't stand it for extended periods of time.

How had her mother done it? Gillian wondered bleakly, not for the first time. Given up her children, just like that? Not that Jolene Bailey was unique in her disregard for motherhood. Mark's mother, Carmen's mother, Suzy and Stacey's mother, along with many others—all of them had thrown away their children and didn't even care enough to inquire what had become of them. As for all of their fathers—well, that was a joke. A singularly unfunny one.

On the other hand, Ashley's father wanted her. Enough to marry her mother. The enormity of that sacrifice was not lost on Gillian. But if she married Devlin, he would be stuck with her, the way her grandparents had been stuck with her, the way the State of Michigan had been stuck with her. Worse, she *knew* he loved Holly though he chose to deny it to her.

Yet how could she deprive little Ashley of a father's love and care, especially after having done so all these months? Whether Devlin loved Holly was irrelevant, Dr. Leah would say in that compelling manner of hers, "Adults can fend for themselves. Children's needs matter most." Dr. Leah fervently maintained that a child needed two parents, and Ashley's father had offered to marry Ashley's mother.

Gillian adjusted Ashley's beloved pink blanket, smoothing it over her small pajama-clad body. She moved the army of stuffed animals to the sides of the crib, lining them up along the rails.

Devlin entered the room. "Brenda and Starr Lynn left, thank God." He came to stand behind Gillian, wrapping his arms around her waist. "I gave them a few of your candles to use, then I picked up some things from my place and brought them over here."

"Dev, you really can't..." Her voice trailed off. The lack of conviction in it was obvious, even to herself.

"Gillian, I really can."

Eight

She closed her eyes, leaning back against him, her body acting on its own instead of taking direction from her mind. Sexual tension stretched between them once more.

"Devlin, don't," she said shakily in another halfhearted attempt to discourage him.

Undeterred, he scooped her up in his arms and carried her out of the baby's room. "Let's go to bed," he muttered softly against her neck.

It seemed so inevitable; he was so sure of her. After all, she'd surrendered so completely in the elevator earlier. Some perverse impulse within her clamored to rebel. "No, I—want to take a shower. I need to. There should still be hot water in the tank, the electricity hasn't been off long enough for it to turn cold."

"Good idea." His instant acquiescence surprised her. "I could use a shower, too."

Gillian glanced furtively at him, and her eyes widened. He was staring at her with fierce fixed intensity, his face taut with a hungry urgency that caused her body to soften in a hot swell of sensual excitement.

But still she resisted. "I'm going to shower alone, Devlin," she announced as he carried her into the bathroom. A vanilla-scented candle was burning on the top of the toilet tank, lighting the small room. Devlin set her on her feet and folded his arms in front of his chest. He made no move to leave.

"Oh, all right, you can take your shower first." Her voice sounded high and breathless and not at all as forceful as she wished. "I'll wait till you're done and then—"

"But there might not be enough hot water unless we share." There was a decidedly wicked gleam in his eyes.

Gillian's mouth went dry as he abruptly whipped off his scrub suit, letting it fall to the floor. Their intimacy in the dark elevator hadn't prepared her for the sight of him nude. She gaped at his lean-muscled torso, the hard chest and long legs covered with a dusting of dark hair. Compulsively, her gaze shifted to his flat belly and then locked on his masculinity, already fully roused and potent. She gulped.

"You look like Little Red Riding Hood eyeing the Wolf after she figured out he wasn't Grandma." Devlin chuckled huskily. "Don't be scared, Little Red." He removed her T-shirt with the same speed he'd shed his clothes, moving so quickly that she'd complied before quite realizing it.

She stood passively, letting him undress her. But she blushed as she stood, naked and trembling, before him. This was very different from their fast, hot passion in the elevator. The dark isolation somehow rendered that time and place anonymous and surreal. Or was that simply her excuse?

There were no excuses now. They were together in her own apartment, the candlelight casting a glow on their bare skin, their baby asleep in the next room.

Their eyes met. Devlin smiled a slow, warm, seductive smile. "In the shower or in bed?" As he spoke, he reached around her to turn on the taps and a torrent of water gushed from the overhead jets.

Gillian couldn't pretend to misinterpret the question. Would they make love in the shower or in her bedroom? He was letting her choose. Liquid desire flooded through her, perhaps temporarily short-circuiting her brain because she never even thought of a third unmentioned option—that they wouldn't make love either place. That he could shower alone and spend the night on the sofa.

Devlin pushed aside the shower curtain that was patterned with brightly colored fish, and stepped into the tub. Ashley's fleet of ducks, in various sizes and colors, were already beginning to swim in the inch-deep water pooling at his feet.

"This must be the admiral." Devlin reached down and picked up the biggest duck, a yellow one wearing a sailor hat.

"No, he's a captain, like your father. Ashley is the admiral." Sweaty and sticky, Gillian couldn't resist the tempting waters and stepped into the tub with him. Devlin yanked the shower curtain across the rod, enclosing them in the steamy wet warmth.

"Do you mind if I use the soap?" she asked politely, though her heart was racing. "Or would you rather—"

"Go ahead. Ladies first."

She reached for the solid white bar and began to work up a lather.

"Ladies first—now there's an old slogan of my dad's that just popped into my head. Would it be considered sexist these days?" Dev's hands were on her waist, then moved to cup her hips as he turned her to face him. "Not to mention politically incorrect, hmm?" He lowered his head and gently brushed her lips with his.

"It doesn't matter." Gillian shuddered with pleasure and admitted achingly to herself that it wasn't only the promise of a refreshing shower that had tempted her in here. "Haven't you heard there's a backlash against political correctness?" She passed the soap to him.

"Does that mean male chauvinist pigs are going to be acceptable again? Can't wait." His palms cupped her breasts, lathering them, his fingers paying special attention to her nipples that were already pointed and erect.

"Oh, Dev, we shouldn't," she gasped.

"It's okay, sweetie. We're engaged, remember?" His mouth fastened hard and hungry on hers, and she clung to him, kissing him frantically as the water sluiced over them.

Both were wild, hot and ready. He found her moist and yielding, and he took her, his fingers closing over her bottom to lift her into his possessive thrusts.

The pleasure rushing through her didn't build slowly but crested into a powerful surge that swept her swiftly to the rapturous peaks. Gillian gave in to the ecstasy, holding him tight while he, too, surrendered to the commanding force of their passion. She felt his searing release deep inside her and was consumed again as the mingled sounds of his hoarse cry and her own sobs of completion echoed in her ears.

"Here's that abominable concoction you ordered, Gilly." Marthea Franklin plunked the paper bag containing Gillian's lunch—hummus, lettuce and salsa on an onion bagel—onto the top of her desk. It was one of Gillian's favorite lunches. She'd eaten it almost every day of her pregnancy and wasn't surprised that Ashley already favored hummus on a cracker. She hadn't been introduced to salsa just yet.

Her stomach growling in anticipation, Gillian tucked the telephone receiver under her chin and began to unwrap her sandwich.

"Still on hold?" Marthea asked, regarding her with real sympathy.

"For the past forty-one minutes." Sighing, Gillian transferred the receiver back to her hand. "They have some horrible music blaring in my ears that sounds like trains derailing. But they're not getting rid of me. I'll get through if it's the only thing I do all day."

"Which it might well be," Marthea said grimly. "I was on hold for a hundred and eight minutes last Tuesday. That's my record so far."

"But did you get the check for the patient?" asked Gillian.

A huge grin split Marthea's face. "I sure did. I beat 'em at their own game."

Gillian smiled, too, vicariously sharing in the triumph, but her smile quickly faded as her extended period on hold was further prolonged. So much of her time on the job—too much!—was spent telephoning various agencies to secure funds for patients' medications and treatments and admissions to after-care facilities. Just getting through to a human voice was an accomplishment, and there always seemed to be endless picayune details required before the proper forms could finally be processed.

No wonder so many patients didn't bother to get the prescribed medication they couldn't afford to pay for themselves or seek the follow-up care recommended to them. They considered the bureaucratic hassles to be hopeless obstacles. Undaunted, Gillian knew how to work the system on behalf of her caseload. Growing up a ward of the state made her an offspring of the bureaucracy, as it were. She could hold her own with the most off-putting government agency any day.

Still, when she finally got through and won the fight—she'd let the testy voice on the other end of the line know that she wasn't *ever* going to give up unless she got the okay for Mrs. Reisman's costly medicines—Gillian felt less victorious than worn out and cynical. It was times like these when she hated her job, when she was even more keenly aware of Ashley downstairs in day care, learning and doing new things every day while her mother was stuck on hold, missing all the cuteness.

Not for the first time did she find herself longing to quit work and stay at home with her baby.

She had never considered that an option because as a single mother no job meant welfare, and she'd been in the system for too many years as a child to ever want to go back there as an adult.

But she was a doctor's wife now. She was Mrs. Devlin Brennan. Gillian glanced down at the plain gold wedding band on the ring finger of her left hand. Though it had been there for three weeks, it still looked strange and unfamiliar. Like she was playing a role and the ring was part of the costume. She often felt that way.

The office staff in the department of medical social work had gone slightly crazy that Monday when she'd come to work and casually announced that she had gotten married over the weekend. To Dr. Devlin Brennan. The new nameplate on her desk, which read Gillian Brennan, had arrived just a day later, courtesy of her supervisor who'd somehow coerced the human resources department to deliver it immediately, as if the new surname printed on the plate would make Gillian's marital status so official it would be irrevocable.

"Are you going to keep working?" Sally, whose cubicle-passing-for-an-office adjoined Gillian's, asked her at least once a day. "The day I married a doctor would be the same day I'd hand in my resignation and get out of this place forever."

"Quit my job? How could I ever give all this up? How could I leave you guys?" Gillian invariably gave Sally the same joking reply to her question.

"Resident doctors' wives who have children usually don't work, Gillian," explained Marthea.

"Are you trying to get rid of me?" Gillian tried to kid them out of their mission—which seemed to be unemployment for her.

"We want the best for you and Ashley," one of her co-workers would inevitably say with such sincerity that Gillian knew it was true.

She was appreciative of her co-workers' caring support that had extended all through her pregnancy and during the first year of Ashley's life. So much so that she'd invited them all to Ashley's first birthday party, to be held next week in her apartment.

In her and Devlin's apartment, Gillian silently corrected herself. Where they had been living as a married couple, as a family, for the past twenty-three days.

Her gaze lingered on her gold ring as her thoughts drifted to their wedding, that quick, efficient ceremony uniting Ashley's parents in holy matrimony. Except the local justice of the peace who'd married them hadn't used the words "holy" or "matrimony" because he deemed them inappropriate for a civil ceremony. In fact, the J.P. had skipped all religious references and stuck meticulously to administrative jargon as he pronounced Devlin Brennan and Gillian Bailey man and wife according to the laws of Michigan. Gillian supposed that was appropriate for the likes of her. The state had always loomed as the major presence in her life.

Dev's sister Kylie had wanted them to have a church wedding, with all the requisite paraphernalia and the entire family present. She'd suggested holding it in the Brennan stronghold of Port McClain and offered to do all the planning herself.

"All you and Dev and Ashley will have to do is to show up, Gillian," Kylie had said during the weekend visit she and her husband Cade made to Ann Arbor, directly following Brenda's revelation.

Devlin had absolutely hated the idea of a big Port McClain wedding. "You and Cade already did the family reunion-wedding extravaganza thing in July, Kylie," he'd told his sister while Cade sat in silence, staring fixedly at a point on the opposite wall. "Why should Gillian and I repeat it? Anyway, we have no intention of waiting to get married. We're going to do it quickly and quietly, and we're not telling anybody till it's over. So please don't mention a word of this conversation to Brenda who, as we all know, will immediately blab everything to everybody.''

"Brenda is busy with Starr Lynn's physical therapy," Cade interjected. "Since the doctors and Noah Wykcoff finally managed to convince the kid she couldn't continue to skate untreated, Starr Lynn has tackled her exercise therapy regime with the same dedication she gave to her skating. Surgery has been put on hold, pending further tests. But her prognosis is looking good."

Cade seemed far more interested in talking about Starr Lynn's progress than wedding plans, but Kylie wasn't about to let the subject drop.

"I loved my wedding, it was one of the happiest days of my life, and I want that for you, too, Dev," Kylie exclaimed with fervor. "What's with the big rush to get married? After all, the baby is already here. So why not take a few extra months to plan a beautiful, meaningful wedding? Even Mom and Dad agree with me on this, Dev. A wonderful family wedding will be a memory that Gillian and all of us will remember forever."

"Unless time is of the essence," Cade Austin interjected, pinning both Devlin and Gillian with a look of laserlike sharpness. "If there is even a remote possibility of yet another little Brennan nine months from now, for God's sake, get married immediately and skip the wedding fanfare."

Gillian and Dev had exchanged glances. The result of their impetuous little interludes in the elevator *and in the shower* had yet to be revealed. Gillian had blushed so deeply and Devlin looked so guilty that Kylie groaned, suddenly aware of their possible predicament. Cade had merely sucked in his cheeks and shaken his head, his thoughts practically stamped across his face. Recalling Brenda's disclosure, Gillian found them easy enough to read: Cade Austin found both her and Devlin exasperating and infuriating, probably put on this earth just to drive him crazy.

Although a traditional family celebration in Port McClain was clearly out, Gillian suggested that the Sinsels and Carmen, not too far away in Detroit, come up for their wedding.

Dev instantly vetoed that idea. "I just want the three of us there, you, Ashley and me," he had insisted.

At last Gillian got the message he was trying to diplomatically impart. Devlin wanted to make this compulsory marriage ceremony to be as unlike a true-love wedding as possible. Forget family and friends being there to wish them well; don't even drag God into it! Devlin wanted no part of a hypocritical charade. She decided she respected him for his honesty. This marriage was temporary but legal—nothing more, nothing less. Why pretend otherwise?

She tried to explain it all to Carmen, who protested nevertheless. "That is *so* not fair, Gilly! Me and you are the only ones who went to church every Sunday with Mom Sinsel, and you and Ash still go. Is Devlin Brennan too cheap or too coldhearted to pay for a nice little church wedding?" Carmen vowed to put a hex on him, should she ever venture into the realm of black magic. Gillian made her swear not to even try.

Mark called and added his own piece. "I talked to a lawyer friend out here and he said *DO NOT SIGN ANYTHING*, Gilly. Without a prenuptial agreement and with a little kid, you can take Dr. Yango for a bundle. And I hope you intend to quit your day job immediately. The doc owes you a nice suburban life-style, Gilly. He really owes you big-time."

Gillian did not agree and told him so. "This isn't a get-rich-quick scheme, Mark. It's important that I keep my independence and that means keeping my job." She didn't dare forget she needed to be prepared for the day Devlin decided their marriage was over.

"But what about Ashley?" demanded Mark. "She's going to be better off as a doctor's kid than a wanna-be actor's kid. That's why *I* signed all those papers Brennan's lawyer sent without even asking my lawyer friend about them. How are those paternity tests going, anyway? Not too many needles for our little cutie pie, I hope."

"Ashley and Dev have had all the necessary tests and she didn't like the needles one bit," Gillian told him. "The results aren't back yet but—thanks again for being her father for a while, Mark. You were there when we needed you to be."

"I always will be, Gilly," promised Mark. "And I am not going to let that yango walk away from you and Ash without shelling out major bucks. That's my blood oath!"

Considering Carmen's hex and Mark's blood oath, and the scandalized Brennan clan, Gillian conceded that the J.P.'s three-minute ceremony with Ashley as the only invited guest had definitely been the safest course.

Their rushed wedding day had ended on a note of irony. After tucking the baby into her crib, Gillian found out that those reckless chances she and Devlin had taken in the elevator and the shower had not resulted in a sibling for Ashley. Gillian was relieved, but getting her period on her wedding night did not strike her as a particularly good omen. Disappointment and embarrassment flooded her as she explained the circumstances to Devlin.

He claimed he wanted her anyway, which embarrassed her more. She'd pleaded cramps and a headache, and he gracefully accepted her no, without even trying to talk her out of it. To her confusion, she was even more disappointed!

So they'd spent the first few days of their new marriage living platonically as roommates. Gillian had plenty of experience sharing a room; she'd had countless roommates during her foster child years and knew all the rules of getting along. Be considerate and neat and quiet. She was careful to be all three with Devlin.

Living with a male was not new to her, either. Over the years she'd lived with more foster brothers than she could remember. She knew there were things that guys didn't do, like pick up towels from the bathroom floor or remove empty containers from the refrigerator or refill ice cube trays, and she did not expect Devlin to perform any of those tasks. She did them herself, along with the food shopping, cooking and vacuuming. She did the dishes and the laundry and took care of the baby herself, too. She knew that was the way things were supposed to be.

"If a woman thinks a man will help with the housework, she's just fooling herself and is in for a nasty surprise when she learns different," Mom Sinsel had counseled her foster daughters. "Don't let anyone trick you into thinking it's any other way, girls. Things only get done when you do them yourself." At the Sinsels, Mom and the girls did all the housework and child care while the male residents took turns mowing the yard and keeping the car running smoothly. The girls grumbled, but didn't protest because they recognized that was simply the way things were.

Since Gillian was not one to be tricked and always tried to avoid nasty surprises, she continued to do whatever needed to be done herself. For the opening days of her marriage, being a wife was somewhat like living at the Sinsels—except the place was smaller and quieter and there were fewer people around.

And then she and Devlin became lovers again. Passion flared

between them every night, their intense sensuality burning, its hot rise ultimately sweeping them both into the seas of sated pleasure. Lying with Devlin in the languorous afterglow, Gillian couldn't seem to not touch him. She would stroke his back or slip one leg over his or simply hold his hand. She learned to fall asleep in his arms, a feat she'd never considered possible because she had always slept on her side curled in a tight ball, her sleeping position as defensive and self-protective as her wakeful posture.

Living with a husband required a new set of guidelines and Gillian paid extra attention to Dr. Leah's broadcast and to the conversations of her married friends at work, trying to learn. She already knew that the intimacy between a husband and wife went beyond sexual because being Dev's wife was definitely different from being his girlfriend. Knowing he was going to be with her every night and still be there in the morning, not having to wonder if and when he was going to call, sharing his bathroom and his bed and refrigerator and feeling that they were hers, too...

Gillian loved the sense of permanence and stability as much as she feared it because she was acutely aware that situations and relationships were temporary more often than they were permanent. One lesson she'd learned well was that change was inevitable; it usually came swiftly, without warning, and often brought great pain.

But she couldn't help savoring the warm feelings of contentment that stole through her as she watched her husband playing with their baby, or during those times when they ate dinner together as a family, or while she and Dev watched television and teasingly challenged each other with impossible trivia questions.

They'd surmounted another hurdle this past weekend when Devlin's parents had flown up from Florida to meet Gillian and Ashley, the newest Brennans. A nervous Gillian greeted them, but Captain Wayne and Connie had been cordial and kind to her while treating Ashley like the adored grandchild they'd been longing for. Dev spent some time alone with his parents, and though Gillian wondered what had been said, she didn't ask. Devlin told her that he hadn't held back any facts, that he felt being fully honest with his folks was the only way to go. Especially since Brenda had already told all she knew to everybody in the clan.

Actually, Devlin was glad Brenda had taken it upon herself to explain the decidedly unusual situation because all he had to add was the reason why Gillian found it necessary to break up with him in the first place. "She had this crazy idea Holly Casale and I were in love with each other," he told his parents, expecting them to find the idea as bizarre as he did. They had spent time with Holly during their visits over the years and knew her well.

"Hmm, Holly," his mother said thoughtfully. "I used to wonder myself about you two..."

"Mom, you're kidding!" Devlin was flabbergasted. "If I were in love with Holly, I'd've done something about it years ago!"

"Yes, I realize that," Connie Brennan agreed. "You've never wanted more than friendship, but what about Holly's feelings for you?"

"Trust me, Mom, Holly is not carrying some secret torch for me." Devlin laughed off the notion.

"But if your wife feels threatened by your friendship with another woman, you know what you have to do, son." Captain Brennan's voice resonated with firm resolve.

"Your primary loyalty is to your wife, the mother of your child. Don't give her reason to ever doubt that."

Devlin quickly agreed. His father was right, of course, and he was eager to end the discussion and rejoin Gillian and the baby. The rest of the visit went so well that Connie and the Captain proposed another trip in late October and asked about holiday plans for Thanksgiving and Christmas.

"You made a big hit with Mom and Dad," Devlin told Gillian that night in bed. "Not that I'm at all surprised." He kissed her lingeringly. "Everybody who knows you is crazy about you."

For a moment she bathed in the sweet surge of warmth his compliment evoked. But Gillian was always one to give credit where it was due. "They're crazy about their granddaughter. I'm glad Ashley has such loving grandparents, I wish they'd been able to know her from the time she was born. I—I wish you had, too, Dev."

"No looking back, Gillian. We have this second chance, that's what matters."

"That is a very Dr. Leah thing to say," Gillian murmured softly. "Except Dr. Leah would add something about not forgetting the past so you won't be doomed to repeat it."

"We are not doomed," Devlin said firmly, then pulled her on top of him. "Everything is going to be all right, Gillian."

He spoke with such confidence and assurance. And when they were together like this, when they were close and making love, Gillian almost found it easy to believe him. That, just maybe, everything really was going to be all right.

Usually their schedules didn't allow them to see each other during working hours at the hospital, but once in a while Dev would call Gillian's office and suggest meeting her in the cafeteria for lunch. Friends would drop by their table to say hello and ask about Ashley, and Gillian would wonder if it were possible to burst with happiness as she sat with her husband, fully acknowledged as his wife.

One friend of Devlin's whom Gillian hadn't seen since their wedding was Holly Casale, though she'd sent them a congratulations card and a gift—an enormous ceramic salad bowl with folk art designs painted on it. Gillian immediately acknowledged the wedding present with a polite thank-you note.

"Good grief, this thing is big enough to serve salad to the entire orthopedic department," Devlin had joked upon examining the bowl.

Gillian was flummoxed. Was that why Holly had given them a bowl that size? Was a newlywed couple expected to entertain the husband's entire department? Was it *required?* She had little knowledge of the class customs and obligations of those with social status.

Of course, Holly knew. Holly would entertain with style and panache, she was probably one of those legendary hostesses.

Gillian looked at the beautiful salad bowl and saw it as a depressing symbol of why Devlin belonged with Holly instead of the woman he'd felt obliged to marry. She could've never explained such a thing to Dev, but Carmen understood. While visiting one Saturday afternoon when Devlin was at the hospital on an emergency call, Carmen deliberately dropped the bowl on the kitchen floor. When it didn't break, she suggested smashing it with a hammer. Or throwing it out the window to hit the concrete below. Gillian nixed the idea. "I think that falls into the category of petty vengeance and Dr. Leah says to stay away from that trap."

But she stored the bowl, that token of her social inadequacy, on the highest longest shelf of the towel closet, out of sight. To her relief, Devlin didn't mention it again.

The day after her Mrs. Reisman triumph, Gillian won another battle with the feds, this one for an eight-year-old's respiratory therapy treatments. As she sat at her desk filling out the requisite reimbursement forms, Devlin strode in carrying a howling Ashley in his arms. He was dressed in green scrubs and looked harassed, the big diaper bag askew on his shoulder. Ashley wore the extra outfit Gillian had packed that morning, and she was waving her small arms and legs in agitation while she cried.

Gillian jumped to her feet. "What's wrong?" She swiftly rounded her desk and reached for her daughter. Ashley fairly leaped into her arms. "She feels warm, she—"

"She got kicked out of the nursery because she's running a fever," Devlin interrupted grimly. "She also threw up her lunch. Her clothes are stuffed in a plastic bag in that zippered compartment. Why don't they send the kids' dirty clothes down to the laundry? Sealing them in plastic only makes them reek all the more and it's damn unsanitary, too."

"The child care center can't use the hospital laundry for personal items, it's against regulations," Gillian explained. "But why didn't Tina or someone on the staff down there call me? They always have before." She rocked Ashley in her arms and the baby began to slowly relax against her, though she continued to sniffle and emit an occasional wail.

"They tried, but your line was busy. Tina said you've been on the phone forever, and my name is down next on their who-to-call list. Apparently, whenever a kid's temp goes over a hundred, they want them out of there immediately. Ashley hit a hundred-two-point-four." Devlin ran his hand through his hair. "I was scrubbing in for a hip replacement and I had to leave, Gillian."

She didn't miss the accusatory note in his voice. "I know all about the center's fever policy. They've always sent someone up here to tell me the baby was sick if they couldn't get through on the phone. I guess they decided to notify you this time instead of coming to get me. You were the one who wanted to be put down as Ashley's father on the emergency card," Gillian reminded him.

"I *am* Ashley's father," Devlin growled. "But I had a patient on the operating table, Gillian. I had med students and first and second year residents there to observe—not to mention the attending physician there to supervise. We've had to postpone the surgery for an hour and believe me, that goes over about as well as testing nuclear warheads in a school zone. I can't make a habit of leaving the OR to run down to day care and—"

"Look after your own sick baby," Gillian snapped.

"If you're trying to insinuate that I'm not concerned about my child's health, I deeply resent it, Gillian."

"You're concerned if it doesn't interfere with what else you happen to be doing."

She conceded it was possible she was being a mite unfair. Maybe even very unfair. But when anyone, even Ashley's father—especially him?—implied that her baby was an inconvenience or a bothersome chore, Gillian took it personally. Clutching her daughter, she reached for the phone. "I'll call and tell Tina to take your name off the card, and that you're never to be called again about anything concerning Ashley."

"Put down that phone," ordered Dev, putting his hand over hers to break the connection. "And drop the attitude, Gillian. I want my name on the card but that doesn't mean I can't voice a legitimate complaint, like being called out of the OR." His fingers tightened around hers. "Right?"

Gillian closed her eyes and inhaled Ashley's baby smell—which was somewhat soured with the smell of the lunch she'd lost. A nice bath for her was definitely in order.

"Gillian, I want an answer." Devlin's thumb began to stroke the inside of her wrist. "Are we allowed to complain and be in a lousy mood sometimes, or do we have to keep a phony smile pasted on our faces every minute, until we're ready to crack?"

As always, she reacted to his touch, his nearness. Response rippled through her. She wanted to lean against him, to feel his strong arms around her. Was it really that simple, Devlin in a lousy mood and complaining because he'd undoubtedly been lambasted by his superiors?

She felt oddly like crying, but successfully held back the tears.

"You...don't have to paste a phony smile on your face all the time," she said cautiously. "I couldn't keep that up, either." She carefully removed her hand from the phone, unlinking their fingers in the process. "I'll take Ashley down to the pediatric clinic as a walk-in patient and—"

"Forget the clinic, I already had Carolyn Kessler look at her."
He mentioned a senior pediatric resident, one of the best, who
was always so busy that it was difficult to get an appointment
with her. But Dev had simply asked Dr. Kessler to see Ashley
right away, and she had.

Gillian was contemplating this good fortune when Devlin's
frown deepened.

"Ashley has tonsillitis. Carolyn pulled the baby's file and I
couldn't believe it's already as thick as a phone directory." Devlin reached over to smooth Ashley's damp curls from her hot little
face. His big hand almost cupped her whole head. "This is her
third bout with tonsillitis. The poor little kid is sick all the time."

"Not all the time." Gillian heaved a discouraged sigh. "Well,
lots of the time," she admitted.

"Carolyn says when babies are grouped together in a place like
the child care center, infections runs rampant among them. We
went over Ashley's case history and everything she's had, all the
colds and ear infections, the tonsillitis and diarrhea and stomach
viruses—all of them—could probably be traced to other cases in
the center."

"You studied Ashley's medical records?" A fiery bolt of heat
scorched Gillian.

"Yeah. I should've done it before." Devlin looked sheepish.
"Carolyn read me the riot act, and rightly so. There's no excuse
for Ashley's father to be unfamiliar with her medical history."

His words swirled around Gillian's head but didn't fully pen-
etrate. The image of the two doctors pouring over Ashley's file,
judging and assessing and evaluating her child and her own role
as a mother, had struck a nerve. Deeply. She felt as if her privacy
had been invaded, as if an Inquisition Team was examining her
life.

Gillian flushed with rage mingled with pain. She'd grown up
as a case file, the details of her life known to anyone who cared
to flip through her records. She'd hated it then and she hated the
specter of it now.

She knew the system so well that she'd learned how to get
things done within it, one of the reasons why she'd chosen social
work as a career. But she'd chosen the specialized area of medical
social work, never child welfare. There were too many memories
to overcome for her to function effectively in the juvenile divi-

sion. Why, merely learning that Devlin had looked at his own child's medical record was enough to access her old demons.

"Are you all right?" Devlin stared hard at Gillian. He tried to put his hand on her face to feel her skin because she looked as hot and feverish as Ashley.

"I'm fine." She ducked his hand and moved away from him, far and fast, as if he were a source of contagion himself. "I'll take Ashley home now. I'll ask to take a sick day in advance because I've used up all my personal days and sick days from the other times she's been sick."

"An advance sick day? Is that allowed?"

"Probably not, but so far nobody's said anything and all the mothers do it." Gillian gathered her things, Ashley tucked firmly on her hip.

"But what if you get sick?" pressed Devlin.

Gillian chose to ignore the question. It wasn't worth answering. "Thank you for picking up Ashley and taking her to see a doctor," she said briskly. "I'll stop by the pharmacy and get her medicine and then—"

"I already did it. The medicine bottles are here in the bag." He slipped the diaper bag over her shoulder. "I was careful not to put them near the barf clothes," he added, so conscientiously that Gillian couldn't contain her smile.

"How thoughtful. Thank you, Dev."

"You don't have to thank me. Ashley is my kid, too." He cupped his hands around Gillian's shoulders and leaned down to kiss her forehead, then the top of Ashley's head. "Whew! She could use a shampoo."

"She'll be smelling like bubble gum by the time you get home," Gillian promised, referring to the bright pink bubble-gum-scented children's shampoo, one of Devlin's many impulse purchases for Ashley.

They walked out of the office together, along the corridor to the elevator bank.

And came face-to-face with Holly Casale. She was dressed all in black—fitted ribbed jersey, thick leather belt, short skirt, dark hose and high heels.

Gillian knew if she were to wear such an outfit, she'd look trashy. Short and trashy. Holly looked sexy and classy. And elegantly tall. Gillian's eyes slid to Devlin, who was also sexy, classy, tall and gorgeous. Once again it struck her what a magnificent-looking couple the two doctors made.

"It's the Brennan family!" Holly announced brightly. She was all smiles.

Ashley burst into tears. Since her wails hurt her already swollen throat, her crying quickly escalated to a full-blown frenzy.

"She's sick, I'm taking her home." Gillian was apologetic.

"Oh, the poor little thing. Do you know what's wrong with her?" Holly tried to stroke some part of Ashley, her head, her little arm, her foot. Ashley managed to dodge each and every attempt at a caress.

"Tonsillitis," Devlin explained. "Carolyn Kessler's treating her."

Ashley's cries were echoing through the halls, and Gillian longed to escape to the sanctuary of her car. Except she couldn't move. Devlin had wrapped his hand around her upper arm, holding her in place, and showed no inclination to let her go.

"Dev, I really think I'd better—" she began but was interrupted by Holly.

"I heard there's an epidemic of tonsillitis in the day care center." Holly frowned her concern. "Laura Kasarian's little boy has it, and the Reardons' two little girls do, too. You know Ned and Rena Reardon, Dev. They're both on my service, second year."

"An epidemic?" Dev was visibly upset by that news.

"Goes with the territory," said Holly. "I remember last winter they had an awful time when strep ran through that place. Laura and the Reardons were terribly concerned but what could they do? They're all residents, they had patients and had to be on duty." She looked at Gillian with concerned, dark eyes. "Did Ashley get strep last year?"

"A few times." Gillian gulped. She felt as if she were being indicted.

Ashley was crying so hard that she gagged. "I have to get her home," Gillian almost pleaded.

Still, Devlin didn't release her. "I realize Laura Kasarian and Ned and Rena Reardon don't have a choice, they have to leave their kids there, but Gillian isn't in the residency program. She doesn't have to answer to the attendings and meet their time requirements."

Gillian shifted nervously. Dev was talking to Holly about her as if she weren't even there. While poor little Ashley continued to shriek.

"I just don't know about this working mother thing." Devlin was scowling now. "It seems like Ashley would be better off staying home with Gillian while she's so little. It's not like I can't afford to support my family."

Gillian's eyes widened. Had Marthea, Sally, and the rest of her department heard him, they would already be cleaning out her desk while simultaneously writing her resignation.

"This working mother thing?" Holly repeated incredulously. "Honestly, Dev, you sound like one of those macho nuts who run around pledging to reassert their male authority and keep the little woman by the hearth. Gillian has a career. You have no right to ask her to give it up. You can't blow off her ambitions because it's more convenient for you to have her at home with the baby!"

Gillian thought how much she would love to stay at home with her baby but didn't dare, not when she was married to a man who didn't love her, a man who could leave at any given moment, having fulfilled what he considered to be his legal duty to his daughter. She longed to tell Holly to keep her opinions to herself but opted to stay silent because she knew that when Holly Casale spoke, Devlin Brennan listened.

She shot a covert glance at Dev to see that his eyes were locked with Holly's, and felt like an outsider, as if she were intruding on a private moment between them. Which she probably was. They had a long-standing relationship that didn't include her.

Devlin shrugged. "I don't think it's good PR for a shrink to rant about nuts, Holly. That's what we macho surgeons do. You're supposed to cure them."

And now she was supposed to stand here and listen to them banter about their respective professional services? Gillian had had enough. She forcibly pulled her arm out of Devlin's grasp. He looked surprised. *Because he'd forgotten she was there?* Gillian wondered peevishly. When that glam-shrink Holly appeared, all other women were rendered invisible—especially his wife who looked nothing less than mediocre in her practical, no-nonsense brown skirt and jacket.

Gillian murmured a quick goodbye and ran into an already

crowded elevator car, pushing her way inside, the baby and the oversize bag giving her extra leverage.

The doors closed, and Devlin and Holly looked from the elevator to each other.

"Did you see how she shook me off?" Devlin tried and failed to conceal the hurt in his voice. "Like a flea on a dog. Like she couldn't stand for me to touch her for another second."

"Dev, the baby was screaming at the top of her lungs," Holly stated. "Gillian had to get her out of here."

"It's not just that. There are times when Gillian can't get away from me fast enough. When she looks at me like...well, like I'm something about as appealing as a used airsickness bag."

"I've never seen her look at you that way, Dev. But she does appear to be very guarded. I guess it's hard to break through her reserve." Holly eyed him curiously. "Assuming that you've even tried."

"Oh, I've tried. And sometimes I actually reach her. We're so close, but then she'll pull back. It's like she catches herself and just—" Devlin broke off, appalled. "Listen to me! I sound like one of those poor saps who call Dr. Leah for advice."

"You've taken to listening to Dr. Leah?" Holly was astounded.

"Since Gillian is always quoting her favorite radio guru, I thought maybe I could pick up a few clues from the program." He shook his head wryly. "Go ahead and laugh, Hol. I deserve to be ridiculed."

"You want to get closer to your wife. That's not something to ridicule, Dev." Holly put her hand on his arm and subtly steered him to the more secluded vestibule a few feet away. "We haven't had much chance to talk since you married Gillian. Are you happy, Dev?"

"God, yes!" Devlin grinned, his face lighting with enthusiasm. "Gillian is the perfect wife, Holly! She's fun to be with, she's great with the baby, she keeps the place spotless—she even met my mom's housekeeping standards—she's a good cook." His smile grew rakish. "And we're fabulous together in bed."

"What a paragon! I think I hate her."

Devlin laughed. "I was in no hurry to get married, Holly, you know that. From the time I was a kid and moving from place to place with Dad in the Navy, I always knew there would be new people to take the place of the ones we'd left behind. When I got older, I applied the same principle to women. There would always be another woman just as sexy and pretty and smart as the one I was with. Maybe even more so. I didn't want to commit to one woman, knowing there was always going to be somebody better out there.''

''Until Gillian? You don't think there is any woman better than she is.''

Devlin's eyes narrowed. Something in Holly's tone unsettled him, though he couldn't quite define it. He recalled Gillian's ridiculous assertions about Holly and himself and frowned.

''I don't care if there is or not. I don't want any other woman,'' he said quietly. ''I only want her.''

''You have her, Dev. You're married to her.''

''It seems like it should be that easy, but it isn't. You know, when my sister and her husband found out about Ashley, they asked me if I could forgive Gillian for keeping the baby a secret from me. You remember, my theory used to be that forgiving a woman for doing something wrong was a big waste of time because there were so many replacement women out there. Why bother with one who'd ticked you off? I guess I sounded so convincing that Kylie and Cade were afraid I wouldn't ever be able to forgive Gillian, that I'd always hold that bogus marriage against her.''

''Do you?'' Holly asked.

''No. Oh, I was mad at first, but I understand why she did what she did. I found it amazingly easy to forgive and even forget. But I don't know if Gillian can forgive me for not knowing, or at least not suspecting, about the baby. I think maybe that's what is keeping her from...from— I don't know.'' He groaned. ''I said she's the perfect wife and she is, but I want even more. That's sheer Devlin Brennan, huh? Wanting more than perfection.''

''You feel she is keeping an emotional distance from you. Of course you want more, Dev. Have you tried telling her what you've just told me?''

''Are you nuts? She'd feel cornered, she'd feel like running away. Hey, I've been there, Holly. I know how it feels when someone wants more than you're prepared to give. I'm not about to put Gillian in that position.'' He glanced at his watch. ''Time for me to hit the OR for a hip replacement. I'm sorry to bend your ear like this, Holly. You ought to charge me for services rendered."

"I don't think I've rendered any." Holly laid her hand over his. "Be patient, Dev. I have this theory—just a personal one, not a scientific one I'd submit for publication—that it's the man who can make a relationship work. A loving, committed male can bring around the most resistant, difficult female to love him and commit to him." She heaved a sigh. "Unfortunately, it doesn't work in reverse. There is very little that a woman can do to get a reluctant man to really see her or to make him love her."

"We ought to run that one by our esteemed Dr. Leah." Devlin was smiling again. He felt buoyed from their little talk. "Thanks for the encouragement, Hol. I needed it."

Holly smiled, too. "That's what friends are for, Dev."

Nine

Ashley was sick until two days before her first birthday party. Gillian stayed at home with her and didn't request advance sick days because Devlin told her not to.

"You're going to end up owing them money. Just take the days off without pay," he insisted.

He didn't seem to care that would mean a lesser paycheck for her, a condition that would've caused Gillian to panic when she was the sole support of herself and Ashley. But she wasn't any longer. And when she fretted about being able to pay their bills, he pulled out his bank book to show that her anxiety was unfounded. And then some. Dev was good at managing money and they lived simply. His salary was enough for all three of them to live on.

Dev convinced her to keep the baby at home until after the party to make sure she didn't have a relapse. "She's doing so well," he said as he showed Ashley how to kick the pink and purple soccer ball he'd bought as a birthday gift. "This past week, she's hardly cried at all."

"Ashley doesn't cry much." Gillian defended her daughter. "You just aren't used to being around a young child."

"Gillian, I've lived here a month, I was used to the baby crying all the time. And after reading that medical record of hers, I know why. The poor kid felt lousy all the time. But she's completely healthy now and I want to make sure she stays that way."

Ashley, a well-practiced walker who rarely reverted to crawling these days, gave the ball a kick and Devlin gave her a rousing cheer and a congratulatory hug.

"Ball," Ashley said importantly, toddling after it.

Gillian smiled. She loved watching Ashley and her dad together.

So did the Sinsels, who drove up for the party, along with Carmen.

"He loves that baby, Gillian," Dolly Sinsel said approvingly as she watched Devlin carry Ashley around the room to socialize with the party guests. Holly Casale was not one of them. Devlin hadn't suggested asking her to the party and Gillian wasn't about to bring her up, either.

"Seems that fake marriage to Mark was unnecessary, after all. When will Devlin be officially declared Ashley's father?" Dad Sinsel asked.

"The tests are all in and the legal papers have been filed. We'll be assigned a court date, probably within a few months." Gillian grinned as Ashley made a spectacular leap from Devlin's arms into Marthea's, then demanded to be returned to her father again.

"Speaking of legal papers, some official-looking letter came for you at the house yesterday," Dolly Sinsel said, then slapped her hand to her cheek. "Oh, darn, I planned to bring it along with us today but I completely forgot about it until just now! I'll forward it to you right away."

"Uh-oh, you're getting senile, Mom," Carmen teased, and earned a good-natured swat for her wisecrack.

"What kind of legal paper would come to your house for me?" Gillian was puzzled.

"We didn't open it, but the return address was an attorney at some law firm." Dad Sinsel shrugged. "I'm sure it's nothing to worry about, honey."

Gillian's heart skipped a nervous beat. She knew she was probably overly superstitious, but simply hearing someone say there was "nothing to worry about" seemed to guarantee that there would be.

"Put it out of your head, Gilly," Carmen said firmly, knowing precisely how her thoughts were running. "This is Ashley's first birthday and you're not going to spoil this party for yourself by going bonkers over some letter. For all you know, it could just be an ad or something that only looked official. It's probably nothing."

Which meant it was probably something. Though Gillian forced herself to put the mysterious letter to the back of her mind while she celebrated Ashley's birthday, the thought of it kept cropping up. A letter from a lawyer contacting her at the Sinsels? Dread quivered through her.

Later that night Devlin lay sprawled on his back in their bed while Gillian cuddled against his side, her head tucked into the curve of his shoulder. He had taken her twice, his desire demanding and fierce, and she had matched his hunger, clinging to him, arching her body to his, her own fire stoking his.

Passion had drowned her anxieties, and the sensual pleasure and release he gave her made her blissfully mindless and drowsy. Her eyes closed, she rubbed against him, luxuriating in his solid, vital presence. She felt sated and safe and very much in love.

"Are you going to fall asleep on me?" Devlin's voice rumbled in her ear.

"Don't tell me you want to have a long heart-to-heart talk about our relationship," Gillian teasingly mumbled, naming what he had once told her was his chief horror.

Dev claimed he liked to roll over and fall asleep immediately after sex. Oddly, since their marriage, he seldom did so. They almost always talked after making love. He often initiated the conversation when she would've preferred to sleep. Like right now.

"You seemed a little nervous today," he persisted. "A little preoccupied."

"I did?" Gillian's eyes snapped wide open. "Was I rude? Do you think I spoiled Ashley's party?"

"No! No, of course not." His arms tightened protectively around her. "I don't think anybody noticed but me. And I probably wouldn't have either except Carmen told me you were freaked about some letter," he added reassuringly.

Gillian groaned. "Carmen shouldn't have dragged you into this, Dev. She was the one who kept telling me it's nothing."

"I don't have to be dragged into anything concerning you, Gillian," he said quietly. "I want to know when you're worried or scared or sad, and I want you to tell me about it."

Gillian felt tears burn her eyes. "I—I think I'm all three," she blurted out.

"Why, sweetheart?"

"A lawyer sent a letter to me by way of the Sinsels. They're going to forward it to me." She swallowed hard, struggling for control. "It must have something to do with my mother or my brother Jody. The Bureau of Family Services is the only agency that could tie all three of us together, plus match me to the Sinsels. And after all these years, it can't be good news."

Devlin digested the information. "Which doesn't necessarily mean it has to be bad news, Gillian," he concluded.

"Any contact from or about my mother is bad news, Devlin, even if she's writing to gloat that she's just won a million dollar lottery prize. But it's more likely that she—that she's dead." Her voice trembled. "Why else would a lawyer contact me? And if it's about Jody, it might say he's dead or in jail or in some state hospital…I just know whatever it is, it has to be bad, Dev."

"My poor little love, you do have a way of looking on the dark side." Devlin stroked her hair. "Gillian, no matter what it is, I'll be there to help you with it, okay? We'll talk it out and if there's anything that has to be decided or something that needs to be done, we'll tackle it together."

She was touched and charmed and swallowed a sob of deep emotion. "Dev, I really appreciate that you'd offer to help with—"

"Don't appreciate it, Gillian," he interrupted, his voice deep with feeling. "*Expect* me to offer to help you. Demand it. That's the way it should be in a marriage, baby. We share the good times and the rotten ones, too."

He sounded like he was making a vow. Something along the lines of for better or for worse. The words she'd heard on their wedding day hadn't really impacted on her at the time; it seemed like they were going through the motions of a TV scene, one that was familiar yet removed from their own reality. But this seemed different, it seemed real. And suddenly the prospect of facing dreadful news about her mother or Jody didn't seem so overwhelming.

"Oh, Dev," she whispered on a sigh, wishing she could express what she was feeling. Wishing she could tell him that she loved him as much as she loved Ashley and she had never, ever thought she could love anyone else that much. But she'd spent a lifetime keeping her thoughts to herself and she couldn't break the habit so easily. What she longed to say went unspoken, but she wrapped herself around him and kissed him deeply, possessively, trying to show how much she cared. To prove by her actions what she couldn't articulate with words.

Mutual urgency flared again, kindling that ever-present spark of passion between them into full blaze. There was no time for talking, no time for anything but to quench the desire driving them. Her legs circled his hips and he surged into her, taking them both to the heady heights of rapture once again, the bond between them growing stronger, growing tighter.

She was still twitching with little aftershocks of pleasure and he was still deep inside her body flooded with wet heat, when he raised himself on his elbows and looked directly into her eyes.

"I want you to do something for me, Gillian. Maybe I don't have a right to ask but I'm going to anyway." He paused. Perhaps waiting for her to object?

Gillian's hands smoothed over the muscular length of his back. She was too emotionally and physically fulfilled to summon a modicum of anxiety. "Ask me, Dev."

"Quit your job. I know you have your career and ambitions, I know it's probably selfish of me to ask you to sacrifice them, but I'm going to. I want you at home with Ashley. I don't want my baby getting sick because she's exposed to every group virus that roars through the center. There's plenty of time for her to catch every conceivable bug when she hits pre-school age," he added wryly.

Gillian lay very still. The tip of her tongue glided nervously over her lips. "I don't think it's selfish, Dev. I don't like leaving Ashley every day," she dared to confess, "but I thought I ought to keep working because—because..."

Her voice trailed off. Telling him that she expected him to drop out of her and Ashley's lives suddenly seemed impossible. Especially when they were together like this, when there were no boundaries or barriers between them, when they were so close that it seemed as if nothing could ever come between them.

His lips feathered hers and their tongues teased. "I'll take care of you and the baby, Gillian. I want to take care of you. I want to give you everything you want, everything you need. Say you'll let me."

Gillian took a deep breath. She felt as if she were about to plunge from an airplane, without being absolutely certain that her parachute was going to open. But she felt an optimism, a kind of reckless courage that empowered her. "I could hand in my resignation on Monday. I, uh, wouldn't mind giving up my career to stay home with Ashley, if you don't mind giving up my income."

"I don't need your income," he said in what Mark would definitely deem yango arrogance. "It's been really good this past week, having you home with the baby, Gillian. Not only is she healthier, but you seem more relaxed."

"Having those extra forty hours a week that I would've been at work does help me get things done around here at a more leisurely pace," she said dryly.

"Sure it does." He agreed so earnestly that she laughed.

He joined in, though he'd missed her own inside joke. "Then it's all settled? You won't go back?"

She didn't even try to pretend she had an ounce of regret. Her co-workers were going to be thrilled for her and she felt a joy of her own tingling through her. For the first time in her life she trusted someone enough not to have Plan B ready to enact in anticipation of failure. There was no Plan B. There was only Devlin's promise that she and Ashley could depend on him always.

Her eyes shone with wonder. "It's all settled."

Gillian loved being retired. She felt as if she were on a wonderful permanent vacation. After two whole weeks of enjoying life as a full-time wife and mother, she had all but forgotten about the letter that had prompted that momentous talk with Devlin the night of Ashley's birthday party. When the letter didn't arrive after it was supposed to be forwarded, she guessed the Sinsels had taken a second look and realized it actually was an ad or something not worth bothering about, just as Carmen had suggested.

One cool fall evening, Devlin waited until after Ashley's bedtime ritual was completed—a bath, a reading of the classic *Good-night Moon* and a bottle—and she was sound asleep in her crib before he sat down on the couch beside Gillian, holding an opened envelope in his hand.

He removed a letter from the envelope, and Gillian's stomach lurched. She instantly knew what it was. The Letter.

"I called the Sinsels the day after you told me about this letter and had them forward it to me at the hospital instead of to the apartment," Devlin explained. "I wanted to read it first, to see what it was about, before you had to deal with it."

Gillian stared at the crisp vellum paper. The fact that he'd waited this long to mention it didn't bode well.

"Don't look so scared." Devlin took her hand in his. He reached for the remote with his other hand and clicked off the TV, interrupting "The Mary Tyler Moore Show" in midsentence.

Every muscle in Gillian's body tensed. Devlin was uncharacteristically serious and without the background noise of the television, silence hung ominously over the room. Whatever was in that letter must be *really* bad news, of that she had not a single doubt.

"There is no mention of either your mother or Jody," Devlin said quickly, seeing the alarm in her eyes. "This isn't even about them, Gillian. The letter is from an attorney who works with your father. Your birth father," he added.

"Craig Saylor?" The name seemed to stick in Gillian's throat like a clot.

Devlin nodded. "Interestingly enough, your dad is an attorney, too."

"He is not my dad." Gillian rose to her feet. "I look on him as an impersonal sperm donor. And whatever he—or his attorney—has to say, I don't want to hear. You can just tear up that letter and we'll pretend I never got it."

Devlin stood up, too. "I can't do that, honey. I've already been in contact with Craig Saylor." He reached for her, but she darted away from him, putting the length of the room between them.

"You can uncontact him then. I don't want anything to do with that person. Ever."

"Gillian, you don't understand. It's not that easy. You see, he—"

"Let me tell you something about Craig Saylor, Devlin, and

then I never want to hear his name again. I went to see him once, when I was twelve years old and stuck in that foster home I described as the world's worst, because it was, in every way. My mother told me when I was little that Craig Saylor was my father, though I'd never tried to get in touch with him because she always insisted he wouldn't want me.'' Gillian drew a deep, shuddering breath.

"But that place I was in was so terrible and so scary, I was desperate. I talked myself into believing maybe I had a chance with him, that maybe my own father would help me. I looked up his address and hitched a ride to his house. He lived in a really nice neighborhood and I'd found out from the Yellow Pages directory that he was a lawyer.''

She flashed a sardonic smile. "You can probably guess how well our father and child reunion went, or maybe Mr. Saylor mentioned it in his letter? Or when you *contacted* him?''

She made the word sound as damning as selling secret intelligence information to a hostile nation.

Devlin folded his arms and watched her, his eyes never leaving her face though she was looking away from him. "Why don't you tell me about it, Gillian?''

"Craig Saylor opened his door that day, and there I stood on the porch. He had red hair, just like me. And he wasn't very tall. Just like me. For a minute we stared at each other, speechless.'' Gillian began to neatly arrange the toys in Ashley's playpen, seemingly more interested in the task than in her toneless recitation of past history.

"Then I told him who I was and he told me— Well, good old Momma Jolene was right. Craig Saylor definitely didn't want me. He told me his fling with my mother had been a disastrous mistake, that she was a disgusting slut and he hadn't known she was as young as she was, which was way too young for him. But he claimed the worst part of that big mistake was her getting pregnant with me.''

"He shouldn't have said those things to you, Gillian,'' Devlin said quietly. "You were just an innocent child.''

"He told me plenty more. He said he gave Jolene money for an abortion but on her way to the clinic, she got sidetracked by a mall and went inside for a shopping spree instead. Then she tried to hit him up for some more cash but he claimed extortion and blackmail and got a friend—a lawyer or policeman or somebody official—to warn Jolene never to bother him again. She must've really been threatened because she didn't dare, and in her few brief moments of maternal concern, she warned me to stay away from him, too."

Gillian shrugged. "Still, I was young and stupid enough to try to explain to him that I was in a dangerous place, and wouldn't he please help me since he was my father? Mr. Saylor told me if I didn't go away immediately, he would call the cops and tell them I was harassing his family, that I was a menace to them and should be locked up like the worthless criminal trash I was. I wasn't so young and stupid not to get out of there fast."

"Honey, I'm so sorry." Devlin was aghast. "What did you do next? How did you get to the Sinsels?"

"I'd lived in enough foster homes to know that the one bit of juvenile acting out every agency took seriously was pyromania. So I got a can of lighter fluid and a box of matches and stood on my social worker's desk and threatened to torch the place then and there if they didn't change my current placement right away."

She smiled slightly. "I got immediate action. I was reclassified as a delinquent and was told that since I was only twelve they would give me one final chance in another foster home instead of shipping me right off to the state reform school. The foster home was the Sinsels'. I told them what had happened and they believed I wasn't an arsonist, though they'd taken in their share of them. It was one of the luckiest days of my life. I stayed with them for the next six years, till I was eighteen and out of state custody."

"Gillian." Devlin moved toward her. "Baby, I—don't know what to say."

He thought of himself at twelve, of his sister at that age. They'd been happy kids, confident of their parents' love, even taking it for granted. He imagined a future twelve-year-old Ashley and vowed she would never experience the abject fear and rejection her mother had.

"Now do you see why I want nothing to do with Craig Saylor?" Reflexively, Gillian continued to back away from Devlin. She didn't want sympathy though she wouldn't be averse to some outrage on behalf of her younger self. "I can't even begin to imagine why he contacted me. He made his feelings about me very clear that day on his porch.''

"But that was fourteen years ago, Gillian. People change, circumstances change. I've talked with Craig Saylor and he feels great remorse for the way he treated you.''

Gillian's eyes narrowed into slits. What she was hearing wasn't even close to righteous outrage. And then it dawned on her. "He wants something from me, doesn't he? Oh, it's so obvious, I can't believe I didn't guess right away. Well, whatever it is, the answer is an unqualified no!''

"Gillian, please! Don't be so quick to dismiss—''

"I'm simply following Craig Saylor's lead and dismissing him as fast as he dismissed me, Devlin. I—I wish you hadn't intercepted that letter. This really isn't any of your business.''

"The letter is about a medical matter and as a doctor, it is my business. Gillian, this is vital, you *have* to listen to me. Your dad, er, Craig Saylor—'' he amended when she shot him a killing glare "—has a fifteen-year-old daughter who was diagnosed last year with acute myelogenous leukemia. She's been given two different courses of chemotherapy that haven't brought remission and her only hope now is a bone marrow transplant. Unfortunately, her parents and thirteen-year-old brother have been tested and aren't suitable matches so—''

"They want to see if I am a suitable match?'' Gillian exclaimed incredulously. "They've come after me for my bone marrow?''

"Gillian, I've already met with Craig Saylor and his wife. They're terrified and desperate about their daughter's condition. Leaving no stone unturned, they—''

"Went looking for me? Expecting to find me, where? Under a rock, like the insect they consider me to be? I mean, if they're unturning all those stones—''

"Gillian, please!'' Devlin huffed impatiently, clearly not appreciating her attempt at levity. "The Saylors hired a private investigator who tracked you to the Sinsels and then a lawyer friend of theirs wrote you to—''

"Oh, they've sucked you right in, haven't they?'' Gillian was scornful. "Those devoted parents, dedicated to helping their poor sick daughter.''

"I met the patient herself yesterday, Gillian. She's your *sister*. Her name is Madeline and—''

"I've always hated that name," muttered Gillian. "Don't even think about buying those Madeline storybooks or dolls for Ashley."

Devlin heaved an exasperated sigh. "This is no time to joke around, Gillian."

"I'm not joking, Devlin." She stalked into the small kitchen and began to rescour the already clean sink. She would've rewashed the dinner dishes, except they were already put away. "For all these years I didn't exist for Craig Saylor and now, suddenly, I'm the long-lost daughter? Forget it. As far as I'm concerned, none of the Saylors exist for me."

He stood beside her at the sink, watching her work. "There is something else you have to be aware of, Gillian. You know all those tests Ashley and I had to prove my paternity? Well, one of those tests shows that Ashley is the closest match so far to Madeline Saylor. Not a perfect match, but as a last resort it could be possible to—"

"No!" Gillian whirled around to face him. "Ashley is just a baby, and as you've said yourself, she's been sick a lot. I will never let them use her as a bone marrow donor. She's too little, her health is—"

"At least be honest, Gillian," Devlin cut in sharply. "It wouldn't matter how old Ashley happened to be or if she'd never been sick a single day. The truth is that you despise Craig Saylor so much you wouldn't give him a fingernail clipping of Ashley's if he begged for one."

"You're right." Her eyes flicked over him in a coolly assessing once-over. "I won't let those people use my baby, no matter what. I refuse to give my consent for any unnecessary medical procedure involving my child."

Her icy detachment riled him more than any burst of temper would have done. "A life-giving procedure is hardly unnecessary, Gillian," he stormed. "And don't forget that Ashley is my child, too. As her father, I can give parental consent to—"

"The court has to declare you Ashley's father and we weren't able to schedule a hearing date till next spring, remember?" Gillian countered defiantly. "Until then, Mark Morrow is legally Ashley's father and he'll do whatever I say concerning the baby. If you don't believe me, call him right now. I promise you he'll side with me."

Devlin had no doubts of that. He tried to maintain the professional, clinical air that served him so well when dealing with patients but he could feel his emotions rising as Gillian continued to freeze him with that arctic stare of hers. To taunt him about his lack of status with his own child.

And there was more. His career was dedicated to curing patients, or at the very least, helping to improve the quality of their lives. He couldn't turn his back on a sick patient, particularly one that he *knew* he could help. He drew a deep, calming breath. How many times did he have to tell patients and their families things that were difficult to hear, things that they did not want to acknowledge? Too many times to count. Likewise, he'd had to convince many patients and families to accept treatments and procedures and outcomes that they did not want any part of. But usually, he prevailed. Certainly, he could succeed with his own wife!

"I share your concerns about Ashley," he said in his most accomplished, soothingly rational physician tones. "She is very young for such a procedure and she has had a history of gastrointestinal and respiratory infections. That does give me pause."

Gillian slanted him a suspicious glance. "What's your point, Dr. Yango?"

Devlin's lips twitched. "I did sound somewhat yango-esque, didn't I?"

She felt herself being drawn in by his charm and tried to steel herself. She already knew that she had a very, very hard time saying no to Devlin Brennan. "Go on, whatever it is, say it and get it over with, Devlin."

"When the Saylors' lawyer wrote you that letter, they were unaware of Ashley's existence. The request was for *you* to please be tested for an HLA-compatibility match for your half-sister Madeline. Will you do it, Gillian? Will you have the test?"

"And if I'm a compatible match, then I'll be expected to donate my bone marrow to her," she said flatly.

He moved to take her in his arms. "Sweetheart, I knew I could count on you to—"

"No." Gillian pushed his arms away and walked into the living room. "I won't do it, Devlin. I won't take the test and I won't let them use Ashley or me. Craig Saylor made his choice years ago when he sent me back to that hellhole and forgot about me.

I needed him then as much as he needs me now. And now it's my turn to say 'I don't care what happens to you. Get lost.'"

She sat down on the sofa and flicked on the TV set.

Devlin felt all objectivity flee as fury rushed through him, displacing any chance of reasonable calm. "I can't believe what I'm hearing! My God, Gillian, this poor girl is going to die without your help!"

"I've been dead to Craig Saylor all these years. Suddenly he's decided to resurrect me so they can harvest my bone marrow, or my baby's, and I'm supposed to amiably go along with the plan? Well, no thanks, we'll pass. Ashley and I are not going to be involved," Gillian said stubbornly.

"Will you at least consider talking to—"

"Someone like Holly? I bet she wouldn't hesitate to open a vein if you asked her for blood. She'd probably happily donate a kidney if you asked." Gillian fairly raced from the living room to her bedroom. She purposefully locked the door behind her with a loud click.

"You don't have to worry about me coming in there after you," Devlin called through the door. "I'm going to the hospital to sleep in one of the on-call rooms."

Ten

Gillian arrived at the lab the next morning for the HLA-compatibility test that she'd scheduled earlier. She brought Ashley with her, and one of the lab technicians held the baby while Gillian was tested. Ashley was friendly and cheerful as she watched the needle prick her mother, though her good mood evaporated when they dropped by the day care center to say hello to Tina and the staff there. The moment they approached the door to the center, Ashley began to wail and cling to her mother.

"You don't have to stay, angel face. I just thought we'd stop in for a few minutes to be sociable," Gillian said soothingly to her child. "Tina will be glad to see us. Unlike certain other people I could name, she doesn't think your mommy is heartless."

Devlin's lack of faith in her still rankled. She had known from the moment he'd broken the news about Madeline Saylor's illness and potential cure that she would have the damn compatibility screening test, that she would be a perfect match and would voluntarily donate her bone marrow to Craig Saylor's daughter. She knew it, but she wasn't happy about it and had no intention of pretending to be.

She was a regular churchgoer, she was a faithful listener of Dr.

Leah, and she knew right from wrong, but she was not a saint. Only a saint could smile benignly and welcome a chance to help the man who'd thrown her out like the "worthless criminal trash" he believed her to be.

"Maybe I should schedule an appointment for myself with Holly Casale," Gillian murmured to Ashley after their brief visit with Tina, as she carried the baby to her former office in the social work department. "That would be a kick, wouldn't it, Ash?"

"Ball," Ashley said knowledgeably, astonishing Gillian.

Her daughter had heard the word "kick" and associated it with the ball her daddy playfully kicked with her. Gillian was a bit awed by her baby's intelligence. And knew she'd better start watching what she said around such a bright little girl. No more cracks about Dev or Holly within Ashley's earshot. She would never expose her daughter to the kind of hateful invectives she'd heard adults hurl during much of her own childhood.

Marthea and Sally and the others were overjoyed to see her and Ashley, and though Gillian was glad to see them, too, she didn't experience a single nostalgic pang to return to her former workplace. Her replacement was already settled in her minuscule ex-office, telephone in hand and waiting on hold. Gillian wished her well.

Next, she and Ashley went to the cafeteria for a snack but Devlin was nowhere to be seen. Gillian told herself she hadn't expected him to be there. His days were filled with surgery and patient rounds and conferences; he didn't have time to hang around the cafeteria. But she had been hoping for one of those happy coincidences that would bring them together in the same place at the same time.

She wanted to see her husband. It had been awful without him in the apartment last night and just as bad this morning when he wasn't there to have breakfast with her and Ashley. He'd been away from her less than twenty-four hours and already she missed him terribly.

Gillian wondered if her marriage was over, feared that it was, and found it strange and grim beyond imagining that Craig Saylor—someone she had never, ever expected to hear from again—was the precipitating cause of its demise. If only she hadn't shown up on Mr. Saylor's doorstep all those years ago, he wouldn't have known she existed. He wouldn't have sought her as a donor and she, in turn, wouldn't have gone ballistic over the out-of-the-blue bone marrow request. And right now, Dev wouldn't despise her for her less than noble reaction.

If only!

Gillian took Ashley home, but the afternoon hours with her daughter that normally flew by seemed to drag interminably. She wondered what she should do. Try to call Devlin? And tell him what? That she'd had the requisite test so he didn't have to hate her anymore?

She tried to guess what Dr. Leah would say and sensed her mentor would not approve of the situation. "He wants you for your bone marrow?" she imagined Dr. Leah snapping across the airwaves. "Hmm, just like your father. What does that tell you about your relationships with men?" Dr. Leah was nothing if not hard-hitting.

"It tells me that I'm useful, not lovable," Gillian surmised aloud. This was hardly news to her. At least Dr. Leah would be proud of her ability to face reality.

If she let herself, she would be aching with pain, but Gillian kept busy cleaning the apartment, doing laundry and preparing dinner while the baby napped. As soon as Ashley woke up, Gillian took her for a walk, and they watched a rousing Barney video upon their return. She was quite adept at keeping hurt at a livable distance and she used those skills to her advantage now.

Devlin arrived just as she was serving Ashley her favorite macaroni and cheese for dinner. Gillian nearly dropped the casserole dish at the sight of him.

"You look like you've seen an apparition," he said coolly. "I had a long day but I hope I don't look that bad!"

He looked wonderful, and she was sure he knew it. Devlin Brennan was one of those people who looked good even with a runny head cold.

"I—wasn't expecting you." She dutifully got him a plate and set him a place at the table.

"I live here, Gillian." He scooped himself a huge portion, smiling at his daughter, without looking at his wife. "I wanted to have dinner with Ashley and spend the evening with her. Then I'm going back to the hospital. To spend the night in one of the on-call rooms," he added meaningfully.

Gillian swallowed back the lump blocking her throat. It felt as painful as ground glass. "Fine," she said in a convincing display of indifference.

He dropped his fork and glared at her. "Don't you care? Are you so cold and so hostile that you'd prefer I stay away rather than have one simple test that could save a young girl's life?"

I'd prefer that you trusted me enough to believe that I would do the right thing, Gillian replied in her head. It was a comeback worthy of Dr. Leah—too bad she didn't have the nerve to say it aloud. But Devlin had allied himself with Craig Saylor. He believed her birth father's assessment of her character and she wasn't going to grovel in an attempt to temporarily win his favor. What was the point? Dev didn't love her and he never would.

"That's just the way we heartless maniacs are," she replied instead with an artless shrug. "We hang on to our bone marrow with a vengeance."

Devlin's expression was chilling. He didn't attempt to speak to her again. Gillian knew he wanted nothing more than to get away from her, but he stayed for two and a half hours to play with Ashley and complete her bedtime routine so the baby wouldn't know anything was amiss. Gillian admired his loyalty to their daughter. Dev was a good father; he wouldn't let his personal animosity toward his wife stand in the way of his relationship with his child.

He stayed away for the next three nights, coming by to have dinner and play with the baby, but leaving as soon as she was tucked in her crib. He made no further efforts at conversation with Gillian, nor did she attempt to break the cold silence between them.

Sometimes she would catch herself remembering how wonderful living with Dev used to be, as compared to this strained state of siege they were currently enduring. She thought about the way they'd laughed and talked and teased and made love. The good memories invariably made her cry, so she tried to block them. Better to think of something else.

Like arranging for Carmen to come stay with Ashley while she was hospitalized as the donor during Madeline Saylor's bone marrow transplant. The results of the test came back revealing Gillian as the perfect HLA match for her younger half sister, just as she'd known they would. Gillian didn't know whether to attribute her prescient knowledge to intuition or irony or pure cynicism, but somehow, she'd just known.

She had been in touch with the Saylors' lawyer and made it clear to him that she would donate her bone marrow to Madeline, but wanted no contact with the family. She didn't kid herself that they would want it any other way. Craig Saylor was undoubtedly relieved to be spared an awkward meeting with the living, breathing biggest mistake of his life.

Devlin came by the night before the surgery, spent his time with Ashley, and then left without saying goodbye. Gillian didn't bother to mention that Carmen would be there when he came over tomorrow evening. After all, his visits were for the sole purpose of seeing Ashley. Certainly, he didn't care whether it was Gillian or Carmen who also happened to be around.

The transplant went smoothly and Gillian was resting in her hospital bed when the only thing she'd asked of the Saylors was not granted. A petite brunette who introduced herself as Elaine Saylor came into her room—right in the middle of an episode of "The Donna Reed Show" that Gillian had somehow missed despite years of TV rerun viewing.

Elaine carried a box of candy, a bouquet of flowers and a cute, stuffed black cat wearing a pointed hat. "The candy and flowers are for you and the toy is for your little girl for Halloween," she said, then burst into tears and grabbed Gillian in a tight hug.

Gillian, sore from the needles, winced, as Elaine Saylor thanked her over and over for "Saving my child's life. The doctors say the match was as good as one from an identical twin. They're extremely optimistic and said Maddie's prognosis is excellent," Elaine said breathlessly between sobs.

"I'm glad," Gillian said politely, easing out of the other woman's embrace. "I'm a mother, too. I know how scary it is when your child is sick."

"But for you to do this for us, after the terrible things Craig said to you..." Elaine began to cry harder.

"He told you?" That caught Gillian by surprise.

"Not until we realized that we needed a compatible bone marrow match for Madeline. Craig had never mentioned he'd had another child before, and then he told me about you. He said you would probably refuse to help because of what he'd done when you were just a child, that one time you came to see him." Elaine seemed genuinely distressed. "I was horrified, Gillian. I couldn't reconcile that cruel person with the man I love. He is a good husband and a devoted father."

Gillian refrained from comment though several pernicious ones struck her. She gazed longingly at the TV set, trying to listen to the dialogue.

"You are the most compassionate, kind and forgiving person I've ever met," Elaine went on, drowning out Donna Reed. "I had to come in here and tell you that, to personally thank you even though they said you'd rather not see any of us. I can't blame you. You have every reason to want to keep your distance from us."

"I think that would be best for everybody," said Gillian. "I—wish the best for Madeline," she added, suddenly exhausted, wanting only to be left alone.

"Craig is extremely grateful to you," Elaine persisted. "He thinks the world of your husband, and he would love to meet you and your baby. He told me to tell you that if you should ever want to talk to him or if you ever need anything at all to please call him." She slipped a small card into Gillian's hand.

Gillian closed her eyes. "If you'll excuse me, I'm very tired," she murmured, and Elaine gave a tearful nod and left the room.

Gillian ripped Craig Saylor's business card to shreds and tossed the pieces into the trash can. His offer was fourteen years too late. She had nothing to say to the man, she neither needed nor wanted anything from him. She was sure that she never would.

Gillian had her second surprise visitor less than a half hour later, just as her dinner tray arrived. This time it was Holly Casale, stunning in a short, red, knit dress, tinted hose and red high heels. She looked like a model in a Victoria's Secret catalogue, one of the fully-dressed-but-just-as-sexy-ones.

And here lay Gillian in a cotton hospital gown and no makeup whatsoever. It figured, Gillian sighed.

"I just saw your name on the patient roster and I couldn't believe it," Holly exclaimed, coming to stand beside the bed. "Dev never mentioned that you were—"

"Why would Dev waste time talking about me when you're together?" Gillian listlessly stirred her stew with a spoon. Was she actually expected to eat this stuff? She hadn't been feeling very hungry anyway, but the dual appearance of Holly and this thick, congealing stew completely killed her appetite.

"You're one of his favorite subjects, you and Ashley." Holly tried to make eye contact, which Gillian deftly avoided. "What's going on with you and Dev? He's spent the past several nights in one of the on-call rooms for first year residents, instead of at home."

Gillian tilted her head to study the beautiful doctor. "Sounds like he's been complaining about his horrible wife to sweet, sympathetic you." Her words seemed to fly off her tongue, independent of her will. She remembered the pain pill a nurse had given her a while ago and wondered if it were actually truth serum.

"Gillian, I don't know what you're thinking but—"

"Oh, come off it, Holly," Gillian blurted. Suddenly, keeping up the usual pretense and defense required more energy than she had to spare. "You don't have to pretend with me. I know you love Dev."

Holly inhaled sharply. "Gillian, I understand your reasoning. You are hypervigilant and while that can be a tremendous asset—after all, people often do have covert motives, and a keen sense of perception will protect you if these motives are threatening—there are times when—"

"I don't want to be analyzed, Holly. My keen sense of perception tells me that you're in love with my husband. And that's threatening."

Holly ran her hand through her thick, dark hair, attractively tousling it. "I do love Dev, Gillian. There, I've said it. Are you happy?"

"Oh, just thrilled! Now the two of you can start making plans. You'll practice at the hospital together and try to claim visitation rights to Ashley every other weekend and—" Her voice broke and to her horror, tears ran down her cheeks.

Holly handed her a tissue from the box on the nightstand. "Dev doesn't love me, Gillian. He never has and he never will. He loves you, he adores you. How can you not know that? I realized it the first time I saw him with you. He was devastated when you broke up with him, though he tried not to show it. I always suspected Ashley was his child. I couldn't figure out why you didn't tell him."

Gillian blew her nose and turned the TV set back on, desperate to escape from this incomprehensible conversation.

Holly boldly turned it off again. "Didn't you think it was strange that you and Dev ended up living across the hall from each other?" she demanded. "Did you really believe that was simply a coincidence?"

Gillian's jaw dropped. Holly had her full attention now. "Are you trying to say it wasn't?"

"I have a friend who works in the housing office. I called in a favor and asked to have you and Dev placed on the same floor in apartments across from each other."

Gillian was stunned. "But why?"

"Because I knew if you both were thrown together it would only be a matter of time before he found out the truth about Ashley. I wasn't sure if you would tell him or if he'd guess, but I did know you two would get back together. I knew Dev loved you and wouldn't give you up again. Which is exactly what happened," she added quietly.

"But that doesn't make sense!"

"It does if you accept that I'm Devlin's friend. I want him to be happy and that means being with the woman he loves. That isn't me. It's you, Gillian."

Gillian knew she should make some response to Holly's astonishing proclamation. But what to say? The two women looked expectantly at each other, each waiting for the other to speak.

Before either one could, Devlin himself strode into the room, heading straight for Gillian's bed. He didn't seem to see Holly, his eyes were affixed on Gillian. Without a word, he grabbed her and held her tight.

For a startled moment Gillian tensed, but then the strength and heat of his body penetrated the terrible chill that had been enshrouding her during the long days and nights without him. She was unable to resist, she began to melt against him. Her arms crept around his neck and she clung to him, desperate to be close to him again, to overcome the seemingly insurmountable barriers that had been erected between them.

"I just came from our apartment." His voice and his breath were warm against her throat. "Carmen told me everything. I can't believe I did it again! Baby, can you ever forgive me?" His expression was agonized. "Please, Gillian. Please, give me another chance."

"Forgive you?" Gillian murmured incredulously. His behavior was as perplexing as Holly's amazing admission a few minutes ago. "For what? I was the one who—"

"For all the truly rotten things I said," Devlin cut in, his voice impassioned and thick with sorrow. "For walking away and believing the worst. After I promised myself—and promised you!—that we would face problems together, I left you alone to cope with the baby and with one of the most difficult decisions that—"

"Getting the test and donating the bone marrow wasn't a difficult decision," Gillian assured him. "There really wasn't a choice. I knew what had to be done."

"I know." He cupped her face with his hands and gazed deeply into her eyes. "I shouldn't have doubted you for even a second."

"I knew what had to be done but I wasn't very gracious about it," Gillian amended. "In fact, I was awful. You saw me at my worst and drew the logical conclusion."

"Don't make excuses for me, Gillian, I don't deserve it. You were hurt and angry and blowing off steam. I would have expected and understood that reaction from any patient of mine and responded accordingly. But with you—" He shook his head self-disparagingly. "I turned into this wrathful, self-righteous jerk and made it impossible for you to talk to me, let alone express any fear or anger. I let you down again and you had to go through the entire procedure alone, just like you went through your pregnancy and labor and delivery without me. I'm never there when you need me."

"Because I don't let you be there," Gillian interrupted softly. "You didn't know about Ashley and you didn't know about this transplant because I didn't tell you." She stroked his cheek. She couldn't stand to see him look so guilty and unhappy. "I don't trust people very easily, Dev. Holly said I'm hypervigilant and—"

Gillian broke off abruptly as she remembered Holly's presence. She looked over Dev's shoulder for her, but Holly wasn't there. Sometime within the past few minutes, she had discreetly slipped away.

Gillian thought about what Holly had said. *He loves you, he adores you. The woman he loves isn't me, it's you, Gillian.* Could Holly possibly be right? She was so smart, possessing the insight and analytical skills required in her profession, and she'd known Dev for a long time.

And why would she lie about him loving Gillian? That would be one of the first questions Dr. Leah would ask if someone phoned in with this dilemma. Dr. Leah always asked questions that cut straight to the heart of the matter and really made you think. Gillian started to really think, putting together the pieces she'd finally perceived of this odd puzzle.

"Holly left," she announced absently. She was thinking of the pivotal role Dev's friend had played in their lives. Holly was practically Ashley's fairy godmother, taking the necessary action to reunite Devlin and Gillian.

A fairy godmother she'd mistaken for a wicked witch! Gillian was remorseful. She'd crossed the line from hypervigilance into paranoia when it came to Holly Casale. And if she'd been wrong about Holly, wasn't it just possible that she was wrong about Dev, too? And herself? That maybe he really did love her because she was a person worth loving?

Devlin dismissed Holly's absence with a shrug. He had other things on his mind. Things concerning Gillian. "I want you to trust me, sweetheart, and I know it works both ways. I have to trust you, too. Let's promise right now that we won't stop trying, that we'll never let anything—or anyone—come between us again."

She lay against him, letting him hold her the way she had wanted to be held for days. "I love you," she said, not waiting for him to say it first, daring to risk telling him her true feelings. "I want our marriage to work, Dev. I love you so much and Ashley loves you and—"

He kissed her then, his lips claiming hers in tender possession that swiftly escalated into urgent need. They were still kissing when the dietary aide came into the room to take away Gillian's rejected dinner. Within moments, another aide came by to refill the water pitcher. The chance of having any real privacy seemed nil.

"I wish we were home." Dev picked Gillian up and carried her to the chair beside the window. He sat down, holding her on his lap. "I don't want to spend another night without you."

"Me, either." She touched her forehead to his. "But I'm supposed to get out of here tomorrow. Carmen said she'd stay with Ashley till I get back to the apartment."

"Till you get *home*," Dev corrected. "And I'm going to take you there."

"Yes," Gillian agreed. "Till you take me home."

"I love you, Gillian." He slipped his hand beneath her starchy hospital gown to rub her back. She shivered with pleasure as his fingers glided over her smooth skin. "When Carmen told me that you thought I didn't, I—"

"Carmen told you that?"

"She told me plenty when I walked in today and demanded to know where you were. I love you, but I've been such a *yango* I managed to forget I'd never actually said it."

"That is more bonehead than yango, I think," Gillian decided.

"I just expected you to know how I feel about you, but you need the words. So do I. Hearing you tell me that you love me makes me realize how much those words mean."

"Do you really love me, Dev?" She allowed herself to ask.

"Do you doubt it or do you just want to hear me say it again?"

"Maybe both," she replied honestly.

"I love you, Gillian." His earnest, intense blue eyes held hers. "Never doubt it. I'll do whatever I have to, to prove how serious I am about making our marriage last forever." He smiled. "Even have a full-blown wedding extravaganza in Port McClain with the entire Brennan clan in attendance, if that's what it takes."

"Carmen did tell all, didn't she? But I don't need that, Dev."

"Suppose I insist on a small church wedding here in town with the Sinsels and Carmen? We could invite my parents, and Kylie and Cade, too." He traced the lovely shape of her mouth with his fingertip. "I didn't suggest the justice of the peace because I considered our marriage to be temporary, Gillian. But I'll admit I wasn't eager to face your family or mine back then. I only wanted to be with you and Ashley, the two newest and most important people in my life. The J.P. seemed the quickest, most efficient way to get married."

"We were kind of in a hurry." Gillian grinned reminiscently. "There was a chance that Ashley was going to become a big sister and we didn't want any countdowns."

"That wasn't the reason I wanted to marry you as soon as

possible, honey. I felt like we'd already wasted too much time apart and I wanted to begin our life together immediately. I couldn't wait.'' He shook his head ruefully. ''Of course, it would have helped immensely if I had told you that.''

''I probably wouldn't have believed you, Dev. I wasn't ready to hear it. It's taken this long for me to finally begin to believe that you could love me.''

''*Begin* to believe it? I want you to *fully* believe it, Gillian.'' He kissed her passionately.

When he lifted his mouth from hers, she smiled seductively at him. ''Let's keep working on making me a total believer.''

A nurse marched into the room to take Gillian's temperature and blood pressure. ''No fooling around with my patient, Devlin Brennan,'' the nurse scolded with mock severity, eyeing Gillian on his lap with her kiss-swollen mouth. ''Let her get some rest.''

''As if anyone can rest in this zoo,'' Dev retorted. ''You have to get out of here to get any rest.'' He and the nurse traded friendly barbs until she left the room.

''I was just thinking about what that nurse said,'' Gillian murmured thoughtfully.

''About getting some rest in here? Forget it, honey. It's a lost cause.''

''No, I mean about fooling around. That's the way it began for us. We were just sort of fooling around and somewhere along the way, we fell in love.''

''Where we will stay, Gillian.''

''Forever, Dev,'' she promised, believing in him, in herself and in their love at last.

* * * * *

Silhouette Romance is proud to present
Virgin Brides, a brand-new monthly
promotional series by some of the bestselling
and most beloved authors in the romance genre.

In March '98, look for the very first
Virgin Brides novel,

THE PRINCESS BRIDE by Diana Palmer.

Just turn the page for an exciting preview of
Diana Palmer's thrilling new tale...

One

Tiffany saw him in the distance, riding the big black stallion. It was spring, and that meant roundup. It was not unusual to see the owner of the Lariat ranch in the saddle at dawn lending a hand to rope a stray calf or help work the branding. Kingman Marshall kept fit with ranch work, and despite the fact that he shared an office and a business partnership with Tiffany's father in land and cattle, his staff didn't see a lot of him.

This year, they were using helicopters to mass the far-flung cattle, and they had a corral set up on a wide, flat stretch of land where they could dip the cattle, check them, cut out the calves for branding and separate them from their mothers. It was physically demanding work, and no job for a tenderfoot. King wouldn't let Tiffany near it, but it wasn't a front row seat at the corral that she wanted. If she could just get his attention away from the milling cattle on the wide, rolling plain that led to the Guadalupe River, if he'd just look her way...

Tiffany stood up on a rickety lower rung of the gray wood fence, avoiding the sticky barbed wire, and waved her Stetson at him. She was a picture of young elegance in her tan jodhpurs and sexy pink silk blouse and high black boots. She was a debutante. Her father, Harrison Blair, was King's business partner and friend, and if she chased King, her father encouraged her. It would be a marriage made in heaven. That is, if she could find some way to convince King of it. He was elusive and quite abrasively masculine. It might take more than a young lady of almost twenty-one with a sheltered, monied background to land him. But, then, Tiffany had confidence in herself; she was beautiful and intelligent.

Her long black hair hung to her waist in back, and she refused to have it cut. It suited her tall, slender figure and made an elegant frame for her soft, oval face and wide green eyes and creamy complexion. She had a sunny smile, and it never faded. Tiffany was always full of fire, burning with a love of life that her father often said had been reflected in her long-dead mother.

"King!" she called, her voice clear, and it carried in the early-morning air.

He looked toward her. Even at that distance, she could see that cold expression in his pale blue eyes, on his lean, hard face with its finely chiseled features. He was a rich man. He worked hard, and he played hard. He had women, Tiffany knew so, but he was nothing if not discreet. He was a man's man, and he lived like one. There was no playful boy in that tall, fit body. He'd grown up years ago, the boyishness driven out of him by a rich, alcoholic father who demanded blind obedience from the only child of his shallow, runaway wife.

She watched him ride toward her, easy elegance in the saddle. He reined in at the fence, smiling down at her with faint arrogance.

"You're out early, tidbit," he remarked in a deep, velvety voice with just a hint of Texas drawl.

"I'm going to be twenty-one tomorrow," she said pertly. "I'm having a big bash to celebrate, and you have to come. Black tie, and don't you dare bring anyone. You're mine, for the whole evening. It's my birthday and on my birthday I want presents—and you're it. My big present."

His dark eyebrows lifted with amused indulgence. "You might have told me sooner that I was going to be a birthday present," he said. "I have to be in Omaha early Saturday."

"You have your own plane," she reminded him. "You can fly."

"I have to sleep sometimes," he murmured.

"I wouldn't touch that line with a ten-foot pole," she drawled, peeking at him behind her long lashes. "Will you come?"

He lit a cigarette, took a long draw and blew it out with slight impatience. "Little girls and their little whims," he mused. "All right, I'll whirl you around the floor and toast your coming-of-age, but I won't stay. I can't spare the time."

"You'll work yourself to death," she complained, and then became solemn. "You're only thirty-four and you look forty."

"Times are hard, honey," he mused, smiling at the intensity in that glowering young face. "We've had low prices and drought. It's all I can do to keep my financial head above water."

"You could take the occasional break," she advised. "And I don't mean a night on the town. You could get away from it all and just rest."

"They're full up at the Home," he murmured, grinning at her exasperated look. "Honey, I can't afford vacations, not with times so hard. What are you wearing for this coming-of-age party?" he asked to divert her.

"A dream of a dress. White silk, very low in front, with diamanté straps and a white gardenia in my hair." She laughed.

He pursed his lips. He might as well humor her. "That sounds dangerous," he said softly.

"It will be," she promised, teasing him with her eyes. "You might even notice that I've grown up."

He frowned a little. That flirting wasn't new, but it was disturbing lately. He found himself avoiding little Miss Blair, without really understanding why. His body stirred even as he looked at her, and he moved restlessly in the saddle. She was years too young for him, and a virgin to boot, according to her doting, sheltering father. All those years of obsessive parental protection had led to a very immature and unavailable girl. It wouldn't do to let her too close. Not that anyone ever got close to Kingman Marshall, not even his infrequent lovers. He had good reason to keep women at a distance. His upbringing had taught him too well that women were untrustworthy and treacherous.

"What time?" he asked on a resigned note.

"About seven?"

He paused thoughtfully for a minute. "Okay." He tilted his wide-brimmed hat over his eyes. "But only for an hour or so."

"Great!"

He didn't say goodbye. Of course, he never did. He wheeled the stallion and rode off, man and horse so damn arrogant that she felt like flinging something at his tall head. He was delicious, she thought, and her body felt hot all over just looking at him.

On the ground he towered over her, lean and hard-muscled and sexy as all hell. She loved watching him.

With a long, unsteady sigh, she finally turned away and remounted her mare. She wondered sometimes why she bothered hero-worshiping such a man. One of these days he'd get married and she'd just die. God forbid that he'd marry anybody but her!

That was when the first shock of reality hit her squarely between the eyes. Why, she had to ask herself, would a man like that, a mature man with all the worldly advantages, want a young and inexperienced woman like herself at his side? The question worried her so badly that she almost lost control of her mount.

The truth of her situation was unpalatable and a little frightening. She'd never even considered a life without King. What if she had to?

She rode home slowly, a little depressed because she'd had to work so hard just to get King to agree to come to her party. And still haunting her was that unpleasant speculation about a future without King...

But she perked up when she thought of the evening ahead. King didn't come to the house often, only when her father wanted to talk business away from work, or occasionally for drinks with some of her father's acquaintants. To have him come to a party was new and stimulating. Especially if it ended the way she planned. She had her sights well and truly set on the big rancher. Now all she had to do was take aim!

* * * * *